Deadly Odds 5.0

Allen Wyler

Deadly Odds 3.0

Other books by Allen Wyler (fiction)

Changes
Deadly Odds
Dead Ringer
Dead Ringer 2.0
Dead End Deal
Dead Wrong
Deadly Errors
Dead Head
Cutter's Trial

Other books by Allen Wyler (nonfiction)

The Surgical Management of Epilepsy

Deadly Odds 3.0 ©2020 Allen Wyler, All Rights Reserved

Print ISBN 978-1-949267-48-8
ebook ISBN 978-1-949267-49-5

Visit Allen online at www.allenwyler.com

Cover design by Guy D. Corp
www.grafixCORP.com

STAIRWAY⹀PRESS

STAIRWAY PRESS—APACHE JUNCTION

www.stairwaypress.com
1000 West Apache Trail, Suite 126
Apache Junction, AZ 85120 USA

Chapter 1—Arnold

"DON'T TELL ME you've forgotten me already? After all of our good times we had together in Vegas?"

Arnold's breath caught. Fear quick-froze his gut. He jumped up from the chair and moved away from the floor-to-ceiling windows, just in case the sniper was back on the other side of the ravine.

Was Chance out on the deck?

Something wet brushed his hand. He jerked it away and looked. His dog was staring up at him with concerned brown eyes and attentive ears, and whimpering softly.

Shit!

He was still holding the phone. He dumped it back in the charger, cutting the connection.

"Awww...Jesus." He dropped to his haunches and pressed his nose to the Malinois. "Chance is a good boy."

He gave the dog a flurry of choobers, the behind-the-ear scratches the pooch loved so dearly. The action short-circuited a bit of the raw anger and panic filling his chest. Naseem was back! Or maybe she'd never left the island. Regardless, she wanted him dead.

He grabbed the controller for the sunshades.

Wait! You really want to do that? What if she's out there watching, looking for your reaction. What will that tell her?

That she struck a nerve?

Right. Probably exactly what she wants.

Maybe show no reaction?

Well, shit, easy enough to say...

Slowly, he stood and glanced around. Nothing looked out of place; on the TV, Al Michaels and Cris Collingsworth were discussing a play. Everything exactly as it was before the phone rang. Reassuring. Sort of.

Still daylight out, all the interior lights off. Meaning if she was watching from the sniper spot, she probably couldn't see in.

But then, why call?

Duh! She's a terrorist. She's trying to make you feel terror.

No, there had to be more to it than that.

Think!

Had hanging up been a mistake? Should he have at least listened to what she had to say?

Why? I know what she wants.

Now what?

First order of business: make damn sure your security is locked down.

Then he was off the couch, heading into the guest room to check on SAM.

Chapter 2—Naseem

"HELLO."

Naseem instantly recognized the Jew's voice.

"Arnold?"

Silence.

"Don't tell me you've forgotten me already? After all of our good times we had together in Vegas?"

She listened closely for his reaction, hoping to pick up the slightest indication of hitting a nerve. Was there shock? Fear? She wanted the Jew to clearly understand that the issue between them was far from settled and that he knew exactly how she intended this to end.

The line went dead.

Ah, so the Jew *was* rattled. Good.

Smiling, she powered down the cell and pushed a straightened paper clip into the small hole on the side of the case, popping out the SIM card, and replacing it with the usual one. She'd toss the just-used card out the window on the H1 freeway during the drive back to the safe house, virtually guaranteeing its destruction. Nawzer argued adamantly and repeatedly against employing this technique to disguise calls, claiming that buying and discarding cheap "burner phones" was far safer. Not her thinking. Burners were more easily found and, if not carefully cleaned before discarding, served as a source of both DNA and fingerprints. A destroyed SIM card—especially one pulverized on a freeway—was infinitely more difficult to find and analyze. Not only that, but SIMs were less expensive.

She raised up on her elbows to continue watching the Jew's house across the ravine. The sky was still light, so he did not turn on the interior lights. This made it impossible to see his reaction. This would soon change. Evening was near. She knew his routine by now, having surveyed the house the past three weeks.

At least twice a day, for example, he drove his dog to one of two parks and sat at a bench or picnic table while the animal ran for a half hour. Each morning before their walk, he stopped at a Starbucks for a breakfast sandwich and grande latté to eat as the dog ran. The Jew's schedule was more regimented than the Japanese railway.

Dusk...for some reason these past days, dusk evoked vivid memories of older brother Fadi, a gentle soul, a grade-schoolteacher rather than a warrior. Fadi died senselessly, a victim of a drone attack. For what reason?

What had he ever done to deserve such a brutal and senseless death

Nothing.

The Americans claimed the school housed ISIS fighters.

A lie.

The moment she'd learned of his pointless murder, her hatred toward arrogant Americans—and their insistence on enforcing their particular political and religious beliefs on those who chose to believe differently—skyrocketed. That hatred had fomented unabated ever since.

And the Jew? Ha! Simply being a Jew intensified her hatred of him. From the start of recorded history, Jews had been the main source of problems plaguing the civilized world. Since the establishment of Israel, their unquenchable expansionistic appetite had done nothing but oxygenate incendiary Middle East politics. Kill the Jews and you will do wonders for bringing peace to this earth.

But Arnold Gold was more than just a Jew. He was directly responsible for her husband's incarceration as well as the deaths of Karim and her brothers in the warehouse. Mere words could never describe the hatred burning in her heart toward him.

She could already taste the delight that killing him would bring.

But the Jew possessed a thing of great value: his computer system's ability to evaluate and predict the outcome of future events, a feat he proudly demonstrated to her in a bout of adolescent bravado. Grave stupidity on his part. For her, learning of his system was a sign from Allah, for it would provide yet another weapon to employ in her Jihad.

But she had blundered by overestimating the spell she cast over him. She'd also gravely underestimated his gullibility. He eventually saw through her fabricated story, and when he did, he attempted to disappear, only to give himself away by making amateurish blunders. It'd been mere child's play to track him straight back to his Seattle home.

Her iPhone vibrated softly, jarring her from these dark memories. She glanced at the screen: Kasra.

"Yes?" she whispered even though she doubted that a neighbor could hear her at normal volume. Plus, a breeze rustling through nearby foliage provided sufficient background noise.

"He is leaving by the front door with his dog, heading for the car."

Naseem wiggled backward a few feet from the crest of the hill to a point where she could stand without being seen from his house.

"Good. I am coming. FaceTime me so I can see exactly what happens. He may simply walk the dog along the sidewalk."

She started working down into the rocky ravine, heading back to her car, one eye on the narrow scree path and the other on the phone.

Naseem smiled.

The Jew would be highly predictable and probably drive his dog

5

to one of two parks. The only thing she didn't yet know was whether he'd contacted the lawyer yet. Nawzer could answer that question soon as she checked with him, a task she planned to do the moment she returned to the safe house.

Meanwhile, there was still a great deal of work to finish this evening.

Chapter 3—Arnold

SHORTLY AFTER MOVING into his Honolulu home, Arnold modified the guest room to accommodate the computers required to rebuild SAM, his artificial intelligence system. The computers that had contained SAM 1.0 were totally destroyed when his Green Lake house burned to the ground. The software, however, had been backed up across multiple clouds, making retrieval practicably instantaneous. The replacement hardware had been easily purchased from Best Buy, but creating a temperature-friendly environment for the system in Hawaii's tropical climate had been the big challenge. This many electronic devices created heat, and heat destroyed electronics.

Of particular importance was maintaining a constant 65 degrees day and night while providing sufficient air circulation to prevent machine overheating. He even went to the trouble and expense of installing an emergency generator in case of a power failure.

His work desk held three OLED monitors arranged in an arc centered on his new state-of-the-art Secretlab 2020 gaming chair. Arnold settled in and adjusted the keyboard. Chance trailed along behind, circled three times, and dropped to the floor with a sigh.

Arnold typed the commands to invoke the self-diagnostic/security routine.

Good move, dude. You're beginning to think rationally again.

His bitter frustration over Naseem began to morph into focused objectivity. This, he decided, was exactly what was needed. Just being aware of this change buoyed his self-confidence.

Do not fall for her shit. She's a terrorist. That's what she does for a living. Incites terror.

Fucking Naseem!

This time their personal fight would be played entirely differently than their prior encounter, because this time Rachael's life was also at risk. This time Team Arnold planned to launch a totally intense take-no-fucking-prisoners offense.

"We're going finish her for good, aren't we, boy?"

Thump thump thump.

"Good boy!"

Arnold reached down and gave him three choobers—a reward for agreeing with him.

With the security routine now churning away, assessing his firewall's integrity, he could relax enough to begin creating a mental checklist of critical items to complete.

Priority one: protect SAM. Underway. Check.

Priority two: protect the house perimeter.

"Launch RAID."

The acronym stood for Remote Artificial Intelligence Drone, an aircraft he built three months ago as an amusing project designed around a totally awesome new Intel chip. He'd equipped the robot with ultra-high-definition light and infrared cameras, a UHF transmitter and a directional microphone. It had been designed with exactly the present use in mind: to search/patrol for threats within the immediate area. It could be launched and controlled automatically by SAM or, like now, by Arnold. Two months earlier, Arnold had used RAID to conduct reconnaissance for the FBI in the minutes leading up to the warehouse fiasco.

"RAID deployed," SAM said in its synthesized androgynous

voice.

SAM spoke with a slight Italian accent, a ripple Arnold added last month as an amusing touch because it sounded way cooler than, say, SIRI or Cortana.

Check: assuring that a secure-house-perimeter precaution was underway.

With a long slow exhale, he wiped his face, and sat back to study RAID's progress. So far, the perimeter appeared clear of intruders, especially the critical spots down in the ravine and up at sniper area.

What next? Ah yes, priority three: Arnold Gold.

Hmmm...no telling what risks he now faced. Naseem wanted him dead. And she wanted SAM. He believed that for the time being, as long as he protected himself, SAM would take care of itself. Although SAM 1.0 had been booby-trapped to self-destruct if used by a person unaware of the tripwires, SAM 2.0 was even better self-protected.

At the moment, Arnold greatest fear was what might happen to Rachael. Did Naseem even know about her? No way to know. All the more reason to get on top of the situation now.

And how do I do that? Well, for starters, think through a couple things. Like; how the hell did she find you?

Chance whimpered, perhaps reading his anxiety.

"Good suggestion, boy. Let's get out of here."

He stood, ready to leave, but decided it might be prudent to double-check the immediate street before stepping out the door.

"SAM, is the perimeter safe?"

"No sign of intruders."

"And the system?" Meaning SAM's firewall defenses.

"No evidence of penetration. Internal security fully invoked."

The instant he glanced down at Chance, the pooch bee-lined for the front door. Arnold detoured to the kitchen to grab car and house keys from the bowl on the polished concrete counter before meeting Chance at the front door.

Chapter 4—Naseem

AT THE BOTTOM of the ravine, Naseem sat on the dirt path watching the FaceTime video from Kasra's phone. She saw the steel gate protecting the Jew's driveway roll aside to allow his silver Mini Cooper to back out. A moment later the Jew was driving down the street with his dog in the passenger seat. The gate began to close.

"Follow him," she told Kasra. "I'll call soon as I reach the car."

Kasra disconnected. Naseem began to scurry down the remaining slope to the cul-de-sac where the car was parked.

From prior surveillance, she knew any direct approach to the house—either from the street or through the ravine—was impossible without being detected by the Jew's security system. But a break-in wasn't the reason for watching the Jew's house this afternoon. Instead, her sole motivation was to judge his physical reaction to her call. She was disappointed at not being able to see this and admonished herself for not waiting until the interior lights were on.

However, the Jew's actions indicated stress, exactly the intended result for the first step of her plan. She'd now do everything possible to maintain and increase this stress to the point of causing him to make a judgment error that would allow Nawzer to penetrate his security.

This time, she believed, their attack would succeed. In two days Nawzer was scheduled to arrive in Honolulu, allowing them to work side by side in the ravine within direct view of the Jew's house instead of 2,300 miles across the Pacific in the decadent comfort of his Los Angeles flat.

Not only would this give her the decided advantage of eliminating miles of fiber-optic cable and satellite links, but it would also eliminate the risk of discovery by NSA or other law-enforcement agencies. This time, Allah willing, she would end up in possession of the Jew's computers.

Then, and only then, would she kill him.

Chapter 5—Arnold

THE DRIVEWAY GATE opened and Arnold backed the Mini into the street, made a tight K-turn, and took off for Chance's favorite park. He felt a surge of relief at physically distancing himself from that fucking telephone, even if just for the time require to drive there and walk the short distance. A break would help clear his mind, allowing him to more critically and objectively assess his predicament.

Chance was sitting beside him, snout out the passenger-side window, angled forward, squinting, tongue flapping in the wind; a perfect example of what Arnold termed UDB—Universal Doggie Behavior. Seeing this small sign of normalcy gave him comfort.

Arnold parked in their usual spot, stepped from the car—Chance right on his heels—and watched him barrel straight for one of his favorite palm trees to relieve himself. Arnold started toward his usual picnic table but froze. Dense foliage surrounded three sides of the parking lot, adding a foreboding remoteness to the area although the park really wasn't that far from the downtown. Early dusk was quickly descending on them with no one in sight. The only light on the picnic table area filtered through palm fronds from a mercury vapor lamp fifteen feet away. Under most circumstances, being this isolated from the rest of the park was precisely the reason for choosing the spot, but now, with...

Fuck no!

No way was he willing to sit over there by himself.

Back at the car, butt propped against the front fender, he scanned the otherwise empty area again and fought a nagging chill of paranoia scintillating up and down his spine. Soon as Chance finished his business, they'd get the hell out of here.

Fucking Naseem!

Well, shit, mission accomplished! She'd successfully punched his buttons. But in so doing, she'd also steeled an angry resolve. This time he'd make goddamned sure to put an end this rise-from-the-dead-terminator-bullshit game of hers. This time there'd be no escaping out a back door of the warehouse. This time she needed to be...what? Offed?

Yeah, offed.

Whoa. This is some serious shit you're contemplating, dude.

He replayed this last thought. *Really?*

Yeah, really!

He gave himself a satisfied nod.

Okay, it was good to lay out a strategy. But even the best strategy would be totally worthless if not built on some serious-as-shit no-nonsense tactics. And whatever plan he came up with would have to include protecting Rachael. And that would be the huge problem. Because he couldn't tell her what was really going on.

Man! The situation was quickly becoming way more complicated. Probably no more complicated than writing bug-free software. And his first step in writing any new program was to map out a flow-chart. He thought about that and realized he lacked one critical piece of information: whether Naseem knew about her.

No way to know. It was one thing to batten down his own security hatches but quite another challenge to protect Rachael without...Jesus, this was going to be a huge problem.

Whoa, dude...think about it a moment.

What's to think about? She needs to be warned. Immediately.

Yeah? How, exactly? A text? Phone call? Shit, neither of those felt...right.

Besides, there was another huge issue in play here: Rachael's previous...stipulation? Was that the right word?

This message had to be delivered face to face. And then, only after careful deliberation. Wording would be everything. He needed to balance her need to know against unnecessarily frightening her. Even if he could summon sufficient diplomacy to walk such a thin line, he wasn't looking forward to her reaction. Two months ago, right on the heels of their Maui trip, she'd made it dreadfully clear that any future relationship would be based on him satisfying a few non-negotiable conditions, the two most important being: give up sports gambling and guarantee that Naseem was gone from his life. Rachael had been stone-cold serious about the Naseem thing.

Well, okay, one thing now seemed clear: he needed to snag a flight to Seattle ASAP. Which left him a shitload of arrangements to take care of, the most important being: arrange boarding for Chance. And then there was the issue of school...

And Fisher! Holy shit. Yes! Agent Fisher needed to be notified immediately. It was just flat-out stupid to not think of this before now.

Okay, but that also meant he needed to talk to Mr. Davidson first. Like right now. He pulled the iPhone from his pocket. Last time they'd spoken was two months ago while he and Rachael were vacationing in Maui. At the time, the lawyer was handling the sale of his Honolulu house to Hans Weiser.

They'd become more like friends than an attorney and his client. A least that's how he viewed it. He suspected they shared a mutual fondness—a father-son relationship of sorts—that had germinated in the immediate aftermath of Howie's murder. In the ensuing year and a half—somehow the span seemed much longer—the intense challenges they weathered together forged and welded that bond.

He glanced at his watch, figured it was just shy of 7:30 p.m. in

Seattle, so Davidson was probably eating dinner. He dialed his home phone.

No answer.

Hmmm...Sunday night.

Okay, maybe he was out to dinner.

He tried Davidson's cell.

Chapter 6—Naseem

"HE TOOK THE Makiki trail," Kasra explained. "I did not follow because it would be too easy to be noticed with so little traffic."

Naseem nodded approval. Kasra was smart. Just one of many reasons she assigned the other woman important responsibilities. The Makiki trail head was usually deserted this late in the day, making close surveillance from anywhere in the vicinity problematic. Her iPhone was set on speaker with the car idling, ready to go.

"Good. Where are you now?"

"At the far end of the access road," Kasra answered.

"Good. Stay right there. I should be able to get to you before he leaves. I'll call when I'm near."

"As you wish, Sister."

Naseem opened Google Maps on her iPhone to refresh her memory of the area. The park was one of the Jew's routine spots. She'd tailed him there numerous times in the past month and although she was confident in her ability to find it without relying on GPS, she didn't want to risk a delay in the waning light.

During her three months trapped on this Sodom and Gomorrah infidel island she'd developed an excellent working knowledge of freeways and main streets as well as the side streets that would be critical if ever there was a need to flee a neighborhood. One never knew when such knowledge might prove crucial to survival. Such as it had the afternoon she had escaped from the warehouse during the firefight.

Tailing the Jew tonight was not particularly critical to her overall plan other than to afford Kasra more hands-on field experience and provide additional evidence as to the Jew's present state of mind.

And this second point was what concerned her now.

The Makiki trail was one of his typical spots. Would a person under stress adhere to routine? No, they should show signs of panic. This was not what he seemed to be doing.

No longer smiling, she drove from the parking lot back into the street, merging seamlessly into traffic. Suddenly, keeping an eye on the Jew was of more critical importance than anticipated.

He was up to something.

She was determined to find out what.

Chapter 7—Arnold

"ARNOLD?" DAVIDSON ASKED.

Davidson's familiar voice was instantly reassuring. Talking with him first was absolutely the right thing to do. His advice and guidance should help protect him from bumbling into a fatal mistake. He glanced around for Chance.

Ah, off sniffing another clump of grass. Fine.

"So sorry to disturb you, Mr. Davidson, but I'm in some serious trouble."

"She found you again."

A simple statement of fact.

"No shit she did."

He suddenly realized his mistake. It hit him head-on. Like an eighteen-wheeler. How could he have forgotten? Two months ago, with all the warehouse shit going down, he *suspected* Nawzer—Naseem's technical guru—had been able to hack Davidson's computers, giving him complete access to all files, emails, texts, and real-time conversations. Major fucking mistake to forget that crucial point.

"Arnold?"

"You wouldn't happen to have another phone handy, would you? One of your burners?"

"No. Why?" Davidson sounded deeply concerned but also a bit...what? Put out?

Oh, shit, have I fucked up somehow?

"Where are you?" Arnold asked without thinking. "Sorry, didn't mean that. I mean, like, did I disturb something?"

"What is going on? You sound very upset."

Arnold couldn't help but glance around again as another paranoia chill burrowed deeply between his shoulder blades.

"We need to talk. I'm not comfortable on anything but a burner."

He hoped Davidson would pick up on the implication.

"No problem. Are you here in Honolulu?" Davidson asked.

Here in Honolulu? Really?

"Yes. Why?"

"Well, that simplifies matters. I am waiting on a table at Taormina."

"You got to be kidding me? Here on the island?"

"Yes."

Holy shit, perfect! A face-to-face would make their discussion sooo much easier. Now it all made sense: Davidson loved to fly over for a few days' stay at the Halekulani whenever his schedule permitted. Taormina was only a block and a half up the street from the front entrance.

Chance came trotting over, perhaps concerned by his tone. Arnold reached out to massage the back of the pooch's head.

"Just out of curiosity, what're you doing here?"

"I am waiting for a table."

"No. You know what I mean. What are you doing here in Honolulu?"

"I just closed on a condo."

"For real! Cool! You finally did it. But back to the point of this. I really do need to talk ASAP. Can we meet, like, now?"

Silence. Chance continued staring at him.

"This cannot wait until morning?"

"No. I'm totally serious. It's important. Totally important."

He immediately felt guilty. Clearly, Davidson was otherwise engaged, very likely celebrating finally achieving his long-time fantasy of owning a *pied-a-terre* here.

"Would you like to join *us?*"

Us?

Oh, shit. Felt like stepping on a warm pile of dogshit. For some strange reason, he'd never given a thought to Mr. Davidson's social life. Why was that? Had he somehow assumed the man existed in a vacuum, shuttling between work and home? How incredibly stupid. Of course Davidson knew people outside of work. Probably had a large circle of friends. It was just that...long as he could remember, Davidson never mentioned a word on that particular subject. Then again, why should he? This only piqued his interest.

"I'm *really* sorry to barge in on your evening...you sure it's all right?"

He knew damn well it wasn't, that he'd just destroyed the man's dinner plans, but what other option did he have? He needed to get Fisher involved tonight, but couldn't do that until he talked to Davidson.

"No problem."

Liar.

"Thanks. I'll get there ASAP."

Naseem

Naseem pulled into the convenience-store parking lot and rolled to a stop behind Kasra's Nissan. Kasra had done a nice job hiding the car from the street by parking between a green Subaru Outback and a black Jeep Cherokee.

Kasra ran to the passenger door and slid into the seat without a word. Then Naseem was rolling again, out of the lot, heading straight to the intersection where the Jew's car should pass in just a few minutes.

Chapter 8—Arnold

AS ARNOLD HEADED downtown, he wondered just how likely it was that Nawzer had actually hacked Davidson's computers. It depended on a few critical factors. Most importantly, how meticulously Davidson and Joyce, his secretary, followed a few basic security steps. The more important question, however, was how the hell had he, Arnold Gold, forgotten to follow through on that particular issue? Well, probably because he figured Naseem wouldn't dare come at him again after the warehouse thing blew up in her face. Wrong! It probably just pissed her off more.

He first became suspicious of the hack when Naseem seemed able to accurately anticipate just about everything Arnold intended to do. This, of course, easily could explain how Naseem knew his phone number and address. The files in Davidson's office held copies of the bill of sale for the house and a record of his Hans Weiser alias. Yeah, it was all making complete sense now.

He figured Mr. Davidson's computers most likely were infected with a RAT—a remote access trojan—as a result of a successful phishing attack. Invisible to the victim, the malware gave the perpetrator full access to the computer from anywhere in the world.

Hmmm....a *RAT*. This triggered a super-cool idea. If Nawzer did, in fact, have a RAT buried in Davidson's computer, was there a way to leverage that into sneaking back into Nawzer's computer? Because, if he could manage that, it shouldn't be much of a leap to then migrate to Naseem's computer. Because, if he could do that...

Holy shit!

He pulled grabbed his phone, opened the Voice Memo app and dictated the idea before another one distracted him sufficiently to forget.

Next question: how the hell did Davidson's computer get infected in the first place? More than likely, he or Joyce was tricked into downloading it. Probably in the immediate aftermath of Howie's shooting, right after Davidson agreed to represent him. That made the most sense.

Would Davidson be *that* stupid? Maybe. Maybe not. Joyce? Well, she was a complete unknown. Could have just as easily been her. But once one of their computers became infected, they all were. Including Davidson's personal ones. Definitely something they needed to resolve soon as possible. In the meantime, he should figure out a way to get a bead on Naseem. *That* was going to be way more difficult.

Well, what about the iPhone she was using last time?

He'd hacked it two months ago.

Naw, she wouldn't be stupid enough to hang onto it after the warehouse ordeal...would she? Hmmm....Okay, say she was; she wouldn't be stupid enough to call him on it.

Okay, say she had called him on it. There were numerous ways to disguise phone numbers. So, unless he figured out her wireless provider, hacked into their records, and then found her account, he was SOL. Bottom line? That particular route wasn't worth the effort.

At least the bright side of this little internal debate was that his brain seemed to be thinking rationally again. This realization helped lessen the panic still smoldering in his chest.

By now he was whizzing along on Kalakaua Avenue, the turn onto Lewers coming up on his right. Chances of stumbling across street parking within reasonable walking distance to the restaurant were beyond astronomical and he wasn't inclined to burn one extra minute searching, so, with a resigned sigh, he decided to simply uncap the KY jelly, bend over, and smile at the totally outrageous parking fee for the Sheraton Hotel garage. The upside, of course, was a guaranteed short walk to the restaurant. Not a bad trade, now that he thought about it.

He hit the turn signal.

Naseem

Naseem watched the Jew's car drive into the back entrance of the Sheraton garage, the one used mostly for delivery and loading and unloading airport shuttles. She pulled to the curb a half block away on Helumoa Road, shifted into Park, engine idling, and made sure to have her phone in hand before slipping out the door.

"Pick me up here when I call," she instructed Kasra.

Kasra climbed into the driver's seat.

"Yes, Sister."

Naseem hurried into the gaping garage entrance in search of the Jew's car, caught the red flash of brake lights, darted behind a square concrete pillar to wait and watch.

Chapter 9—Arnold

ARNOLD FIGURED NO one would mess with the car with Chance inside, so routinely left all windows lowered but the door locked. Not only would a car-jacker have to deal with Chance, but also the car alarm if he tried to open the door without the key.

He leaned in the window.

"Daddy has to go. Chance stays."

He threw in a few behind-the-ear choobers for good measure, then walked toward the same entrance he just came in. The walk along Helumoa Road was pleasant. Although the sun had settled completely below the horizon, the surrounding concrete was still radiating heat from the day and the salt air remained laced with the scent of coconut-oil suntan lotion. All very pleasant, if it weren't for the deep burrowing gut pain Naseem's call triggered.

A half block from the restaurant he recognized Davidson on the sidewalk by the front door, chatting with a woman. And wow, what a woman. A drop-dead stunning knockout! Gorgeous silky black hair, bewitchingly beautiful face, dark completion, terrific body sheathed in a clingy pink and white dress printed with tropical flowers. She looked to be what, mid-forties? Yeah, a bit younger than Davidson. Exotic.

Yeah? And how old is the dude?

No clue. But Davidson's age was beside the point. Point was...well, actually there were a couple points. The first being, he was witnessing a totally new facet of the man's life: a social life. This only intensified his guilt over disrupting their dinner plans.

The counterpoise to this, of course, was an immediate surge of relief at having a trusted friend—a lawyer with whom he could hash things through—on his side. Davidson's opinion mattered greatly. Davidson would help him navigate this clusterfuck.

As always, the lawyer was looking *tres* dapper in tropical white linen slacks, blue and white Tommy Bahama Hawaiian shirt, and light-gray Mephisto low-top kicks sans socks. Might not make the cover of *GQ*, but, hey, what the hell did it matter? Arnold paid absolutely zero interest to style.

Arnold extended his fist.

"Mr. Davidson."

The two men did their fist-bump thing, a routine they'd fallen into during the last debacle.

Davidson gave a nod toward the woman.

"Arnold, Martina."

She beamed, extending her hand.

"A pleasure to meet you, Arnold."

An accent? Italian? Arnold blinked, blinked again, realized he was staring, and dropped his eyes.

"Ahhh...nice to meet you too."

Really dude? That's the best you can come up with? Pretty fucking lame!

A chill tickled the base of his spine.

We're being watched.

He spun to look back the way he just come, quickly scanned the sidewalk and licked his lips. The feeling grew more intense.

"Arnold?" Davidson said.

Arnold returned his attention to him.

"Look, I apologize for barging in like this, but..." Then to Davidson: "Mind if we have this discussion down the street to

25

where, uh...just the two of us can talk?"

He flashed Martina an I'm-so-sorry smile.

Davidson hesitated, shooting him a decidedly curious expression.

"Yes, we can do that." Then to Martina: "This should not take long. If they call, go ahead, take the table and we will join you shortly."

She beamed at him.

"No problem. Take care of business. I'll hold the fort."

Arnold liked how she said it. Familiar, endearing, something way further along the comfortable scale than first-date acquaintances. So, what did this say about them? Arnold's interest meter pegged.

None of your business, dude.

Davidson was flashing him that weird look again.

"What?" Arnold asked.

"Where would you like to talk?"

Once again Arnold scanned the sidewalk for someone watching but milling pedestrians were making it impossible to pick up on anyone who might be singling them out. What they needed was a less congested spot.

"How about down there," he said, indicating Helumoa Road.

Helumoa Road—a narrow, block-long afterthought, more alley than road—connected with Lewers at a right angle. Its obvious advantage was sparse foot traffic, which eased Arnold's pucker factor. Slightly. Nonetheless, Arnold still did a quick three-sixty. No one within a hundred feet and only one vehicle—a panel truck—parked in a loading zone twenty feet further on toward the Sheraton garage, with no one around it. Ah, mucho better.

"This works," Arnold said.

Davidson planted his feet, straightened his posture, crossed his arms. All business.

"Proceed. Tell me exactly what happened."

Another tingle squirted down his spine. But he refused to give in to it and look.

If that's Naseem, fuck her!

"Please turn off your phone."

Davidson shot him a double take, opened his mouth, hesitated, then retrieved his mobile from his pants.

"Is it that serious?"

Growing more nervous, Arnold couldn't resist another quick down the street. Fucking feeling just wouldn't let up.

"No, no joke. I can't shake a super-creepy feeling of being watched."

Arnold watched Davidson power down the phone.

"There you are. Off." Davidson held it for Arnold to see. "Now, tell me exactly what happened."

"Nothing to tell, really. Phone rings, I pick up, and it's her. Naseem Farhad."

No need to say her name, but he wanted to leave no doubt to whom he was referring.

"What exactly did she say?"

Arnold repeated Naseem's words to him verbatim.

"What did you reply?"

"Nothing. I hung up."

Davidson started kneading his right shoulder, seemingly in thought. Finally, he said, "Damn it. I thought we were finished with this...this..."

This was the first time he'd seen the lawyer at a loss for words.

"...this bullshit."

Whoa. Davidson rarely swore, which only lent more impact to the few times he did.

Davidson pointed to the dead phone toward the end of the alley.

"And the reason for all this secrecy?"

"Overkill? Yeah, I totally get it. Maybe it is. Then again, maybe it isn't. Back there, outside the restaurant? I got this totally weird creepy feeling of being watched."

Davidson nodded.

"To tell you the truth, so did I."

That was a relief! I'm not the only one totally freaked by this.

"And the phone thing just now? What's that all about, you ask?" Arnold continued. "Well, remember a couple months ago I suspected your computer was infected?"

"I do. Distinctly, too."

"Well, we never checked that out, did we?"

Arnold hoped the use of "we" somehow diluted his sole culpability for the oversight. If forced to bet, he'd put money on Davidson not knowing how to search for, and remove malware.

"I see," Davidson said, his face taking on a totally foreign expression.

Uh-oh, don't like the sound of that.

Nor the look.

"I simply assumed..." Arnold said, realizing there was nothing to say at this point to excuse the mistake.

Davidson said, "It is what it is. Just one more thing we must deal with now." Pause. "Anything else you remember about the call?"

Arnold welcomed moving the conversation to a more productive topic.

"Nothing. The entire call lasted probably a whooping five seconds. I think it's her way of telling me nothing's changed."

"Remind me, that business at the warehouse, was that two months ago?"

"It was."

"In other words," Davidson continued, "you believe she obtained your number from my computer."

Davidson didn't look pleased.

"Yeah, exactly."

"That certainly complicates things."

Arnold shrugged.

"Perhaps. Perhaps not."

Chapter 10—Naseem

NASEEM STOOD FIFTY feet from the Jew and his lawyer on Helumoa Road, hidden by a large palm in a planter at the rear-entrance alcove to the Halepuna hotel, watching them talk. The spot provided a perfect view through the palm fronds while hiding her. The Jew cast occasional glances in her direction but it became obvious the large palm sufficiently shielded her from being seen. Excellent. The Jew's apparent nervousness confirmed that the phone call served its purpose. She felt relieved.

And if the Jew came toward her? She'd simply slip through the automatic glass doors, dash down a short hall, through the lobby, and on out the front onto Kalia Road, placing her just a short distance from where he must walk to reenter the garage. Yes, Allah surely must be smiling upon her.

It came as no surprise nor mystery to see the lawyer here either, for she knew all about his recently purchased condominium. She knew, in fact, every detail of the transaction, right down to unit number, building floor, unit floorplan, and total cost. Thanks to Nawzer, she even knew his inbound and outbound seat assignments and scheduled departure time.

It was a truly amazing luxury to possess the in-depth intelligence Nawzer could reap from the lawyer's computers, both office and personal. As an added bonus, he could obtain the man's phone texts. Naseem didn't understand—nor did she wish to listen to—Nawzer's complex explanation of how he'd accomplished such magic. She only concerned herself with the results. Yes, she harbored many serious issues regarding the decadent lifestyle Nawzer had slid into since relocating from New York to LA, but most of those distractions were easily ignored just as long as all his work effort was focused on supporting of the Jihad.

As she watched the Jew and the lawyer huddle in conversation, she made another prediction: the Jew and Davidson will phone FBI Agent Gary Fisher. Probably within the next half hour. She smiled at this conviction, for it provided both power and a decided advantage. Almost as if she could actually listen in on their conversation.

Yes, this time her mission would not fail.

This time Allah would surely grant her victory.

Chapter 11—Arnold

"DAMNIT! YOU KNOW my computers contain extremely sensitive information! *Your* file, for example. This needs to stop immediately. It is difficult to comprehend how we could have forgotten something so critical."

Arnold liked his use of "we," on account of evenly dispersing responsibility for the mistake. Although he appreciated this kindness, he also realized the lion's share of blame rested squarely upon his shoulders. Assuming, of course, the computers were infected.

"Can you fix this tonight?" Davidson asked.

Arnold had never seen the lawyer this upset. Ever. It was...well, a bit scary.

"You mean, like, right this minute?"

"Yes, right this minute."

Arnold scanned the alley for the umpteenth time.

"I could, but let's chill waaay down and think about this a moment, Mr. Davidson." He made a lower-your-voice motion with his hand. "Let's consider the ramifications before we react and possibly destroy a potential opportunity."

He had yet to devote any serious thought toward how to effectively weaponize Nawzer's malware—if such a strategy existed—against him, but knew instinctively that the possibility to was viable. He simply needed a focused block of uninterrupted time to work out a plan.

"There is nothing to consider, Arnold! This is an egregious invasion of privacy affecting not only me but every one of my clients. This cannot be allowed to continue!"

A passerby on the sidewalk turned to stare in their direction, prompting Arnold to flash the quiet-down signal again.

"Yeah, no problem, I can take care of it..." Arnold said, purposely lowering his voice. "Probably from home. But bear with me a minute and hear me out before we step on a potential landmine. Okay?"

Davidson kept slamming his fist into his palm, *smack smack smack*, red face pinched into obvious angry frustration. Arnold glanced toward the parking garage again, then to the back entrance to a hotel. Nothing.

Yeah? So what? Naseem or one of her lieutenants could easily be in either of those spots, watching, yet obscured from sight.

He turned back to Davidson.

"Here's the deal. We both know how we want this to end, right? We want that bitch put away for good."

As in dead.

"That we do."

"And if there's one thing we've learned from our past experience with her, it's just how slippery she can be." He paused briefly to let this sink in. "We also know this game's for real, that things aren't going to end well for one of us. Right?"

Davidson said nothing.

"What I'm saying is, whatever we do next, it needs to be planned with extreme caution on accounta we'll only going get *one* shot—if we're lucky—at her. I want to be goddamned sure that shot hits her right between the fucking eyes. Understand what I'm saying?"

Davidson laughed at that—which seemed to drain a bit of tension from him.

"So...what I'm thinking," Arnold continued, "is our first priority is to bring Agent Fisher up to speed on this. Right?"

Davidson sighed and nodded.

"You are correct, of course. But allowing him continued access..." He shook his head in disgust. "I at least need to know how he was able to get in there."

Goddamn it! That creepy eerie feeling just would *not* go away. He refused to look again and give whoever—Naseem or one of her accomplices—the satisfaction of seeing him so rattled.

"We can remove it at any time we choose, but before we do, let's talk to Fisher, see if he wants their cybercrime dudes in on it. They might be able to learn something we can't."

"That is a valid point, but..." Davidson appeared to rein in his emotions. "You are sure there is a virus on my computers?"

"I'd put money on it. And I also guarantee we'll get rid of it at some point."

"You understand, this paralyzes my office until it is removed?"

"I don't see why that is. What's changed in the past five minutes? You've been using those computers every day. Nothing's *really* changed in the past hour, right?"

Davidson didn't look like he was buying that.

"Look of it this way," Arnold said, scrambling for an argument the lawyer might buy. "That malware's a crime scene. As such, it shouldn't be touched until after it's been thoroughly investigated and documented. Make sense?"

"Point made," Davidson said grudgingly.

"Okay, so we call Fisher now?"

Davidson sighed.

"Yes, but I suspect this will end up requiring more than one brief phone call. I have Martina to consider."

Oops. Completely forgot about her.

"Tell you what. Go back," Arnold said. "Enjoy dinner and I'll call Fisher. We can touch base after you're done."

Not his first choice, but if this were Rachael...

"Goddamnit!"

Davidson spun around and began walking briskly toward Lewers. Arnold hurried to catch up.

"She live here on the island?" Arnold asked.

Davidson reached Lewers, turned right, then slowed as he approached the restaurant, Arnold trailing behind. Martina was out on the sidewalk waiting.

"We have a table on the second floor," she said, smiling. "I asked them to set it for three."

She looked directly at Arnold now.

Again, Arnold found himself totally enchanted. Most definitely a keeper.

Davidson shook his head sadly.

"Sorry, M, I am afraid a serious matter needs immediate attention. You mind if I walk you back to the hotel and call after we resolve it?"

She flashed an absolute killer smile.

"No problem, but I'm starved, so if you don't mind, I'll just catch dinner at Orchids and maybe you will join me for a nightcap later?"

She spoke with a suggestively raised eyebrow.

Wow! Arnold certainly could appreciate the magic.

Nice choice, Mr. Davidson.

Davidson said to Arnold, "She is at the Halekulani. I will return in...say"—he glanced at his watch, "ten minutes."

Ten minutes? The walk should take, like, maybe five, tops. Interesting. His antennae sensed a super-intense energy of something stronger than casual friendship. This realization jolted him with another pang of guilt for having destroyed their dinner plans. However...

"Where is your condo?" Arnold asked him.

"Over by the marina. Why?"

"Did you park nearby?"

"No. I took an Uber."

Well, that simplified things.

"Okay, so how about this;" Arnold said. "I parked at the Sheraton. We walk Martina to the hotel and then I drive us to your place."

Clearly less than thrilled with the suggestion, Davidson held his tongue. He turned to Martina.

"Sorry, M. I will explain later."

Seeing Davidson and Martina in such intimate contact brought home how intensely he missed Rachael. Frequent phone calls and Skype chats helped bring them together but could never come close to the satisfaction of personal contact. He couldn't allow Naseem's appearance to destroy his dream of eventually being together...

First things first. Speak with Fisher, get this under control, then worry about long-term repercussions.

The only thing he knew for certain was that something bad was about to happen.

Chapter 12—Naseem

NASEEM SLIPPED QUICKLY from her hiding place through the hotel, out the front entrance, then through the Sheraton garage to the circular drive serving the hotel. At the curb, head bowed to prevent security cameras from recording a full facial shot, she dialed Kasra.

Several questions now swirled through her mind: Who was the woman with Davidson? Did she represent a threat? Could she be weaponized to manipulate the Jew? Or was she simply an insignificant player? These questions fed her growing suspicions that Nawzer had been slacking off from actively monitoring the lawyer's computers. Either that, or he wasn't informing her of all developments. Which raised an important issue: why had he failed to provide concrete details about the Jew's girlfriend? Name? Place of residence, employment...she wanted answers. Tonight.

Kasra answered.

"Yes, Sister?"

"Pick me up in front of the Sheraton."

"Two minutes."

Naseem terminated the call. On any cellphone, even an encrypted one, she deliberately kept calls brief as possible, a point she hammered home to every one of her followers as an ultra-important security rule. Phones were used only for the most basic communications that, if intercepted and monitored, could yield little if any substantive information. All other discussions were to be held only on a special Dark Web service similar to Skype and known only to a trusted few. Such rules were designed and enforced to make it almost impossible for NSA, CIA, or FBI to monitor them.

She texted Nawzer: *Davidson is with a woman. Who?*

Thirty seconds later a reply came back: *A friend. No worry.*

Perhaps. Perhaps not. Time would tell. But definitely a topic for in-depth discussion after he arrived. But he was not her only source of information. She would contact a Seattle sympathizer for more information on the Jew's girlfriend, Rachael.

Kasra braked at the loading zone. Naseem opened the door and quickly slid into the passenger seat.

"Pull around to the entrance he used."

"Yes, Sister."

Kasra continued around the circular drive and back onto the street from which she entered only moments ago.

Chapter 13—Arnold

ARNOLD WAITED PATIENTLY across the street from the gaping entrance to the inviting Halekulani lobby of glossy white marble, rich wood paneling and tasteful Zen decor. He watched Davidson wrap his arms around Martina as they exchanged an abbreviated but meaningful kiss. It was obvious to anyone but a brain-dead observer that the kiss contained more than a perfunctory good-night peck. Way more. Way interesting. Just one more facet of Davidson he'd never witnessed.

They exchanged words before she turned and disappeared into the cavernous lobby. Davidson watched for a moment before ambling back across the street toward Arnold.

"I like her," Arnold offered as Davidson drew within earshot.

Davidson responded by checking his watch. All business. Arnold totally got it.

"Where do you suggest we make the call?" Davidson asked briskly. "If we believe my computer is not secure, the condo is out of the question. How does right here sound?"

"Why the hell not? Naseem probably knows exactly what we're up to, so I don't see that we have anything to lose, do you?"

"Nothing."

Arnold readied the cellphone.

"All set?"

Naseem

Naseem watched the Jew talk into the phone, but his hand obscured his face, making lip reading impossible. The purpose of the call, she believed, was of little mystery or importance. The lawyer and the Jew were surely speaking with Fisher.

Exactly as planned.

Well, not exactly. The plan's first iteration didn't take into account Davidson being in Honolulu. The end result, however, really didn't change; in response to their conversation with the FBI, the Jew and his lawyer would either fly to Seattle or Fisher would come here. Either course of action would likely correspond with Nawzer's arrival.

She preferred the Jew not be in Honolulu when Nawzer attempted to hack his system and program the bomb's triggering mechanism, but if he were, she had a contingency plan mapped out.

Nawzer argued that there was nothing to be gained by being in Honolulu, that he could accomplish the same things more effectively in Los Angeles where all his tools were available to him.

She countered that thus far, each of his attempts to penetrate the Jew's security ended in miserable failure, so why not try a fresh approach in the vicinity of the Jew's house? Besides, it was too risky to ship the bomb's triggering mechanism. He then argued that he was at risk of being identified at a TSA checkpoint. He refused to believe the claim of Kasra—a TSA agent—that no travel alert had been issued for him, and argued that she couldn't be 100 percent certain of this.

His arguments did not change her mind.

She interpreted his reluctance to travel as nothing more than evidence of how deeply corrupting his soft, convenient American life had eroded his resolve. His belief in Allah might remain strong, but his appetite for jihad was clearly not. To make matters worse, her

LA sources had sent her photographic evidence that his lover was a non-believer.

None of which really mattered *if* he was able to give her the pleasure of stealing the Jew's treasure before taking his life.

And if Nawzer failed to produce the expected results?

He'd be forced to watch his blond California lover beheaded in the moments before meeting the same fate.

Chapter 14—Arnold

FISHER ASKED, "WHERE the hell are you?"

Arnold's cell was set to speakerphone so that Davidson could participate. Arnold flashed Davidson a "what-do-I-say-now?" look. Davidson responded with a "he's-got-to-know" shrug.

"Yo, Gold, still there?"

Man up. Do it.

"Honolulu," Arnold admitted sheepishly.

"Are you shitting me!"

Arnold rolled his eyes.

"I shit you not. I'm in the same house."

"Jesus Hieronymus Christ, Gold...please tell me you're joking." Arnold said nothing. "That's right up there as one of the all-time stupidest moves I've ever heard of, and believe me, in this job, I hear a lot."

Davidson made a circular hand motion; get on with it. Arnold flashed pleading eyes at Davidson. Davidson just shrugged.

"You've made your point. Can we move on to point of this call?" Arnold said.

"Do you have any ideas how she tracked you down so easily?" Fisher asked.

Uh-oh, he was about to step in the dogshit again.

Davidson leaned closer to the phone.

"Palmer Davidson here. We suspect—and I emphasize we *do not* have confirmatory evidence—yet—that someone in Naseem's cell hacked my computer. All his contact information is contained there."

"Ahhh, makes sense," Fisher said. "So, help me out here...why are *you* there?"

Davidson quickly summarized the coincidental circumstances.

"A new condo in downtown Honolulu! My oh my, did I go into the wrong end of law enforcement. Must be nice kicking back with a Mai Tai and a few malignant melanomas."

Arnold sliced a palm, stopping Davidson from the sarcastic reply he figured was coming.

"What we have here is your classic good-news, bad-news situation," Fisher continued. "Bad for Gold, because he's obviously at risk again. Good for us, because we now have another shot at her. And as long as we're on the subject, have any idea where that call originated?"

"Thought about that on the drive over but don't have anything concrete. I'll put some work in on it later."

"No background noise or static...anything of value?"

"Not that I can think of."

"You didn't happen to record the number, did you? Area code? Anything like that?"

"No. I was watching the game when it came. The caller ID showed ANONYMOUS, so I almost dumped it. Still not sure why I even bothered answering. I'll see what I can dig up once I'm home, but if I do track down a number, I suspect it's spoofed."

"I agree, but check into it anyway."

"Roger that."

"Excellent. This is how I want us to proceed..."

42

Naseem

Naseem watched the Jew and the lawyer talk to Fisher, which of course, meant the FBI would once again focus their attention on Honolulu and raise local security to the highest level. She'd been enjoying the temporary lull following the warehouse disaster, for it allowed her sympathizers to operate more freely.

It had also lulled the Jew into a false sense of security, making it much easier to surveil him over the ensuing weeks. As her intelligence grew, so did the granularity of her plan. She now knew his daily routines, preferred routes, stores, even the brand of beer he drank.

In spite of all this knowledge, one crucial unanswered detail from two months ago constantly nagged her, weighing down her mind, making sleep even more problematic: exactly how did the FBI locate the warehouse?

Had a sympathizer turned traitor?

Or had the FBI somehow discovered and penetrated their communication network without Nawzer detecting it? This was just one more item on the ever-growing list of topics she intended to discuss with him upon his arrival. It also served a perfect example of the need to meet in person.

Of all her sympathizers, who had the most to gain by sabotaging her plan?

For weeks, one by one, she'd been carefully eliminating members through careful analysis of their behavior and through her intelligence members. However, a handful remained to sort through.

The other very real possibility, of course, was that it had been the Jew who discovered the warehouse and turned the information over to the FBI. This raised the question; if able to capture him alive, should she interrogate him before killing him? These unresolved questions represented the only loose ends to her plan.

However, if Nawzer could penetrate the Jew's security, she

believed these loose ends could be easily eliminated.

Her attention returned to the scene playing out before her. Once again, the Jew was proving to be extremely predictable, so at this point she saw no further need to risk discovery.

"We return to the house now, Kasra."

"Before we see more?"

"There is no need. I know exactly what will happen tonight. Besides, I have much work to finish this evening."

Having a talk with Nawzer now took the highest priority.

Chapter 15—Arnold

"SOON AS WE'RE off this call," Fisher said, "I'll notify our Honolulu counterterrorism that she's back in play. They'll issue a BOLO to every fucking law enforcement agency from ATF to Fish and Game. We know she was in that warehouse just moments before the shit hit the fan and that realistically, her only way off the island was by air. We clamped down on that route tighter than a whale's asshole. I suspect she's been holed up with sympathizers since then."

"In the meantime, what should we do?" Arnold asked.

"Just hang tight and I'll catch the first available flight. This case is turning into an epic pain in the ass for every one of us. I want to close the sonofabitch for good."

"Whoa, hold on before you do that. We're coming there ASAP."

Davidson cocked his head, mouthed, *Really?*

"When and why?" Fisher asked.

Arnold's mind was back to rabid bat speed, tossing around ideas to entrap Naseem. He had a general idea, but a shitload of fine-tuning was necessary before it would be ready to lay out for Fisher.

He said, "Davidson needs to be back in the office," and raised eyebrows at Davidson. Davidson gave an if-you-say-so shrug.

"Plus, we need to check out Mr. Davidson's computers,"

Arnold continued. "Any chance of having John Chang assigned to this?"

Chang was an FBI geek assigned to the counterterrorism team. Arnold worked with him briefly in the immediate aftermath of Howie's murder, when the Naseem saga was in its infancy and the Green Lake house had not yet gone up in flames.

"I'll look into Chang's present responsibilities. If he's available, great. If not, I'll get another tech from that unit. But before touching anything on Davidson's computers, we need to coordinate efforts to make sure we don't step on each other's toes."

"I agree," Arnold said, feeling vindicated for talking Davidson down from taking immediate action against the suspected malware. "The main reason *I'm* flying over is to warn Rachael in person. She's at risk too and needs to understand that. I'm worried if Naseem knows about her..."

"Good point," Fisher agreed. "Be in my office by Wednesday morning. Otherwise I need to be there. Get me an answer by nine tomorrow at the latest. We can't afford to delay this."

Oh man! Was that it possible to arrange?

"Look, Mr. Fisher. I'm *seriously* worried about Rachael. There any way you can protect her until this thing stabilizes?"

"You have evidence to indicate she's under direct threat?"

"No, nothing directly. But if that malware's in Mr. Davidson's computers, Naseem has to know about her. That alone guarantees she's at risk."

"Sorry, Gold, but we simply don't have sufficient manpower to expend on your girlfriend. How you want to handle her security is your responsibility. If you're really worried, I suggest hiring security. This simply underscores the necessity to find Naseem. So, how about it: can you two be in my office Wednesday morning? Davidson?"

"I am scheduled for return Wednesday. I will try to move it."

Davidson raised his eyebrows at Arnold.

"How about you, Gold?"

Jesus, the man wasn't kidding.

"I'll see what I can do and get back to you."

"All right. In the meantime," Fisher said, "it's critical to know if Davidson's computers are infected or not. Can one of our techs access your office tomorrow morning, Palmer?"

Arnold immediately jumped in with, "I can probably settle that tonight." He asked Davidson, "Is your laptop with you?"

He would be surprised if it wasn't.

"It is."

"Can you access your office from it?" Arnold asked.

"I can."

"In that case," Arnold said, "if any one of his computers are infected, they all are. I can see if his laptop's infected soon as we hang up. What do you think, Mr. Fisher?"

"Do it," Fisher answered. "Call me soon as you have results. Then let me know your travel plans. Tonight. I want to roll on this ASAP. Remember, in my office no later than nine a.m., Seattle time. Oh, before we go, you checked *your* computers yet, Gold?"

Damn good question.

"I have security running all the time, but right when she called, I started a full system scan. That takes about an hour, so I'll have results when I get home. I seriously doubt Nawzer's been able to penetrate my firewall."

Strange how certain events radically change the way we live our lives. Before this Naseem thing embroiled him, he'd never been a team player. Now he loved being part of the team.

"Excellent. Once more, just so we're all on the same page, here are your assignments: Gold, check Davidson's laptop and report back straightaway. Then both of you make arrangements to be in Seattle Wednesday morning. Got it?"

"Sir, yes sir!" Arnold saluted.

Davidson laughed at that.

Chapter 16—Arnold

DAVIDSON FLASHED A wry smile.

"Guess we just received our marching orders."

With a laugh, Arnold returned the phone to his pocket.

"True that. But actually, I'm super amped he's taken charge of this. I feel safer already."

"I agree. However, it might not kill him to smooth off a few edges to his messages." He made an after-you-Alphonse motion toward the back entrance to the parking garage. "Shall we?"

Arnold started walking.

"We shall."

As they approached the Mini, Chance had his head out the passenger window as far as possible out without falling, his whines growing in volume and frequency the closer they came, tail going like sixty, swinging his entire rear side to side. He gave two staccato barks as Davidson reached for the passenger door. Rather than a serious don't-mess-with-the-pack bark, this one was his long-time-no-sniff bark.

Arnold opened the driver-side door.

"Back seat."

Chance jumped to the rear with his tail still fanning the thick humid air. After an unsuccessful attempt to brush doggie hair from the passenger seat, Davidson slid in. He was barraged with sloppy doggie kisses and returned the love with a bout of behind-the-ear choobers.

Arnold made a mental note to run the Mini through the carwash on Kapiolani soon as (make that, *if*) life returned to normal. The seats and floor mats needed serious vacuuming and all the side-windows were smeared with doggie nose art in spite of being down most of the time.

"Don't let him become a nuisance," Arnold warned. "You know what a mooch pooch he can be for attention."

"No problem. It comforts me to know he is still with you."

"Always. So, where we headed?"

"Straight out Ala Moana Boulevard and follow my directions. It is easy. The garage always has a few empty guest stalls, so no need to worry about finding street parking."

They drove in silence, Chance's head out the rear window; Davidson facing straight ahead, apparently deep in thought.

Having Davidson riding shotgun instead of 2,600 miles across the Pacific felt comforting. Not only that, but their proximity brought into focus how much he missed their easy camaraderie and friendship. Which, now that he thought about it, seemed totally strange given their generational difference. Did Davidson miss their bond too or was he just another client?

"Stay in the right lane up ahead. It turns onto Atkinson Drive," Davidson said, breaking Arnold's train of thought. "I am in the building to our right."

As he rounded the curve, Arnold glimpsed the building; a generic, architecturally ho-hum high-rise, stereotypically seen in large cities, especially nearby expansive marinas and beaches; San Diego, Miami, and Fort Lauderdale, for example.

"Slow down. Up ahead on the right is a short drive that takes you straight into the parking garage. There always is one guest spot available."

Arnold did as instructed.

"Your turn is coming up...right...now, then straight into the garage."

Ahead loomed the entrance to an expansive parking garage linking twin towers. He realized he'd passed this apartment complex countless times without ever noticing it.

Then again, why should I? Never had reason to.

So typical...we spend our lives processing only a fraction of the various surroundings until an event gives one cognitive significance. Must be an adaptive brain filter.

Before closing his door, Arnold asked, "Okay for me to bring Chance?"

Sure, he could keep him in the car again, but after leaving him in the Sheraton garage he preferred to take him, especially not knowing how long this might take.

"I'll keep him on leash," he quickly added, hoping to influence the decision.

"No problem. This building seems extremely pet-friendly. One sees dogs in the elevators all the time."

"Awesome! I like it."

Chance shot out of the car like a rocket.

The lobby struck him as generically sterile and bland as the exterior: polished concrete floor, darkly stained concierge desk, sparse and uncomfortable-looking furniture, mailbox alcove, elevator alcove. As they passed through the front door, the concierge—a surfer-looking dude in a scarlet palm frond Hawaiian shirt—glowered at Arnold from behind the desk.

"Keep your dog on leash."

Arnold saluted.

"Yes, sir," without breaking pace.

A brightly lit elevator awaited. Davidson thumbed the button for the thirty-first floor and the doors glided noiselessly together.

"Wow," Arnold said. "You got to have a one killer view, right?"

"It certainly has that. Sorry about the dog Nazi. I have had minimal interactions with him, definitely nothing more than perfunctory hellos."

"Hey, not a problem."

Arnold gave Chance a few choobers for good measure.

He found himself curious to see what the interior looked like. It couldn't possibly rival Davidson's Queen Anne home. This was, after all, a getaway rather than a primary residence. Besides, he just took possession of it, so...

Compact. One bedroom, one bath. Pretty much what was expected given the building's yawn-evoking exterior. Functional utilitarian floorplan. Neutral light-gray walls, no artwork (yet), beige carpet, matching beige tile. Uncharacteristically Davidson. The showstopper, of course, was the killer panorama of the expansive marina directly across Ala Moana Boulevard from the living room and bedroom. Being night, only streetlights and the well-lit marina were visible, leaving the ocean a black void. The hotel-bland interior made Arnold suspect the unit's prior life was likely a rental or timeshare. Undoubtedly, over time, Davidson would transform the it into his own style.

Arnold scrambled for something positive to say, but ended up with; "Great view! How many days have you been here now?"

Davidson accordioned open the glass doors to a small balcony off the living room.

"Four. It will obviously require numerous trips to transform it to my vision, but it serves as a wonderful start. No buyer's remorse at all. I say this in complete honesty; I am thrilled to have finally taken the first step. Thanks to *you*, by the way...your pep talk broke my inertia. That was all I needed."

Pleasing to hear, because in a small fractional way, Arnold had finally given something back to the man who'd done so much for him.

"Is it okay for Chance be on the balcony?"

"Precisely the reason I opened the door. He can guard the harbor for us."

Chance needed no invitation. The moment Arnold released the leash, he trotted out, pressed his nose to the glass balustrade and settled down to gaze out over the harbor and freeway.

Davidson remained at the threshold, facing the living room.

"My first order of business is to find a few nice pieces of art, preferably by local artists. Once I have those, I will begin to replace furniture." He gave a sweep of his hand. "For the time being, this serves me adequately."

Arnold turned his attention to the business at hand. Davidson's open MacBook Pro sat on a small coffee table in front of an L-shaped couch. For a paranoid moment, he wondered if Naseem's sympathizers had been able to plant a monitoring device in the condo before Davidson could move in. After all, if Naseem knew about the purchase...*those fuckers!*

Then again, what difference did it really make at this point?

Probably moot if Davidson's devices were already compromised. And that particular issue would be settled in a matter of minutes. He dropped onto the couch.

"It asleep or off?"

"Asleep."

Davidson folded himself into a club chair to the right of the table.

Arnold tapped the space bar to waken the machine.

"And your PIN?"

Chapter 17—Arnold

SHOCKED, ARNOLD SLUMPED back in the couch and began to massage his temples.

Could it be true?

Davidson stiffened.

"What is it?"

"This machine doesn't have any antivirus software, but I'm not really all that good with Macs. Am I missing something?"

"You are correct. I did not install any," Davidson replied somewhat defensively.

Arnold studied him.

Was the man joking?

Nope, Davidson looked dead-ass serious.

He scrambled for a diplomatic way to tell him that was flat-out stupid, but couldn't dredge up any. The room went silent except for a barely perceptible hum of the laptop fan and muted intermittent road traffic thirty-one floors below.

Davidson finally cleared his throat.

"Your expression...did I do something wrong?"

Arnold realized he was frowning. A perfect example why he never played poker in person.

Now what?

"I have been led to believe viruses attack only PCs and not Macintoshes," Davidson added defensively.

How many times had Arnold heard that bit of digital folklore? Not so often in recent years but still...

With a shrug, he said, "There's no way I can settle the question without installing an antivirus package. You okay with that?"

He'd be shocked if Davidson objected at this point.

Chapter 18—Arnold

ARNOLD LEANED BACK on the couch, thinking through a way to answer the questions without interfering with whatever strategy they developed during future discussions with Fisher.

Call him and ask if he should bounce his next steps off John Chang?

Was Chang even assigned to this case? One small mistake potentially could tip Nawzer that they were on to him—assuming, of course, he was the asshole who infected Davidson's machine. On the other hand, at the moment, Team Arnold needed clarity: Were Davidson's computers infected or not? Fuck it. Just proceed with extreme caution and gather as much information as possible.

"Do we have a problem?" Davidson asked.

Another chill tapped the trigger spot between his shoulder blades. Arnold pushed off the couch and nodded toward the balcony.

Once outside, he whispered, "Did you check this place for bugs?"

Davidson recoiled in shock.

"No. Did not even consider it, it being new. Why?" Then immediately added, "Yes, I get it. You are absolutely right. If they know about this condo..."

"It's a bit late to worry about it now, on accounta what we've already discussed, but no harm in being super careful moving forward."

"I agree. How shall we proceed?"

Arnold scratched his head while blowing a breath.

"Here's the issue. Although we *assume* the computer and phone are infected, we need to actually prove it. And the only way we can do that install antivirus software. Follow me?"

"I do."

"Here's the rub: if Nawzer happens to be watching your computer when I run the antivirus scan, he'll know that we know the machine's compromised, right? After all, why would you suddenly be protecting this machine now?"

Davidson nodded.

"Ahhh...I see. Interesting conundrum. What is your solution?"

"I assume you have wi-fi in here, right?" Arnold asked

"Correct."

"Just your unit or is it common to the building?"

"It is for just my unit. It is bundled with the cable and phone."

"Is it password-protected?" Arnold asked.

"It is."

"Okay, so here's the plan. I disconnect your router only for as long as it takes to run the scan. If we find something, we don't touch it. Then, once the scan's finished, I uninstall it and restart your modem. Nobody's the wiser and next time he checks, everything looks exactly the same as before. You okay with this?"

"Absolutely. Do what is best."

"Good. When we're back inside, don't talk. What's your password?"

"Mycondo with an uppercase M."

After double-checking that a copy of Norton was installing on Davidson's Mac, Arnold motioned him to hand him his phone. A quick scan of the apps revealed none of the well-known traps. In fact, the iPhone contained only a few apps. Next, he inspected Settings.

Interesting...he motioned Davidson back to the balcony.

"Do you use this"—he held up the phone—"as a personal hotspot?"

Davidson shook his head.

"I do not know what that is."

"Didn't think so. Second question; do you make calls through your iCloud account?"

Davidson appeared equally baffled.

"Not that I know of. I only use the phone to call and text and have never changed a thing on the phone since removing it from the box. Why?"

"In that case, someone's made a few changes for you."

"How?"

"Long story short, Nawzer can do it from your computer by linking them."

Davidson slumped against the railing, visibly shaken. Arnold reached out, held onto his left arm to steady him.

"Whoa, watch it, Mr. Davidson. Everything will work out. This is nothing we can't work around. We just need to be careful moving forward. C'mon, there's still have a ton of work to do. Including our travel arrangements."

The computer indicated the antivirus had just downloaded, so Arnold started a full system scan to identify—but not remove—any threats. Once that was underway, he motioned Davidson back to the balcony.

"The scan's running. Our next item is to establish secure communication until this is over."

"Are you thinking burners?"

Arnold nodded.

"Yep."

"Damnit, mine are in Seattle."

"Let's make a short shopping trip."

Chapter 19—Arnold

ARNOLD AND DAVIDSON said nothing on the ride back up to the thirty-first floor, both of them now carrying out-of-the-box TracFones primed with prepaid twenty-five-dollar, five-hundred-minute plans. Before leaving the store, they'd activated the phones, programed each other's number into speed dial, and confirmed that the devices functioned properly. This last step was probably overkill, but Arnold wanted to verify they worked, especially if needed in an emergency. He firmly believed in not taking technology for granted.

As Davidson was about to unlock the door, Arnold touched his arm.

"Hold on, what's our game plan?"

"We discussed this in the car."

"We did, but just for drill, humor me and tell me one more time."

Davidson withdrew the key and folded his hands.

"We act normally. Any discussion concerning the computer will be conducted on the balcony."

"Okay then, let's do it."

Davidson opened the front door. Arnold beelined for the computer while Chance wandered back out onto the balcony to resume his role as harbor guard dog. Davidson opened the wine fridge, stepped back to study the bottles.

The scan completed during their trip to Target, so Arnold flashed Davidson a thumbs-up and went to work, but more slowly than if it were a PC. His highest comfort level was with Windows or Linux—SAM's operating system—having only infrequently worked with the Apple operating system.

"Might I interest you in a glass of wine?" Davidson asked.

Without looking up from the screen, Arnold said: "Is a bear Catholic? Does the pope shit in the woods?"

"I take as a yes."

"You are correct."

"Unfortunately, my current selection is quite limited. I have only been wine shopping once and that was at Costco. Against all odds, I did manage to find one or two drinkable cabs."

"No problem."

Arnold continued to work full-out in an effort to limit the computer's downtime in the off chance Naseem wanted Nawzer to increase surveillance following her call.

A moment later a glass of wine appeared on the table to his left.

"Still a little cool from the wine fridge, but give it a couple minutes."

Davidson then held up his glass in a toast. Arnold paused to clink glasses with him.

"To health and happiness," Davidson said.

"To health and happiness," Arnold echoed before adding, "and Naseem's destruction."

Davidson shot him a surprised, questioning look.

Gotta watch it, dude.

Five minutes later, Arnold pushed up from the couch and, glass in hand, nodded toward the balcony. Davidson pushed the slider shut after joining him at the railing. Chance paid them no attention whatsoever.

"Well? What did you learn?" Davidson whispered.

"Surprise-surprise, you're infected." Arnold paused for an initial sip of wine, having ignored the glass until now. He held it up but couldn't really appreciate the color and clarity out here on the dark balcony. "Hmm...not bad. What did you say this is?"

"And you left it there, just as discussed?" Davidson said, ignoring the question.

"Yep. I also copied it to a flash drive before uninstalling Norton. Everything's back on-line now, looking the same as it was an hour ago. If, by sheer bad luck and unfortunate timing, Nawzer *did* try to monitor you while it was disconnected, all he'll know is that your wi-fi was down for an hour and that's innocently explained for any number of reasons. I mean, hell, you just moved in, so, like, maybe you had a reason to unplug the router when rearranging things. And when he examines the machine, nothing's changed."

"Shall we update Fisher now?" Davidson asked.

"No, I'll do that on the way home." Arnold checked his watch. "Jesus! There's still a shitload to do tonight, like arranging our flights." He paused for one last sip. "Before I jet, let's go over our next steps to make sure to not overlook anything."

"Good idea."

"First, I apologize again this shit came along at such a bad time for you, what with your inaugural visit and all."

"Not to worry. It is a valid reason. Besides, my vacation pales in comparison what you face. Now that I have this condo," Davidson pointed toward the living room, "I can pop over whenever my schedule permits. Which I suspect, will be more often now."

"Thanks for understanding," Arnold said. "Okay, back to our to-do list; your first priority is move up your return. Tuesday works best for me. Soon as you nail that down, call me with the details and I'll see what I can do. Ideally, I'll shot for the same flight, but if that's impossible, I'll somehow do my best to be in Fisher's office Wednesday morning. We good?"

"We are." Davidson swirled his wine in the glass. "I'll call the airline straightaway."

"Can't thank you enough, Mr. Davidson." Arnold gave him a good-natured punch on the shoulder.

"All right then." He opened the slider. "C'mon, boy."

Arnold led Chance to the front door, setting the unfinished wine on the kitchen counter along the way.

"Thanks for the tour," he said. "You done good, getting this place."

Chapter 20—Naseem

NASEEM DROPPED INTO a chair at the kitchen table while Kasra busied herself at the stove, heating water for tea. After waking her laptop, she logged into the Dark Web message board used exclusively for secure communication between sympathizers.

It would be simpler to call Nawzer on his encrypted cellphone, but he refused to use it, arguing that if it ever fell into the hands of law enforcement, they could use it to locate her. She suspected this was nothing but a convenient fabrication to further shield his degenerate LA lifestyle from inopportune interruptions. She never challenged him with this suspicion, choosing instead to bide her time and wait until he'd served her purpose. Then she would she take executive action.

Good as Nawzer was at maintaining the group's digital security and intelligence-gathering, no one was indispensable.

Certainly not him.

Seeing the lawyer with the Jew caused her to realize that it had been days since Nawzer last updated her about Davidson's activities. Yes, she knew of his condo purchase and trip here, but now, with him and the Jew actively working together, Nawzer should monitor his computer much more closely. Nawzer would, of course, be arriving in Honolulu the day after tomorrow, but she wanted an update this evening. Waiting another forty-eight hours was unacceptable.

She logged onto the message board under one of her many pseudonyms, posted a short message for him to call immediately, and cut the link. Her online time amounted to a mere thirty seconds. She sat back to plan her next steps.

"Is the tea ready, Sister?"

Arnold

Arnold slipped into his usual spot at the scarred picnic table while Chance explored tree trunks and shrub for scents laid down since their last visit. Coordinating with Davidson and Fisher felt reassuring, knowing they had just taken a first step in formulating an offense.

He dialed Fisher.

It rang twice before, "Yeah, Gold. What news you got for me?"

"Just finished on Mr. Davidson's laptop and on my way home, so don't have anything on her phone call, but it shouldn't come as any big shocker that his laptop *is* infected. This, of course, means that every piece of his office equipment is also infected."

"Any reason to believe Nawzer knows you were in there?"

"Seriously doubt it. I took the computer completely offline, so, we should be safe."

"Excellent. You do anything with it?"

"Hell no! Didn't touch it. I did, however, make a copy. I plan on a closer look at it later tonight."

"Excellent! Let me know what you come up with. Anything else before we sign?"

Typical Fisher, all business.

"Nope. Just expect another call later tonight."

"No problem. I'm open for business twenty-four-seven."

Nawzer

The computer beeped a distinctive signal: an urgent message just arrived in his in-box. Only one person would use that route of communication to reach him urgently: the bitch herself!

Nawzer faced a conflict: check the message—which would undoubtedly require a response and perhaps some research first—or finish the game? The two-minute warning just stopped the Rams' drive; they were down one point and on the Dallas 40-yard line. He had a hundred bucks on the Rams to win, no spread. He shook his head in disgust.

For the love of God...

That woman had no life. Pitiful. Not only was she a pathetic human being, but she possessed not one-tenth of the leadership qualities of her husband. If not for her marriage to him, she wouldn't have been appointed their leader as he began an extended stay in federal prison. He knew he wasn't alone in his dislike for her. None of his male comrades respected her either.

With a sigh, he carried the Stella Artois to the small study, settled into his desk chair, and paused for a refreshingly long pull before reading Naseem's message. Typical. She wanted—no, demanded—to know what had taken place in the lawyer's computer during the past forty-eight hours.

For the love of God, why?

The man was on vacation enjoying a new home. Why would he be conducting important business under such circumstances, especially on Sunday evening?

He thought better of what he was about to type: that nothing of importance had taken place. Hmmm...what would be gained by lying? Nothing. More importantly, was this a trap? To catch him in a lie? Did she know something he did not? After all, she was in Honolulu, the same city as the Jew and lawyer. The risk just was not worth the few seconds it would take to quickly look at lawyer's computer. Yes, he would look, but only after the final two minutes of play. Fuck her.

Game over, Nawzer wandered back to his desk and opened up the lawyer's office computer. As he suspected, nothing appeared changed from the last look. Next, he typed the command to take him to Davidson's laptop. But this time the message DEVICE NOT AVAILABLE flashed on screen.

Nawzer perked up.

Why was the computer suddenly unavailable? Had the lawyer turned it off? Yes, that was a possibility, but he usually only put his computers into Sleep mode. More importantly, had Naseem asked him to check because she knew something important? Thank God he did not lie!

He paused to consider this confluence of events. Somehow it must involve the Jew. But why would the Jew be in the lawyer's computer, and why tonight?

Ah, the lawyer must have contacted him. That made sense. After all, both of them were in Honolulu. Yes, but that still didn't explain why the Jew would be on the lawyer's computer. Did Davidson discover the trojan? Or was the problem all a simple mistake, perhaps a mistyped command? He should double check before responding to her.

Once again, very carefully, Nawzer reentered the commands to transport him to the lawyer's computer. Satisfied that he made no typos, he tapped the enter key as he watched the screen. The Dark Web was excellent for providing anonymity, but at the cost of severely degraded speed even in spite of a high-speed fiber-optic connection. He waited and...

Ah...this time he was seeing the directory of the lawyer's laptop. He breathed a deep sigh of relief. This could only happen if his malware remained intact. Wonderful!

A cursory check of the contents showed that nothing changed since last visit. Business as usual. He logged back onto the bulletin board and sent Naseem a brief message assuring her that the computer contained nothing of interest, especially any communication between the Jew and his lawyer.

By now the postgame analysis was finished, so he checked the time. If he left his flat immediately, he might be lucky enough to still secure a table for two before the restaurant filled with the usual crowd.

Melissa would be joining him in thirty minutes.

Chapter 21—Arnold

ARNOLD FRESHENED CHANCE'S water and slipped him a peanut-butter-flavored doggie biscuit, then checked that the sliders between the kitchen and back deck were securely locked and all the sunshades for back windows were down.

He rarely implemented such security precautions, preferring to keep all shades up and sliders wide open to allow lovely evening breezes to continuously freshen the air in the house. Naseem's call totally derailed that routine, especially with his paranoia needle now bent around the peg. Before visiting SAM, he paused in the kitchen to run a mental checklist:

Chance taken care of: check.

Extra security precautions invoked: check.

Fisher brought up to speed on developments: check.

Okay, time to start work.

Arnold whipped up a cup of steaming hot chocolate and carried it to his desk, settled into the chair and plugged in his airpods.

"Good evening, SAM."

"Good evening, Arnold."

Although disembodied and synthesized, SAM's voice sounded surprisingly human, giving Arnold the sense of being with another person.

Allen Wyler

"Security report, please."

"System is free of threats. No attempted intrusions in the past twenty-four hours."

He fist-pumped the air. The first good news of the day.

"Launch RAID for a level-four perimeter patrol. Please provide me a complete report when finished. Then have him fly constant reconnaissance patrols between charging."

RAID—the acronym for robotic artificial intelligent drone—was the name he devised for the aircraft he built and programmed as part of a just-for-fun kick-ass personal robotics project. The name was a tad corny, but hey, you got to name him something, right? RAID "lived" on the roof and was capable of self-docking and charging in a landing pad, similar to Roomba vacuum cleaners.

Two tasks now topped his priority list: analyze the malware and take a deep dive into Naseem's phone call. Which to tackle first? Well, the phone call might yield a hint of her location, whereas the malware sure as hell wasn't going anywhere, sooo....

Naseem's call had come in on his land line, making it easy to track down the number of the caller by simply opening the webpage, logging into his account, and looking at the call history.

There it was!

He jotted down the number.

Okay, what now? Investigate it further on the off chance he could squeeze out additional information or simply hand it over to Fisher? Hmmm...there was nothing he could do with it that the FBI couldn't. Sure, he could dial it to see what happened, but doing so would invite risks he wasn't prepared to take at the moment. Besides, odds were, the number was spoofed, so why bother? Naw, definitely best to let the FBI waste their time on it.

He paused to sip his hot chocolate.

Ahhh, perfect temperature.

Fisher had also requested whatever information he might still have on the iPhone Naseem used in the days leading up to the warehouse incident. Searching this took ten minutes. Satisfied that he had the information Fisher requested, he dialed the FBI agent's number.

"What else you have for me, Gold?"

He could not hear any extraneous background noise, so he figured Fisher was still in his office. The guy seemed to go totally into heavy-duty machine-mode when working a case. Arnold gave him the information.

"Good work. Keep at it. Anything on the malware or travel plans?

"Not yet. Haven't heard back from Davidson yet and the malware's my lowest priority. Am I wrong?"

"No, you're right. Just asking. Let me know when you come up with something."

Chance wandered in, circled three times, plunked down on the floor next to Arnold's chair. Arnold leaned over, gave him a few choobers.

"Roger that."

Call finished, he wasted a few more minutes on giving Chance a serious dose of behind-the-ear choobers. He knew he'd have to board him if he and Davidson ended up flying to Seattle, so wanted to give him as much attention as possible before leaving.

Thump thump thump.

Next item of business; the malware.

Chapter 22—Arnold

THE SAFEST WAY to analyze a potentially virulent form of malware is to "air-gap" the computer; that is, completely isolate it from other devices. After all, Arnold *suspected* it had spread to Davidson's laptop from his office machines, perhaps via either a flash drive or logging in remotely. The route of infection was irrelevant and, by now, could never be nailed down.

He planned to do the analysis on his laptop after disabling all connections to SAM even though he kept SAM constantly updated with state-of-the art protection.

He made another hot chocolate. Moments later, he confirmed that his antivirus software contained the most recent updates, then turned off the laptop's wi-fi connection, air-gapping it. Good to go. Because the flash drive contained only the malware copied from Davidson's computer, the analysis went very quickly. Pretty much exactly what Arnold had expected.

He picked up the phone.

"What you got for me this time," Fisher asked by way of greeting.

"Couple things. First of all, that's one nasty-ass RAT on Davidson's machine."

"The fuck's a rat?"

"Remote Access Trojan. It allows the plantee—in this case most likely Nawzer—complete control of the infected computer. Ever called tech support for help with a computer problem?"

"Unfortunately, yes."

"Well, if they sent you a link to allow them remote-access to your computer, that's what you got."

"Huh! Any ideas how it got there?" Fisher asked.

"No, but I bet that either Davidson or his secretary were sucked in by a phishing attack. Once it infected any one of those computers—office or home—it spread to all the others just like the Coronavirus. But that's only speculation on my part."

Fisher fell silent.

Then: "Good. Least it's a start. You'll be happy to know Chang's now assigned to this case and the priority's been bumped up, so we have his undivided attention. I'll pass along to him what you just shared. If he needs more granularity, he can contact you directly. Otherwise the two of you can coordinate efforts when we meet in person. And while we're on that subject, have your travel plans nailed down yet?"

"That's just one of the things I still need take care of. Still haven't heard from Mr. Davidson. I'll call the minute it's settled."

"Excellent. Soon as I have that, I'll arrange things on this end."

"Oh, and my security scan showed there's been no recent attempt at penetrating the firewall and my system's secure."

"Good to hear."

"Oh, one final thing: Mr. Davidson and I bought a couple burners earlier."

"Nice! But think that's necessary?"

"I do, on accounta..." Arnold went on to explain why he thought Davidson's phone was also compromised.

"Good to know. Changes a few things. I agree, picking up burners was absolutely the right thing to do."

As Arnold was about to hang up, his TracFone pinged: Davidson texted.

Allen Wyler

Chapter 23—Arnold

DAVIDSON'S TEXT WAS concise: Hawaiian Airlines flight Tuesday.

Wow, that was a relief.

Arnold worried that Davidson's only option would be to fly out in the morning. Now—assuming he could nail a Tuesday flight on any airline—he'd only have thirty hours, tops, to finish things up before taking off.

He logged onto Hawaiian Airlines and, to his great relief, scored—sort of—in a good-news bad-news way. The sole remaining seat was a full-fare (aka phenomenal cost) first-class ticket. He booked his return for Thursday, giving him only one full day in Seattle. In spite of wanting more time with Rachael, he felt obliged to limit the time Chance would be at in kennel.

Then, as if to spit in the face of the travel gods, he called the airline help desk to dish out an egregiously bold-faced lie. He was truly shocked and, well, a bit guilty, when the agent switched two seat assignments, allowing him to be next to his terminal father-in-law to manage his multiple health issues including medications.

Call finished, he exhaled a long sigh of relief, sat back, and polished off the not-so-hot-anymore chocolate.

Thump thump thump.

He reached down, gave Chance a few seconds of behind-the-ear choobers before calling Davidson's TracFone.

"Good news. We'll be sitting together on the flight."

"Seriously? How the hell did you manage that?"

"You don't want to know."

"You are probably right, but nevertheless, I am delighted with the arrangement."

What next? Chance. He dialed the veterinarian clinic after-hours number, only to end up on hold listening to a mindlessly repetitious tune for seven interminable minutes, but he managed to book Chance for a four-night stay in spite of his scheduled return on Thursday. He figured it'd be best to reserve the kennel for more nights than needed just in case an unexpected complication arose in Seattle. You never knew what curveball Fisher might throw your way. He hated being away from Chance, but was comforted in knowing the vet and her staff treated him extremely well.

What next? Rachael. He checked the time, figured she was still at work so decided to text her that he'd be home Tuesday and Wednesday nights.

Home? *Hmmmm...*

That word gave him pause. This place was home too.

Stop stalling. Get on with it.

He texted: *No ur at work. Quick call?*

He leaned back in the padded chair, mulling over how to justify such a precipitous and short stay without disclosing the real reason for the visit. That particular bit of news needed to be delivered in person.

Christ!

He certainly wasn't looking forward to breaking the news, especially in view of her stipulation if they were to continue a serious relationship. The thought of losing her...

Stop it! Think of something productive.

Such as coming up with a fail-safe strategy to once and for all stop Naseem from being a threat to everyone he loved. Okay, but wasn't that really the FBI's responsibility? Shouldn't he simply assist them with whatever help they needed?

Most definitely...*but*, and this was a mondo *but*: what happens *after* the FBI takes her into custody?

What then?

Good question.

He thought back to articles he'd read about other terrorists arrested in the United States, how everything was turned upside down so dramatically in the aftermath of September 11, and how prosecuting suspected terrorists totally changed. The problem was, prosecuting a terrorist meant they needed to stand trial, and any trial carried the possibility that the defendant might walk....

Ping.

Rachael. His heart fluttered.

She texted: *On break now.*

He dialed.

"I'll be back in Seattle Tuesday evening. Any chance we can see each other after work?"

"You're coming here? To Seattle? Yes, of course! I'm scheduled that evening...it's too late now to trade shifts with someone...but I can arrange to leave early, maybe around eleven. Wow, this is sudden. Why so sudden?"

Oh man, it was so damned good to hear her voice in spite of daily phone and Skype chats.

Now came the tricky part.

"I need to walk through the house with the interior designer."

True, but...he jotted a reminder to email her in the off chance he could shoehorn in a meeting, but knew he wouldn't be able to any set time on account of no knowing how long the meeting with Fisher might take.

"Oh, for some reason I keep forgetting about that. What a wonderful surprise."

You have no idea.

"Came up sort of last-minute..." He figured it would be

pressing his luck if he said much more, so, much as it pained him: "Sorry to cut this short, but I have a ton of things to finish up tonight. I'll text before I go to bed. Love you."

"I love you too, sweetie."

Whew! Dodged a bullet on that one.

He downed the last of the cold chocolate, sat back.

What next?

Oh crap! School.

He pulled up the university webpage and waded through various sections until finally dredging up the rules for dropping a class. Turned out that if he remained enrolled any longer than two days, dropping the course would result in an automatic incomplete. Unless of course, he could prove one hell of a valid reason, such as...what? Terminal cancer? A dying parent?

How about having a terrorist wanting to kill me?

He doubted that last one would fly. Besides, how long would this Naseem thing take to play out? No idea. He hated to walk away from the hours already invested in that class, but...what the hell. Just drop the puppy and walk away without penalty. He could reenroll in the same course once this situation stabilized. And next time, he'd have a head start on the class.

Big fucking consolation.

Chapter 24—Naseem

"WHY ARE WE wasting all this effort on this one Jew?" Kasra asked, pouring two small fluted glasses of steaming brown chai, one for each of them.

The aromatic fragrance of cinnamon mixed with cardamom hung heavily in the kitchen air.

Naseem inhaled the familiar, pleasant scent. Kasra had learned quickly to flavor and prepare the tea to her preferred strength and taste before serving it. Naseem would stir in exactly the right amount of sugar, then wait patiently for the liquid to cool to perfect drinking temperature before downing it in two savory swallows.

Kasra brought the glasses on their matching saucers to the kitchen table, placed one in front of Naseem, and settled into her chair. Naseem sprinkled the precisely measured spoonful of sugar in a clockwise pattern into the steaming chai before slowly stirring it with a figure-eight motion. Satisfied, Naseem set the small silver spoon on the saucer to wait while watching the steam rise lazily from the brew, its density an indicator of proper drinking temperature.

Kasra knew enough to not speak during this ritual. Naseem ignored her, preferring instead to stare at the chai and inhale its delicate fragrance. How could she possibly explain her hatred for the

Jew? Hatred compressed into multiple layers of dense emotional bedrock forged in the twenty months since first encountering the man. The Jew initiated contact through her website with the intention of paying money for the right to selfishly use her body to satisfy his sexual urges over a five-day period. Jews! They were nothing but Zionist expansionists harboring intense hatred toward anyone of Arabic descent.

Unless, of course, they want to fuck them. Then, no problem.

The moment she set eyes on him in his fancy Bellagio suite she knew, in spite of his Toby Tyler alias, he was a Jew. She had almost turned around and walked away from his money. It was one thing for him to be a kafir, but quite another thing to be a *Jew...*

She'd realized, of course, that her repugnance for him should not obstruct or distract from her crucial role in their jihad. So, she selflessly and flawlessly played her part in the belief that Allah would be with her during the ordeal. Besides, the Jew was paying handsomely. Money she gladly used to support their cause. And after the Jew, she would be on to the next man, fishing for someone who might benefit their fight by carelessly dropping scraps of important intelligence to bolster their fragile male egos.

And this was exactly what the Jew did. In a burst of adolescent bravado, the naïve infidel boasted of his computer's ability to predict the outcome of certain events. Essentially, to predict the future. She immediately realized the benefits this could provide their cause if properly directed.

Was it possible?

Could such an outrageous claim actually be true? She needed to find out, so she flattered him into proving his claim by betting a few horse races. To her astonishment, he won all bets. From then on, controlling the Jew's system became the sole mission in her personal jihad.

At first, she offered to buy the computer for a vast sum of money. Like a stubborn donkey, the Jew refused, forcing her and Firouz to begin applying other pressure. Still he refused.

When neither the carrot nor stick budged the stubborn donkey, they searched for an alternative strategy for appropriating his system. From the little he explained about how it worked, the computers resolved complex problems by analyzing massive amounts of readily available public information garnered from extensive internet searches.

The obvious and most direct strategy for stealing his system was to simply break into the Jew's house when he was away and physically carry away the computers. But after their disastrous attempt at that in Seattle, they realized the job required a more sophisticated approach. There was also Nawzer's dire warning of a very real potential danger: that a complex system such as his might be extremely tricky to use, especially without specific instructions by the programmer. In addition, the software might contain booby traps that, if inadvertently triggered, would destroy the program. A much better approach, he suggested, would be to hack directly into the system and, over time, copy the software while documenting exactly how to use it.

This made sense, they all agreed, so Naseem asked Nawzer to proceed along that strategy. Nawzer tried unsuccessfully to trick the Jew into unwittingly infecting his computer, as he had done with the lawyer. Nawzer then tried to hack the system remotely through the internet. It was during this attempt that Karim was horrifically burned alive in the Seattle house. To this day she became nauseated just thinking of it. Just one reason why she hated the Jew so viscerally.

Firouz's arrest had followed a few days later. Again because of the Jew.

At this point she vowed that the Jew could never keep his precious system even if it meant destroying his house again. She would make one more attempt to rob him of it before resorting to such a scorched-earth approach. Yes, Nawzer had attempted to break into his system, but only remotely, from a 3,000-mile distance. He'd never worked within a proximity that did not require an internet connection.

That was about to change.

She'd established a mental timeline. Nawzer would either succeed in copying it remotely or not. If he didn't, the Jew or his girlfriend would be taken hostage and he would be forced to surrender his system. Whatever the outcome, he would be killed. Preferably, slowly and painfully, over days. And if this proved too difficult, a simple bullet to the back of the head would suffice. This had become very personal.

This was why she was devoting so much effort on this one Jew. Kasra could never understand.

Chapter 25—Arnold

ARNOLD DROPPED TO his haunches and cupped Chance's head in both hands and looked into those intelligent brown eyes.

"Daddy has to go. Daddy will be back. Chance stays."

Chance wagged his tail and planted three wet doggie kisses on Arnold's cheek. He understood.

"We'll take good care of him," the veterinary assistant said.

"I know you will. It's just...I hate to be away from him. He and I are pack."

She nodded, gently taking the leash from Arnold's hand.

"Daddy loves Chance."

Arnold threw in a few bonus choobers before hurrying out to the Mini, already way behind schedule.

"Mr. Gold?"

"Yes!"

"You couldn't have cut it any closer," the ticket agent said at the boarding gate. She quickly scanned his ticket and returned it with a forced smile. "Seat 3B. Have a good flight."

The cabin door whooshed shut right behind him as the flight attendant muttered a few words. He made his way down the aisle as other passengers eyed him while Davidson flashed an obvious look of relief.

"I was debating whether to call Fisher," Davidson said. "I worried something might have happened to you."

Arnold blew a long sigh, sat, and settled back against the seat. Eyes closed, he tried to relax but immediately began to worry about Rachael's reaction to the news.

On one hand, he longed to see her (even if just a few hours) after two months of separation; to wrap her in his arms, smell her hair and...on the other hand, there was the Naseem issue to discuss. Well, not just an *issue*. A *huge* fucking issue.

Just how the hell was he going to break *that* news?

He was dreading it.

The Boeing 777 jerked backwards as a tractor pushed it from the gate.

Chapter 26—Arnold

"A BLOODY MARY is the perfect way to start a long flight. Or any flight for that matter," Davidson said as the 777 began leveling off at altitude.

The words jolted Arnold from brooding rumination over his future—or lack thereof—with Rachael. Would she even speak to him after he disclosed this latest...latest what?

Development? Disaster? Wrinkle? Threat?

Two months ago, as they sat on a chunk of Maui beach coral, Arnold proposed that she move to Honolulu so they could spend more time together. Preferably cohabitate. After a moment of serious thought, she said that in spite of wanting to do exactly that, she could never feel comfortable with him as long as Naseem remained a threat.

Although disappointed, he understood. He suggested perhaps, with the FBI still actively searching for her, Naseem had given up on him and moved on to another city and target. Rachael wasn't buying it, but proposed the following compromise: if, at the end of a six-month trial period, all went well and Naseem remained out of the picture, she'd quit her job and get her own apartment in Honolulu.

The second month of the trial period had just ended when, *wham*, his world came crashing down on him. One fucking phone call!

Arnold turned to Davidson. "Sorry, what'd you just say? I was, ah, distracted."

"I can see that."

Davidson took a sip from his Bloody Mary.

"How do you suspect my computer contracted the malware? It would be helpful to know so we can prevent the situation from reoccurring."

Arnold swallowed.

"Didn't we discuss this the other night?"

"Humor me. Go over it once again."

Arnold shrugged.

"More than likely it was infected months ago, when we first suspected it. Too much time has passed to stand any shot at tracking down the cause, but if you're asking for my best guess, then I'd say you or Joyce clicked on an infected email."

"A phishing attack?"

"Exactly."

By the look on his face, Arnold could tell Davidson wasn't satisfied with this explanation.

"You disagree?"

Davidson hesitated.

"You are undoubtedly correct, but I find this unnerving. Unless I know the exact cause, I cannot be sure of not repeating the error."

"Tell you what," Arnold said. "Odds are you picked it up from an email. When I get back home, if you give me your password, I'll see what I can find out. But don't get your hope up, okay? The simple rule of thumb is to not open any email from an unknown source."

Home?

Once again, he asked himself which of his two houses was "home." He'd grown up in a classic Tudor that was now being replaced by a contemporary cube. In addition, he also owned his beloved Honolulu home. So, which one was home? And now that he thought about it, when did owning two homes become okay?

I mean, seriously, dude?

The Arnold Gold who innocently walked through the back door of the old Tudor carrying a nicely warm, fabulous-smelling, fresh-out-of-the-oven, double cheese-and-pepperoni pizza the night Howie was shot to death, viewed such blatant materialism with clear disdain. The same disdain he felt watching the mega-yacht *A* moor at Pier 91 refueling dock en route to the Mediterranean. He considered the small ship an over-the-top brazen display of excessive wealth.

Which begged the question: when did this principle begin to erode? When first stumbling on how much money he could rake in from betting on sports events with SAM's help? Yeah, probably....

"Would that mean you need to look through my emails?" Davidson asked warily.

"And Joyce's."

Davidson pursed his lips.

"I do not think I realized that until just now...I need to think about this." He stirred the Bloody Mary again. "How did Rachael react to your surprise visit?"

"She was thrilled. It came as a total surprise."

"Have you told her the reason for the visit?"

"Uh...not exactly."

Silence.

Arnold added, "I will. Tonight. Though I'm really really dreading it."

"But you *will* tell her?"

"I have no choice. She's at risk too." Arnold said. "Did I tell you about her ultimatum?"

Davidson raised his eyebrows.

"Ultimatum? No."

Arnold went on to explain.

"Well, stipulation might be a better word for it, but the result's the same."

"You have to admit, this is beginning to wear a bit thin on all of us," Davidson said when Arnold finished.

"No shit."

Davidson sipped the Bloody Marry and waited.

"The other part of it was to stop gambling. She thinks it paints a big red bull's-eye on my back." He shrugged. "She definitely had a point, so stopped that. But this Naseem thing..."

He shook his head.

"Perhaps this time Fisher will capture her."

Chapter 27—Arnold

"YOU MENTIONED YOU have other tasks to tend to while in town. Care to elaborate?" Davidson asked.

Arnold eyed the in-flight menu.

"The big one is to meet with my designer at the Green Lake house."

"Oh, right, right...that completely slipped my mind." Davidson chuckled. "A couple months ago, when tracking you down, I stopped by the property and was surprised to see the building site. I must admit to being amazed that a man your age could afford a project that scale. Especially considering you already have the Honolulu place." He locked eyes with Arnold. "Apparently your online gambling was much more lucrative than I ever imagined. You are paying taxes, are you not?"

Arnold felt his face redden at the not-so-subtle jab.

"No worries. I learned my lesson last time."

"Good. Which brings me to my next question. If, in fact, you ceased gambling, how *do* you support yourself? That is, if you do not mind me asking."

Arnold smiled, paused for a sip of his own Bloody Mary.

"The stock market's always interested me, so last year I did some serious research about Quants...you know, those dudes on

Wall Street who come up with all the cool algorithms for buying and selling shit for fractional gains. So, I nurdled around with a few of my own ideas and started trading options." He shrugged. "That's my thing now."

Davidson's voice was tinged with surprised awe.

"You actually make money doing that?"

Arnold laughed.

"You think I'd still be doing it if I didn't?"

Davidson nodded.

"Touché. Regardless, I find it hard to fathom a man your age making sufficient income to support your lifestyle. However, if you are doing so within the law, well then..."

He let it hang.

"Enough on that," Arnold said. "I want ask about your Queen Anne home. Did you build it?"

Arnold fell in love with the place the first moment Davidson opened the door from the garage into the kitchen. Until then, a home was nothing but a dwelling to support necessities of daily living: eating, sleeping, entertainment, and, in his case, working. It certainly didn't influence the occupant's mood or emotions. All that changed the moment he set foot in Davidson's kitchen. Especially the view. He could sit and gaze out at it for hours.

"I bought it. Why?"

"I guess on accounta it feels so new."

"That is because it was when I purchased it," Davidson said.

"I love that place. So, all those furnishings...did you or a decorator pick those out?"

"I worked with a designer. She chose some but others are my choice. I have to admit, there were times when her suggestions just felt wrong so I nixed them."

The discussion was helping Arnold solidify a few ideas he'd been wrestling with.

"Give an example of something you didn't like?"

"She suggested a chair she thought was fun." Davidson made

finger quotes as he said "fun." "I explained to her I do not do *fun*. She got the message, so she stopped suggesting the f-word pieces. I tend toward minimalist contemporary and she leans toward traditional, so it took some give-and-take before she finally understood my taste. Once that happened, we clicked. Why do you ask?"

"I can't seem to get my designer to understand the look I'm after. I think it'd be more effective if we can discuss it in person while walking the interior."

"How did you manage to decorate Honolulu?" Davidson asked.

"That was all Loni."

"Do you envision your new place having a similar feel?"

"Entirely."

"Well then, that should make it easy," Davidson said. "Send her pictures of that interior."

"Already did, but still think it's a good idea to walk the space together."

"That certainly will not hurt. Do you still see Loni?"

"No."

Arnold summarized their last, aborted, date at the Sicilian restaurant.

"In other words, asking her for advice would be out of the question."

"Most definitely.

"Does this mean you are exclusively attached, so to speak, to Rachael?"

"She's always been *The One*. That's the reason I'm so damned worried about how she'll handle this latest, uh, issue."

"Do not sell her short, son. From everything I know about her, she is reasonable. She could very well surprise you."

Time to change subjects.

"Your friend, Martina...what's the story there?"

Davidson cracked a faint smile.

"We have been very close for years."

Arnold waited for Davidson to elaborate.

He didn't.

"What does that mean? Friends?"

Davidson nodded.

"Presently."

"Christ, Mr. Davidson, what's that supposed to mean?"

After appearing to weigh a decision, Davidson sighed.

"We were married for ten years before divorcing five years ago. For whatever strange reason—I really cannot explain it—we do better as a couple this way. Yes, I realize it may seem a bit strange, but it is what it is."

Wow!

That answered a ton of questions as well as adding a completely new spin to the man.

Chapter 28—Arnold

MOMENTS BEFORE TOUCHDOWN, Davidson closed his book and turned to Arnold.

"Are you planning to stay with Rachael?"

"I wish! No." Arnold sighed. "We discussed it, but she works until eleven and I need to be up early, so we decided it'd best for me to stay at a hotel. I snagged a room at the Hyatt Place off Denny. It puts me close enough."

"In that case, why not cancel the reservation and use my guest room?"

Arnold thought about it.

"Thanks, but we plan to see each other tonight and it'll be late."

"No problem. I will give you security privileges." Davidson referred to his extensive system. "You know where everything is, so just be quiet when you come in. This way, we can be sure to arrive at the meeting together."

Made sense.

Besides, he loved the guest room. Much better than a hotel room.

"In that case, I'm in."

Naseem

Naseem lay motionless on a sun-baked patch of reddish lava-rich dirt, propped up on elbows, patiently staring across the ravine at the back of the Jew's house. Although the sun was just kissing the horizon, the dense humid air still held the day's heat in spite of a gentle breeze.

An hour had ticked slowly past since the hike up here to the very spot they had shot and killed FBI agent Rios. Over that hour, the ground had grown hard and uncomfortable but she ignored this, fearing that any unnecessary movement would increase the risk being spotted by either a neighbor or the Jew's elaborate security system.

The two times she'd attempted to approach his house on foot, she'd been detected before she crossed the property line. The first attempt ended when the Jew fled from the basement and escaped down this same ravine. The second time she threw poisoned hamburger into the courtyard, but the infidel's dog, for unknown reason, failed to eat it. She blamed the security system for both these failures.

Not complete failures, however. They had yielded useful information. Of greatest value, she now had a very good estimate of the police response time: approximately ten minutes. Plus, she now knew exactly where his multiple sensors and cameras were located.

Ideally, once Nawzer arrived to examine the property in person, he could discover a weak spot in the system to exploit. If so, this would allow them to disable the alarm remotely before physically breaking into the house. But if that proved impossible, they could simply smash in the basement door, seize the computers, and be down the ravine before the police could respond. After all, they would be well down in the ravine before the police would get to the front door.

Yes, this time her mission would succeed. This time Allah was smiling upon her.

Kasra was stretched out to her left, shielding the sun's glare from her phone while reading the Honolulu *Star-Advertiser*. Naseem sensed Kasra's impatience. But patience, she knew, was essential for them to succeed.

Movement caught her eye. An object gained altitude from the flat roof of the Jew's house.

"Down!" she whispered to Kasra.

She pressed flat against the lava to watch a drone ascend to perhaps ten meters above the solar panels before it began a lazy enlarging spiral centered over the launch site. Ah, the Jew also employed aerial surveillance to supplement the stationary movement sensors. This was good intel to share with Nawzer when visiting the site. Military surveillance drones, she knew, kept in constant communication with their handlers. Although she didn't understand the electronics, she instinctively suspected that such a communication link might provide a potential access point for Nawzer, one they'd never considered until this moment, a revelation that underscored the value of making repeated reconnaissance trips no matter how boring they might seem.

She studied the drone more closely, mentally noting its behavior. Yes, she'd use this to drive home to Nawzer the value of working within eyesight of the Jew's property rather than from a Los Angeles flat. She smiled at this argument.

"We are seeing nothing for an hour now. No dog. No Jew. So, what is this we are seeing?"

She placed an index finger to her lips, whispered, "A drone."

Was the aircraft capable of sensing and recording voices?

"Yes, I can see that, Sister. What I am asking is, do you think someone is actually in the house?"

"I don't think so."

"But if not, who controls it?"

"I don't know, but it may be the Jew's computer. Or, perhaps it can be operated remotely like the Air Force."

Kasra's phone vibrated; an incoming call. She whispered an answer, listened, nodded, disconnected.

"My sister."

"The one at SeaTac?"

"Yes. She just saw the lawyer and Jew walk off the flight together. We now know for certain he's there."

"This is good. This means we have at least twenty-four to seventy-two hours to finish our mission before he can return."

"This seems to be so, but what exactly is our mission now?"

Tell her? No, she has no reason to know.

Although Naseem believed the FBI knew nothing of Kasra or her sister, the fewer people aware of the details—no matter how trusted—the less risk of a leak. Now that the Jew and his lawyer were halfway across the Pacific, she could kill the Jew and, in so doing, deflect the attention from her. She knew exactly where the Jew would be during the Seattle trip. Once again, she thanked Allah for smiling on her.

With the Jew away from the island, she grew ever more anxious for Nawzer's arrival. For if, as planned, the Jew died in Seattle, no one would care what happened to the contents of his house.

"Sister Naseem," Kasha said, "we must go now. Don't forget, I'm working tomorrow."

"Yes yes, we go, but first I need to make one phone call. Just not here."

Naseem slowly pushed onto her knees, allowing an initial dizziness to pass. The sky was now dark enough to not worry about the drone spotting her. She thumbed on the iPhone flashlight to help navigate the rocky path they'd ascended more than an hour ago. After descending into the ravine ten meters, she dialed the number.

"Yes?" answered Sheena, a sympathizer in Seattle.

"They just stepped off their flight at SeaTac."

"I will be waiting so will keep an eye out for them."

Sheena terminated the call.

With a smile, Naseem resumed the climb down the rocky terrain to the cul-de-sac where their car was parked. She knew the Jew's new Seattle house wasn't finished yet, meaning he'd either stay at a hotel, his girlfriend's, or with the lawyer.

Eventually, however, the Jew would meet his girlfriend and she was, at the moment, a crucial link to her plan's success. More importantly, though; he and the lawyer would visit the lawyer's office tomorrow either before or after meeting with Agent Fisher.

Chapter 29—Arnold

AS A ROUTINE security measure, Davidson always hired Evergreen Town Car to shuttle him back and forth from the Smith Tower to Sea-Tac Airport rather than from home. Tonight was no different. The moment the driver dropped them in front of the building, Arnold summoned an Uber for the trip to Davidson's house.

The Uber just pulled into Davidson's driveway as Arnold's phone dinged: an alert from SAM. He read the message.

"Jesus! Check this out!" Arnold said, handing Davidson the phone.

On it was a still image taken by one of RAID's cameras.

Davidson squinted slightly, spread his fingers to enlarge the picture, and studied it a moment longer before returning the phone.

"You think this is Naseem? I am unconvinced."

"Sure as hell looks like her. Especially stretched out like that, watching the back of my house. I mean, who else could it be? Soon as we get inside, I'll bring up the infrared for a better look, but man, if it quacks like a pope and shits in the woods..."

"I will notify Fisher. If HPD can dispatch a car in time, we might be able to solve one huge problem."

After checking his watch, Arnold changed priorities. Only

forty-five minutes until Rachael was expected home and he wanted as much time as possible with her. Besides, there was no real reason to look at the infrared images tonight. Who else would be watching his house? Had to be Naseem. He knew it, Davidson knew it, now Fisher knew it. Davidson was already talking with him by the time he was rolling his luggage through the front door.

Soon as Davidson hung up, Arnold said, "I'll wait on the infrared but will check out your computer before heading over to see Rach."

After dumping his rucksack on the floor, Arnold settled into the desk chair, took a moment to tip and rate and the Uber driver, then turned his attention to the computer.

"Hey, Mr. Davidson, need your PIN."

Davidson walked into the study.

"Fisher said HPD's on its way. Hopefully they will catch her."

He leaned over Arnold's shoulder to type in his PIN.

As the antivirus software began downloading, Arnold checked the time, decided it was time to call Uber for the trip to Rachael's and that he'd check the scan results before hitting the sack later. But, for him there was no mystery as to what the results would be.

"We need to set you up with security access," Davidson said.

Arnold checked the Uber, saw it was still four minutes out. Plenty of time to establish his voice analysis, retinal scan, and fingerprint login. Yeah, overkill for sure, but probably wise.

"That should do it," Davidson said with the satisfied tone of a proud father. "Just to verify you are in the system, go outside, close the door, wait ten seconds, then come back in."

A minute later, Arnold successfully navigated the security without setting off an alarm.

"Very good," Davidson said.

Arnold's phone dinged.

"Uber's here. I should be back in...oh, forty-five minutes to an hour."

As much as he wanted to hang with Rachael for longer than that, he needed to be at the top of his game with Fisher and Chang in the morning.

"Keep in mind, we are to meet him in the lobby at seven o'clock."

Fisher had emphasized the punctuality.

"Yes, Mom."

Davidson laughed.

"I am just saying..." Pause. "Before you leave, what did you learn from the computer?"

"Software's still downloading. The scan will be finished when I return. I'll update you the morning. But you know it's there, right?"

Chapter 30—Naseem

KASRA WAS PULLING away from their parking spot at the bottom of the ravine as headlights rounded the corner two blocks ahead and approached slowly. Curbed vehicles to either side along the narrow residential street made passing an oncoming car impossible, trapping them in the cul-de-sac. As the vehicle drew closer, Naseem could see it was a police cruiser.

"Sister!" Kasra said.

"I see it," Naseem answered. "Pull over, let them pass. Do nothing to attract attention."

Naseem opened the glove box and removed a black Glock 40, cold and heavy in her hand.

Kasra slid the Nissan at the open space in front of a driveway so the patrol car could pass.

But the HPD cruiser did not pass and instead rolled slowly alongside to a stop, blocking them in. A female officer stepped from the driver side, approached, and motioned Kasra to lower her window. Naseem slid the gun between the seat and the door, where it couldn't be easily seen by the officer.

Kasra's window whirred down. The officer leaned in and quickly swept the interior with a flashlight.

"Evening, ladies."

"Evening, officer," Kasra answered.

The officer nodded at the surrounding homes.

"You live here, ma'am?"

"No, just visited a friend."

"Uh-huh. May I see your driver's license, please?"

"Yes, it's right here in my purse."

"Fine, but first please set the purse on your lap where I can see it before you slowly open it to remove the license. Do you understand?"

"I do."

Naseem could see the officer's eyes darting between the two of them, so kept her hands folded in her lap in plain sight while Kasra complied with the request. The officer accepted the license and straightened, saying, "This'll only take a minute."

She returned her vehicle.

With the officer in the patrol car, Kasra opened her mouth to speak.

"Shh! Not a word, sister," Naseem whispered, eyes still fixed straight ahead, her heart hammering. She struggled to keep from hyperventilating. A firefight wasn't how she envisioned her mission ending, but if need be, she'd use the element of surprise to her advantage. The police car would prevent them from fleeing but would also serve as an excellent barricade against other vehicles approaching within a half block of the cul-de-sac. This should give them adequate time to scramble back up the ravine toward the Jew's house, then across the first accessible property to the street. Once on pavement, they would have perhaps ten minutes to split up and disappear.

Yes, the police would use Kasra's car to track her down, but so what?

She knew none of the other network sympathizers nor any details of her plan. Her biggest risk at the moment was being wounded should a firefight break out. Especially if the wound required emergency care.

A minute later the officer returned, handing Kasra her driver's license. She bent down, pointed her light directly at Naseem.

"And you, ma'am. May I see your identification, please?"

Naseem nodded and unzipped her fanny pack.

"Here you are."

She passed the officer the fake California driver's license Nawzer supplied three months ago. The officer studied it a moment before returning it.

"I'll move my car so you ladies can get going. Sorry for any inconvenience."

Chapter 31—Arnold

RACHAEL WAS WAITING a few feet from the concierge desk when Arnold pushed through the glass doors into the now familiar lobby. She rushed to his arms for an embrace, tempered only by the prying eyes of the gnome at the desk pretending not to watch.

"I don't have much time," he whispered.

"C'mon, then," she said, pulling him toward the elevators.

Only two words, but from their Maui vacation he knew their implication well. An erection was in full bloom before the elevator doors finished closing.

Ten minutes later: "Oh no...I think I just gave my ass a bad case of rug burn." Rachael rolled onto her left side. "Did I?"

"Naw..." Arnold touched the red spot. "A little pink maybe, but in my esteemed medical opinion, not a certifiable case of rug burn."

"Whew!"

They were sprawled on the carpet at the foot of the couch, clothes strewn haphazardly from the front door to the scene of the crime. Well, except for his socks.

Shit!

His face started doing the space heater imitation. He had no idea what proper spontaneous-sex clothes etiquette might be, but seriously doubted the black-socks-dude-look was the coolest choice he might've made. The situation never arose in Maui because socks were not part of their daily dress code.

She stood, began to gather her clothes and vanish into the bedroom. He began to dress too, dreading the conversation ahead.

A moment later Rachael walked back in the living room swathed in a white terrycloth robe, finger-combing her short black hair.

Christ, time to drop the big one.

He swallowed hard and prepared himself mentally, but at the last second wimped out.

"Before I forget...were you able to change shifts?"

She flashed her drop-dead gorgeous smile.

"Yes! So..." Her smile widened. "I'm free tomorrow."

Fantastic!

"Then how about going out to dinner. I should be done by late afternoon."

If all went well. Well, not entirely true.

He'd try his damnedest to be back here in time to...

"That'd be nice. What're you thinking?"

Actually, he hadn't given it a thought other than to simply spend time together, so snapped up the first thing that came to mind.

"How does Chinese sound?"

"You know me...always up for that. Where?"

"Uptown." Pause. "Mind if Mr. Davidson joins us?"

"Not at all...just as long as we have some personal time."

Her smile held that excitingly devious expression he loved.

"Sit down." He patted the couch next to him. "There's something we need to discuss."

Her smile evaporated. She dropped onto the cushion to his right.

Oh fuck! She knows.

He inhaled deeply.

Her eyes grew coldly serious.

"This have something to do with Naseem?"

Well, shit, no way out of it now. He opened his mouth to speak.

C'mon man, cowboy up.

He licked his lips and nodded.

"Yes..."

She just stared at him with rapidly changing emotions flashing through her eyes.

Finally she said, "I suspected...this sudden trip...you being so damned evasive." After a resigned sigh, she said: "Tell me what happened."

Not good. Not bad. At least she wanted to hear the details.

"Okay, so, I get this phone call..."

He took her through what was said, and his meeting with Davidson in Honolulu. He wrapped up by explaining that the primary reason for the sudden trip was an all-out, all-hands-on-deck strategy session with Fisher and Chang in the morning to hammer out a rock-solid, failure-is-not-an-option strategy for finally taking down Naseem.

When he finished, she asked, "Why am I getting such a strong déjà vu?"

Uh-oh! Don't like the sound of that.

"You shouldn't, because this time it's different," he blurted, and cringed at how lame that sounded.

"How, exactly, is it different, Arnold?"

"Well..."

He knew damned well he was dead in the water and sinking fast.

"Well?" she demanded.

"A lot of things are different. Most importantly, we're not going to let her to take the initiative."

Wow, he liked how that sounded: emphatic, calculating, determined. But believable? Wasn't so sure about that part.

"This time we have that advantage," he quickly added. "Plus, we have the entire weight of the FBI and all the other law-enforcement agencies—federal and municipal—behind us."

He waited for a reply but she remained perfectly still, seemingly deep in thought, as if weighing a very important decision.

Uh-oh, not good.

Her face solidified into an amalgamation of expressions: resolve, resignation, sadness, and something unidentifiable and, well, a bit scary. She stiffened. Her eyes hardened.

Oh, shit!

"So, how does this affect us?" he asked, worried as hell.

No answer.

"What you said on Maui...about this, ah, problem in my life..."

"*Your* life?" She was glaring now. "What about *my* life? *Our* lives? *Chance's* life? Arnold, that woman intends to *kill* you...maybe kill all of us. Including Mr. Davidson. Who knows what's fomenting in her twisted terrorist mind?"

Then she was up, moving to the window. She stood before the thick glass staring out at the myriad city lights.

Not good. Not good at all.

How would Davidson handle this? He'd know exactly what to say.

"I *knew* this was going happen, goddamnit! I just *knew* it," she muttered.

"Okay, but I thought...."

"No, that's the whole goddamn problem, Arnold...you didn't think. Did you *actually* believe your little Hans Weiser bullshit story might fool someone? How totally crazy insane was that?"

When he didn't respond, she said, "I worried about how I'd deal with this when this day finally came because I knew it would. Well, here it is, and I need to make a really big decision."

A decision? Decide what?

Fear exploded into panic.

"Please don't do this, Rach. Please."

He fought the urge to reach out and put his arms around her but her body language made it diamond-clear he'd be in even deeper shit if he so much as touched her.

"We can work through this. Everything will be all okay. Have faith."

She started slowly shaking her head side to side without saying a word.

"Tell me something," she finally said in a strangely soft voice.

"Anything. Just talk to me. Rach."

"Your system...that's the reason you're in this mess, isn't it."

Was that a question?

He decided not to answer.

Still facing the window, she continued, "What would happen if you just give it to her?"

He swallowed.

"Yeah, I could...but it gets more complicated than that."

"Why? Seems very straightforward to me, Arnold."

Oh, Christ.

She never called him Arnold.

"Well, for starters," he said, mind racing. "She wants to kill me. There's also the whole terrorist-angle thing. The only reason she wants SAM is to use it for planning more effective attacks. I mean, we're not dealing with a Nobel Peace Prize laureate here. You understand this, right?"

"Of course I understand it! That's the point. Why do you think I'm so goddamn angry, Arnold!"

He backed up a step. Then another.

"Shouldn't she be the FBI's problem? *They're* the terrorist experts. I get it. She wants you dead. But why couldn't that change if you negotiate a deal for SAM?"

He reached out, took hold of her shoulders. She shrugged him away.

"Don't dare touch me! Just answer the question."

He backed up a step again, giving her more space.

"Sure, I could hand over SAM, but that's not going to change the personal vendetta she has. She has it in for me."

Rachael turned to face him but didn't step away from the window.

"Why not?"

He backed up another step.

"Because too much has happened since this all began. The woman's dyed-in-the-wool Old Testament, Rach...all that eye-for-an-eye, tooth-for-a-tooth-type shit. She's not going to walk away from this until she exacts some serious payback for Karim and the warehouse and a bit more just out of pure spite."

"That, Arnold, is *exactly* my point!" She stepped closer; they were now face to face. "Where does that leave me? And Chance? She knows about me too, doesn't she!"

"We don't know that."

"Maybe *you* don't, but I do. I saw a seriously creepy woman watching me leave work tonight. It gave me this...really freaky feeling. I *know* she's watching me for Naseem. Don't try to palm off a load of crap on me, Arnold. You and I both have bright neon bull's-eyes painted on our backs now."

Chapter 32—Naseem

"WE'RE JAMMED UP at the moment," said the manager behind the counter, "so no way can we start on it tonight. We close at ten o'clock, so you might want to bring it back in the morning. Even then, it won't be finished till late tomorrow afternoon."

Kasha and Naseem were in the front office of Sparkling Auto Detailing, their vehicle just outside the front door.

"We both have the early shift at the restaurant," Kasra said. Naseem stood behind her, sun hat pulled low, obscuring her face much as possible. She was also turned as if watching traffic pass outside. She said nothing.

Kasra asked, "Could we leave the car and pick it up tomorrow after work?"

"Sure," the manager said with a shrug. "If you want. But just so you know, it'll be parked over there." He pointed out the dusty side window to a small asphalt lot surrounded by an eight-foot, flimsy cyclone fence that, at best, might take all of thirty seconds to climb over. "We'll, of course, make sure the keys are locked inside there." He nodded toward a substantial combination safe up against the back wall, its legs bolted to the cracked concrete floor.

"That's nice to know. It'll work best for us to leave it overnight. What time tomorrow should we plan to pick it up?"

The manager paused to dig at his right ear with his pinky, which was as heavily tattooed as the rest of his exposed body.

"All depends. Which package we talking about?"

Kasra quickly scanned at the garishly painted menu on the wall behind the desk and zeroed in on the most expensive choice.

"The Super Fresh detail."

The manager did a reappraising take.

"Ma'am, that one's the top of the line...so it's going to set you back five hundred bucks. You sure you're up for that one?"

The not-so-subtle implication being that her piece-of-shit Nissan didn't warrant throwing so much coin at.

"Oh, yes," Kasra beamed. "Anabelle's my baby!"

With a shrug; "In that case, it's probably not gonna be ready to until, oh, nine, nine-thirty or so tomorrow evening. Still work for you?"

Kasra pursed her lips a pensive moment.

"And the shop closes at ten?"

"That's right, ma'am."

"In that case," she beamed, "why not keep her an extra day, just to make sure she gets all the time she needs in the beauty shop. Besides, won't that make things a lot easier on you?"

The manager appeared relieved.

"Yes ma'am, that helps us a big bunch. Thanks. See, we usually only do Supers on advanced bookings, but since we don't got none on the schedule, you're in luck."

Kasra smiled at him.

"That's so kind of you."

He beamed back.

"Will that be cash or credit card, ma'am?"

"Credit card."

"I was really fond of that car," Kasra said to Naseem when they were a half block down the sidewalk from the detailing shop.

"It's safer this way. I didn't like the way that cop checked us out, or her tone of voice. Something really weird about it made me uneasy. There's a used-car lot over off Hickam. We'll buy you a replacement tomorrow."

Arnold

Arnold audibly exhaled.

"I honestly don't know if she knows about you."

Bullshit!

With access to Davidson's computers, Naseem undoubtedly knew exactly who Rachael was and, perhaps, even where she lived. And for sure knew about Chance, having attempted to poison him once. And if Rachael *did* see someone watching her leave work...

Rachael's glare burned directly through his retinas.

"Oh, don't you dare try to lie to me Arnold Gold! You're a terrible liar. We both know she knows. Admit it! And that woman...I didn't fucking hallucinate that."

Checkmate. Totally and completely screwed.

"What are not telling me?" Rachael asked. "What are you leaving out?"

He scrambled to answer as truthfully as possible without admitting just how dire the situation actually seemed. He felt like gerbils were running wind sprints through his gut, their sharp little claws digging into his gastric lining. His hand pressed against his belly, but that didn't ease the pain as he scrambled (unsuccessfully) for a few reassuring words.

"Arnold?"

Up went both hands in surrender.

"Okay, so here's the deal. Somehow Nawzer—actually I guess it *could've* been some totally different dude, but that's doubtful—was able to hack Mr. Davidson's computers and...that's how she found out where I live."

He purposely edited out the part about suspecting this months ago on account of it being irrelevant at the moment. Maybe it always would be.

Rachael, fists on hips, continued to glare.

"In other words, she knows *exactly* where I live."

Arnold's hands were still raised in surrender.

"Whoa, let's not get ahead of ourselves, Rach. We don't know this for sure."

Again, total bullshit!

"I assume by *we* you mean you and Davidson. Because it certainly doesn't include me. I know."

"Well, let's be truthful here. No one knows for sure yet except Naseem."

"Wrong," Rachael said, her voice growing in volume. "*I* know she does and I damn well don't like it! This is exactly the type of crap I was afraid might happen. It's exactly why I said..."

Fists now balls of white knuckles, she spun around to face the window again, her whole body vibrating intense anger, frustration and God knows what else.

Wow! He had never seen her this enraged. At anything. Go to her? And say what, exactly?

In her reflection on the glass, he saw her cheeks glisten with tears. Had to do *something*.

He stepped close and set both hands gently on her shoulders again.

"Oh, Rach honey...I'm so sorry..."

She shrugged herself free and spun around.

"Do *not* patronize me, you self-centered son-of-a-bitch. I'm not the same little girl you knew when we were twelve. Saying you're sorry doesn't change a goddamned thing. Your gambling put us in this mess, goddamnit."

For one moment, she skewered him with dagger eyes before storming into the bedroom. The door slammed.

She yelled: "Make sure the door's locked on your way out."

Fuck!

He took one step toward the bedroom door, hand out for the

knob, thought: *Wrong!*

He stood at the door feeling as helpless as he had when first learning of his parents' senseless murder. The only difference between then and now was that their deaths could never be reversed. This? Surely, her rage would blow over. Perhaps a strategic retreat would be best. Bleak situations always looked less bleak after a night's sleep. Check in with her in the morning after meeting with Fisher, when he could at least tell her their plan.

He shifted from foot to foot, cleared his throat again, knuckled the door softly.

"We still on for dinner tomorrow night?"

Dude! Really? That's it? Your best shot?

"No! Just leave, Arnold."

"Okay, okay...but I'll call in the morning, after we meet with Fisher and I know our plan. I love you, Rach. Don't forget that. I'm going to do *every*thing in my power to end this...this situation with Naseem. I mean, like, forever. She'll never threaten us again. I promise."

Silence.

He paused at the front door for one last look around the apartment, a strange, uneasy gut feeling having replaced the gerbil claws.

But he had tomorrow. He'd call soon as his meeting with Fisher was finished.

In the hall now, door knob in hand, he leaned back into the apartment, "I love you."

Silence.

He checked to make sure the door was securely locked, just as she requested.

Chapter 33—Arnold

"THANKS FOR THE ride. I'll rate you a five," Arnold said to the Uber driver.

"Thanks. Likewise."

Arnold stepped from the Corolla and proceeded to Davidson's front porch, where he waited for car to leave before starting in on the security system. The Uber app pinged on his iPhone. He rated the ride and gave the driver a five-dollar tip.

To either side of the front door were large lush rhododendrons, the sight triggering a memory of a seemingly distant evening just two months ago when he sought refuge in the shadows there while awaiting Davidson's return. In retrospect, it amazed him how little had actually changed since. In fact, not a goddamned thing was substantially different from a year and a half ago when fleeing Las Vegas. Well, that wasn't entirely true if one actually kept score: Karim dead, Firouz imprisoned, the Green Lake house burned to the ground, two terrorists shot to death in the warehouse firefight. Yet Naseem remained a clear and present danger. All significant events. The only new ripple in the equation was Rachael. And this caused him serious worry.

His fault. All because of some adolescent need to impress a high-priced call girl. An escort. A prostitute. Jesus!

With a sigh, he started working his way through Davidson's elaborate security.

Arnold stood just inside the front door, listening for any sounds of activity. Silence. Davidson had retired, leaving on the desk lamp in the guest room. Thoughtful.

After deciding to shower in the morning, he changed into his extra-large well-worn Seahawks t-shirt—his favorite nightwear—and slipped between the crisp sheets of the Murphy bed and flicked off the bedside lamp. Curled up on his right side, he gazed out the floor-to-ceiling windows at the twinkling city lights rimming the inky harbor.

He needed sleep but knew it might be difficult to come by, especially with Rachael weighing so heavily on him. The thought of losing her...

Had to admit, though, she did make a valid point; as long as Naseem Farhad was hunting him, every being in his immediate circle remained in danger.

He saw only one way to extricate himself from this clusterfucked epic saga: kill The Bitch.

Could he actually do it? In the final analysis, he'd killed Karim, so why not her? Well, Karim's death was provoked and under entirely different circumstances. Karim was on the cusp of killing *him,* making it a case of flat-out self-defense.

Yeah, okay, so why doesn't that apply to Naseem? After all...

Had to think about that. Naseem knew—or perhaps rightly suspected—that if he wasn't alive to disarm the tripwires that were likely programed into SAM, the system would self-destruct the moment Nawzer attempted to use it. So, if she really intended to use SAM for her jihad, she needed him alive. Initially. Once Nawzer knew enough to disarm the tripwires, it would be game over.

The flaw to this logic was, of course, Rachael. Because, if Naseem used her as leverage to force him to hand over SAM intact...

Which brought him back to square one. His best option—his

only option, really—was to kill Naseem before she had the chance to take Rachael hostage because the FBI never negotiates for hostages...

Yeah, but could he actually do it? Not only *could* he, but, *how* could he? A gun? Hell, he'd never fired one in his life. And, truth be told, he couldn't see himself using one in cold blood. A knife? He shuddered at the thought.

No, whatever method he came up with would have to be more, ah, hands-off and less up close and personal. Like a car bomb. Hmmm...that one had a nice ring to it.

Moreover, he'd need to make sure there was absolutely no evidence to implicate him.

Perhaps make it look like the work of a rival cell? Might work. She undoubtedly has created a modest number of enemies in her line of work.

Fuck!

He pounded his pillow, rolled onto his left side and closed his eyes.

Sleep, goddamnit, sleep!

Naseem

Naseem grabbed the cellphone before it could ring a second time. Sheena. Had to be of extreme importance for her to break protocol and call directly.

"Yes?"

"I finally have some news on the Jew's woman. She is in an apartment downtown. I followed the Jew from the lawyer's house."

Ah, yes, the girlfriend.

The Jew's Achilles' heel.

"Well done. Send me what information you have."

Meaning through their secure Dark Net link. Naseem terminated the call.

Smiling, she leaned back in the chair to stretch. She'd been considering an alternative plan for forcing the Jew to cooperate since first learning of this girl, Rachael. Simple and effective; kidnap her and demand his system as ransom.

As easy as this sounded, if it were to be successful it'd entail a flawless series of risky steps. Each layer of complexity increased the risk of an unforeseen error resulting in a disaster for the entire project, and potentially the entire mission.

For this very reason she rejected Kasra's suggestion of capturing the Jew to waterboard the password from him. Yes, he was soft and ill-prepared for an "enhanced interrogation," and would, she predicted, quickly surrender the information.

But Nawzer warned—based on nothing more than educated suspicion—that the system was not only complex but certainly booby-trapped, making it problematic to operate without inadvertently sabotaging the result. She believed him.

The ideal scenario would be for Nawzer to engineer clandestine access into the Jew's computer. If successful, this would allow him to learn the intricacies of operation while, bit by bit, copying the software to his own computer. Although this sounded like a solid idea, so far over the past eighteen months Nawzer had failed to produce any results, forcing her to doubt that he could outwit the Jew.

Would bringing him here to Honolulu alter that?

Perhaps.

Perhaps not.

But because doing this appeared to carry the least risk to their jihad, it remained worth one more try. But, to hedge her bets, she always searched for an alternative. Since learning of the Jew's woman, using her as a bargaining chip assumed higher priority, a strategy definitely worth analyzing in greater detail.

One way or another, she would win this struggle.

Chapter 34—Arnold

FISHER MET ARNOLD and Davidson just inside the front doors of the office building at precisely seven a.m. After checking Arnold's Surface tablet, Fisher escorted them to the elevator and then to the conference room three doors further down the hall from his office. Arnold and Davidson were already familiar with this room, having spent time here during their last run in with Naseem.

John Chang was sitting at the long oak conference table working on a laptop. Another open laptop—Fisher's, Arnold assumed—glowed beside Chang's.

Beaming, Chang stood, came around the table for a bro-hug.

"Good to see you, bro!"

"You too, dude. Damn shame it's under these circumstances, though."

Fisher settled in with, "Now that the kumbayas are finished, let's get to work. There's much to cover this morning. We'll start with you, Gold. Walk us through everything you know and remember about your telephone conversation with Farhad, every detail including what you were doing at the time and your conversation."

Arnold finished the story, surprised at not being interrupted.

Fisher asked, "I realize you and I already discussed this, but did you pick up anything on the call that might be of help? Background noise? Anything at all?"

Arnold pointed to his Surface.

"May I show you my security video now?"

"Is it relevant to what I just asked?"

"It is. Here, let me show you..." He rotated the tablet and slid it across the table to him. "My surveillance caught her watching the house."

After studying the series of images, Fisher and Chang returned the Surface to Arnold.

"Have to admit, that certainly resembles her. But for now, let's get back to the actual phone call. Pick up anything worthwhile from it?"

"Like?"

Chang's turn.

"A number?"

"Yeah, I did and," Arnold said, turning to Fisher. "I emailed it to you that night, right?"

"You did, but I haven't had a chance to share it with John yet."

Arnold shrugged.

"Hold on." He opened his notes, found the number and read it to them. "I suspect it's of no help, that it's either a burner or spoofed."

Chang again: "I agree, but we can't afford to overlook an angle no matter how slim. Did it come in on landline or mobile?"

"Landline."

Chang raised an eyebrow.

"Didn't have you pegged as a Luddite. Any particular reason for having one?"

"Couple reasons, actually. Mostly, to eliminate any chance of someone monitoring my calls with a Stingray." It was a device capable of eavesdropping on nearby cellphone traffic. "And that's probably all on accounta owning one. I know firsthand how effective they can be. Also, it was cheaper to bundle it into my internet charge. I mean, why not? Turns out to be a screaming deal, actually."

Fisher motioned Chang to continue, making Arnold believe they'd scripted the interview strategy.

"You don't happen to have her old iPhone number on you, do you?"

"No, but I can dig it up later today, if you want."

Fisher said, "Do that, please, and pass it on to him." He glanced at his screen a beat. "Let's move on to the malware on Davidson's laptop. Tell us again why you suspected it and what you did to confirm it." Before Arnold could answer, Fisher added, "Yes, you told me that too, but I want to go through it again for John's benefit."

Arnold walked them through the reason he became suspicious and that yes, he found malware on Davidson's laptop and home computers but had not yet checked the office machines. Chang agreed that the trojan had undoubtedly replicated itself in those computers too.

Arnold concluded with, "I didn't touch a thing. I wanted to discuss how to proceed with you guys before doing that."

"Believe me, we appreciate that," Chang said.

"You're the one with the most experience with these shitheads," Fisher added. "You think Nawzer's still their go-to guy for tech?"

Arnold nodded.

"Until proven otherwise."

"Where do you grade his skill set?" Chang asked. "On a scale of one to ten?"

Good question.

"Hmmm...never thought about it before, probably on accounta never had any serious concern that he could actually hack my security. So, I have to ask myself, why think that? Let's work through this; he's tech-savvy. I'll give him that much. But, based on the tactics I've seen him use, he's no wizard. If forced to put a number on it, I'd give him a seven-point-five, best case."

Chang typed into the laptop.

"Good information to know."

Arnold spoke.

"We open to suggestions now?"

Fisher motioned Chang to answer.

"What're you thinking?"

"Last night, I got this thought as I was trying to go to sleep; it's your basic honeypot trap to first catch Nawzer, and then leverage that to track down Naseem. The tricky part is pulling it off without tipping our hand. Goes like this; far as they know, we haven't tumbled to the malware on Mr. Davidson's machines, right?"

Rhetorical, but Fisher answered anyway. "That's a safe assumption."

"What if we plant some sort of a file in Mr. Davidson's office machine, one we make so irresistible that next time Nawzer's in there nosing around, he can't help but open it."

"Promising," Fisher said.

"The trick is to make it," Arnold quickly added, "enticing without being suspicious."

"I like it. I saw a similar setup work," Chang said enthusiastically. "How about this for a nice little twist, a little flair to make the trap look legit: when we plant it, we remove his trojan and bolt down security just enough to make it look like the work of an amateur...but not tight enough to keep him from hacking in. That should make it appear more legit, don't you think?"

Arnold applauded.

"Love it! But how about this: we tighten security enough to keep him out and force him to try another spear-phish attack. We'll have it all set up that when we take his bait, it actually infects him."

"You just lost me," Davidson said.

"I'll explain later, Mr. Davidson."

"What do you think would be good bait?" Fisher asked Arnold.

"How about an official FBI report in PDF form...something to do with Naseem..."

"...or you," offered Chang, clearly growing more excited with the plan.

Arnold turned to Davidson: "We load the PDF with our malware so that when he opens or downloads it, *his* computer becomes infected..."

"...with a RAT that'll give us access to his computer," Chang finished the thought.

"I fucking love it!" Fisher slapped the table and stood. "Let's take a quick break before hammering out the specifics."

Chapter 35—Arnold

"GOT A MOMENT?" Arnold asked Chang as Fisher and Davidson exited the room. "I have a couple questions, if you don't mind."

Chang sank back into his chair.

"Sure. What up?"

"What's your background? I mean, how'd you land this job?"

Chang eyed him.

Curiosity? Something else?

"And you're asking because?"

"On accounta your job...it's so super cool; a White Hat catching Black Hats thing. Very cool, indeed. What's your degree?"

Chang laughed.

"Degree? I don't have no stinking degree."

Whoa.

"Seriously?"

"Seriously. Freshman year I was doing all the basic computer-science required shit, still undecided what I'd actually end up doing other than it'd eventually be something to do with cybersecurity. About midway through my second quarter I met a couple *friends*"— he verbally italicized the word, which, to Arnold, implied hackers— "who convinced me the best training was in the military, in particular, the Air Force."

"No shit?" News to him.

"I shit you not, bro. Did some serious digging and came to find out other knowledgeable friends totally agreed with that. I really wasn't happy in school, so I signed up for a four-year stint. Never looked back. But, far as this particular job goes, although the online recruitment notice claims you need at least a BA to apply, they look very carefully at military training and experience too. In essence, they hire you based on performance and not what initials follow your name."

"The military, huh...interesting." Arnold said, although he couldn't see himself going that route. "Why do you think military training's superior to a university?"

"Because those dudes *always* play for keeps. If they're not one step ahead of the bad guys it's game over. Hell, they encounter shit every day that most professors won't even hear about for years, if ever. And if the professors don't know about it, how the hell they going to teach you how to deal with it?"

Made a lot of sense.

Chang gave him a I-know-what-you're-thinking look.

"Why you asking, bro?"

"I applied for two cybersecurity gigs, but was turned down on accounta no degree."

"You have any killer references? Any track record?"

Arnold felt his face reddening.

"Unfortunately, no."

"Okay, there's the reason you were dinged. A degree had nothing to do with it." Chang paused. "What kind of work you looking for? Specifically."

Great question.

Until now, Arnold had only been thinking in generalities. Perhaps he needed to hone it down some.

"I'm totally into AI. So, ideally it's something along the lines of merging AI with cybersecurity."

"There's a super-cool project that DARPA"—Chang was

referring to the Defense Advanced Research Projects Agency—"is working along those lines, but I have no idea what their requirements are. Hey, don't let that discourage you...there're tons of jobs out there for someone like you."

"Such as?"

"Don't know off the top of my head, but if I were you, I'd seriously check out starting my own business, something along the lines of searching out network vulnerabilities then finding ways to correct them. I tell you, bro, it's low-hanging fruit."

Wow! Cool idea.

He was stoked.

"If you want, I can point you to a few people already doing that sort of gig."

"My man!"

They fist-bumped just as Fisher and Davidson came back in.

Chapter 36—Naseem

KASRA BRAKED THE car to a stop in front of the Holiday Inn Express off Kuhio Avenue, where Nawzer was waiting at the curb.

Naseem lowered the passenger window.

"Welcome to Honolulu, Brother. Use the back seat."

She wanted to spend as little time in the open as possible. She wore on reflective Ray-Bans and a wide-brim floppy sun hat that barely fit inside the car.

The moment the back passenger-door clinked shut, Kasra was moving into the flow of traffic again. With the pickup completed, Naseem turned off her iPhone.

"How was your flight?" she asked, not really giving a shit.

"Long and uncomfortable. I was stuck in a middle seat."

She pictured Nawzer, refugee-thin and a half inch over six feet, folded uncomfortably into a narrow seat, but felt no sorrow or empathy for him. You did whatever job was required in the fight against the infidel. A few hours of personal suffering paled in comparison to the greater glory of the Jihad.

"You took the bus from the airport?" she asked.

As she had instructed. She didn't want to risk a cab driver identifying him to an FBI agent at some later time. In contrast, airport buses were perpetually stocked with harried drivers and exhausted travelers anxious to reach their destination, thereby allowing one to remain relatively anonymous.

"I did."

"We will talk later."

That ended the conversation. Although Naseem considered Kasra one of her loyal and dedicated sympathizers, she didn't know her for as long or as well as Nawzer, meaning she'd continue to be extremely cautious over how much information to share with her. Naseem applied the same rule to all local sympathizers.

Ten minutes later they turned into the Parking Lot B at Daniel K Inouye airport. Kasra pulled to the side of the road, shifted into park, set the brake, and stepped out, allowing Naseem to push up over the console into the driver's seat, knocking off her hat in the process. Once seated, she promptly replaced the hat after fastening her seatbelt. God forbid she should be pulled over for not wearing it.

"You will pick me up after my shift, Sister?"

Naseem nodded.

"I will."

Naseem maneuvered into the flow of traffic, reversing the route Kasra just drove. With only the two of them in the car, she felt free to talk with Nawzer about the mission.

"I am happy to see you again, Brother."

"Yes. It is being four months since you are in Los Angeles?"

"Close to that, I believe. Being face to face makes discussing our plans much safer. I worry about security when we use electronics of any type."

"Yes, this is always a worry. Always. We are being lucky, I think."

"It was good work, you finding the Jew," Nassem told him. "Very good work."

"I am thinking he is being very stupid using the name Hans Weiser both places."

"True, very true."

"But I am being confused. What is the reason I am flying here? What am I doing here that I am not doing in Los Angeles?"

The question was annoying. They'd discussed his complaint multiple time over the last three weeks. Yet he still complained. *What did he not understand? He was growing softer than she ever imagined.*

"You must find a way to bypass the Jew's security system."

"This is what I am not understanding," Nawzer whined. "What are you believing I am doing here that I am not doing there? The Jew's firewall is being too strong to defeat."

"Have we not discussed this?" Now even more pissed at him. "I am quite aware you haven't been able to breach his *internet* security. But what if we can discover a way to physically enter his house to put something directly into his computer? Think what you might be able to do then."

Nawzer appeared to think about that.

"You may be right, but I am thinking we are wasting too much time and effort on this one Jew. He is not being so important to our cause. There are other things..."

"There is no other thing more important than this, Brother!"

Chapter 37—Arnold

AFTER THE BREAK, Fisher, Chang, and Arnold began to toss around the contents of the PDF that Arnold would plant in Davidson's computer as bait. Something that would clearly entice Nawzer. The title of the PDF—the cheese for the mousetrap—would be the first compelling lure.

"It should exactly look like an official FBI report," Chang suggested.

"Perfect!" Arnold replied.

"I agree," Fisher said. "John, why don't you take point on that part. With that now settled, let's talk contents. I suggest we throw in a few choice bits of critical disinformation...things Nawzer would find highly inflammatory."

"Interesting," Arnold said. "You obviously have one in mind. What?"

Fisher smiled.

"Our evidence suggests that Nawzer *never* set foot in that warehouse, and most likely wasn't even in Hawaii when the incident went down. Yet your surveillance showed two or three people, probably more—one of whom was definitely Naseem—inside in the moments the incident blew up. Yet, only two bodies were recovered, meaning a least one person—I suspect more—escaped soon after the firefight erupted. One of those escapees had to be Naseem."

"Yeah, that part still pisses me off..." Arnold said

"Point is, bet you Nawzer has no fucking idea what actually went down in there."

"Okay, so the punchline is?"

"His cousin, Bijan, ended up shot point-blank in the back of his head by someone inside. We have credible evidence that points to Naseem as the shooter."

"Wow! For real?" Arnold was shocked. "*She* offed him?"

"Fuck if I know who actually pulled the trigger," Fisher answered. "I'm just saying we add that choice tidbit in the dummy report and make it incontrovertible."

"The mockup will appear exactly like a copy of an official report," Chang added. "We don't have much deep background on Nawzer, but we do know that his culture values family very highly. So, if there's anything we can possibly do to stir the pot with him, this might just be our best shot. I don't see that we have anything to lose by adding it. Do you?"

Davidson, Chang, and Arnold agreed.

Fisher made a point of checking his watch. A busy man with a busy schedule.

"There anything else any of you want to add?" Fisher asked.

No one spoke up.

"In that case," Fisher continued, "let's review our individual tasks. You two"—he pointed to Arnold and Chang—"work on cleaning-up Davidson's computer and baiting the trap. I want all of you to communicate freely and move ahead independently but do so while keeping me in the loop. I'll be available anytime you need. Otherwise, just let me know when you finished with the trap and are ready to proceed to the next phase."

One point still bothered Arnold.

"Uh, Mr. Fisher...sometimes my methods aren't exactly kosher, right?"

"Hey, Gold, how you get your information is your business. Officially you're our CI. We just have to find a way to use any critical intel you come up with in court."

Court? Court? Who said anything about court? No way was that bitch going to end up in court!

"We good, Gold?" Fisher asked, eyeing him suspiciously.

"Absolutely, solid." Arnold said.

"Good. Once everything's set to go," Fisher continued, "I want Gold to remove the malware from, and make appropriate changes to, Davidson's computers. Notify John when you finish because at that point, the clock starts ticking. We clear?"

"I am," Arnold said, looking at Chang.

"So am I," Chang said.

"In the meantime, there's a BOLO out on the island for her. Any questions?"

When none were raised, Fisher stood, apparently ready to leave the meeting.

"John, will you please escort these gentlemen out when you're finished?"

"Hey, before you go, have a couple quick questions," Arnold said.

Fisher nodded but continued to stand. Davidson began to get up, but Arnold motioned him to wait.

"Is Firouz still in prison?" Arnold asked, referring to one of terrorists who attacked him almost a year and a half ago.

"Yes."

"Where?"

"That information's classified."

This gave Arnold pause.

Why classified?

"So, here's the point; he's got to be contact with Naseem, right?"

"We suspect he is. That's why we've heightened surveillance on him this past month, but so far, nothing's turned up. Which leads us to suspect they're communicating through other inmates' family members. So far, we've had no success sorting that out."

Figures.

"Last question: the two bugs the electrician planted in my house. What happened to them? What'd you find out?"

Fisher took a moment to answer.

"Ah, yes, those. You were right. They were intelligence-grade devices that"— he used finger quotes—"went missing."

"Went missing? From whom?"

Fisher shook his head.

"That, Gold, is way above my pay grade."

Fisher plunked his attaché case on the conference table and popped the latches.

"Oh, almost forgot. This is for you."

He handed Arnold and Davidson what, at first glance, looked like Samsung Galaxy cellphones. On closer inspection, they were CryptoPhone 500s: ultra-secure cells with bulletproof encryption algorithm. Meaning no fucking way could Nawzer—or anyone else, for that matter—listen in on their conversations with a Stingray.

Sweet!

Fisher said, "Only our numbers"—he pointed to Chang and himself—"are in—or can be programmed into—memory. From now until this situation is resolved, I want all voice communication between us on these. No exceptions. Except a flaming emergency. Understood?"

Holy shit.

He wished he hadn't wasted money on shitty little TracFones. These sweet little CryptoPhones set the taxpayers back a few bucks.

Arnold stood to fist-bump Fisher.

"Thanks for..." *For what? Doing your job trying to hunt down terrorists?* "...everything. I got a very good feeling we're going to nail her this time!"

With Fisher gone, Arnold asked Chang, "Once everything's set, I plan on analyzing the trojan offline. Have any problem with that?"

He was pretty sure he wouldn't, but felt it politic to inquire anyway, on account of Chang being FBI and all. With a grin, Chang reached in his pocket.

"I anticipated you'd be tempted to do that. Here." He tossed Arnold a flash drive.

"Awesome."

"Once you copy it to that flash drive, call an Uber to run it over here and I'll do an independent analysis. Look forward to comparing notes with you. Soon."

Chapter 38—Nawzer

"THAT IS HIS house," Naseem whispered, pointing up the sloping jagged bank of reddish lava to four I-beam pylons encased securely in a substantial concrete foundation sunk into the slope.

Nawzer leaned back to study the underside of the deck. From what little he could see of the actual house from this angle, it appeared to be two stories. A dusty footpath just to his left snaked up the steep slope to a basement door, putting the main floor at street level. The house appeared no different from all the others they passed on the hike up here.

Nawzer—winded from the climb and midday heat—wiped the back of his hand across his forehead, more intent on settling his oxygen debt than studying the back of the Jew's house. What could he possibly learn from looking at a concrete basement? Naseem was a fool to make him climb all this way for nothing.

After sucking a deep breath, he asked, "We are looking at the Jew's house for...?"

His peripheral vision caught the hard look she flashed in response but he pretended to not see it. *Fuck her.* Fact was, she needed him more than he needed her. This thought made him smile.

"What?" she demanded, having caught that too. *Bitch!*

"I am simply asking why are we being here looking at a

basement?"

"Because you have never seen it before," she whispered, clearly irritated.

"This is true, but what am I seeing now," he said, pointing at the house, "is helping me how?"

"That's for you to determine," she said with an exasperated sigh, as if trying to reason with a petulant adolescent. "The more firsthand information you have, the more likely you can solve the puzzle. After all, you've not been able to solve it from Los Angeles, have you?"

He rolled his eyes. *Stupid pig.* Since beginning her very personal jihad to steal the Jew's computers, her technical ignorance resulted in nothing but unreasonable and fruitless demands and wasted effort. Effort better spent elsewhere.

"Don't do that!" Naseem ordered.

"What?" he asked with feigned innocence, finally turning to face her, still unable to mask the faint smile.

Her eyes tore into him.

He understood that it might benefit him to play along by displaying pretend deference but he refused to stoop to such levels. Yes, she was their titular leader. But only because Firouz, her husband, was presently in federal lockup, certainly not because of any merit on her part. No woman—especially her—should be in charge of the group. Women became too easily bogged down emotionally and distracted by petty slights and grievances. This obsession with the Jew served as a perfect example.

He simply stared back in feigned innocence.

Suddenly, he saw a flicker in her eyes that had never been there before. What? Hate? He stiffened, realizing its unstated implication. Perhaps it might be wiser to placate her until his plan was completely ready to execute.

"Watch this." Nawzer raised his iPhone so she could see the screen, then opened Settings, then scrolled to wi-fi, as if demonstrating a magic trick.

"Look," he said, pointing to the list of signals it was picking up. "Four networks are being available. We are standing below the Jew's house, so this one, being strongest, is being his. I am not being surprised it is encrypted."

All true, but absolutely useless information to now have. He gave her a triumphant look.

"Yes yes! See? We *did* learn something coming here. Now you must find a way to defeat the encryption."

She seemed truly excited over this finding. He simply nodded, happy to have defused the situation.

Stupid cow.

"Yes," he said, suppressing a sigh, "but this is not being easy. We are traveling this trail before, when we are in Seattle, and it is yielding us nothing."

Now more questioning than demanding.

"Yes, but you will work on it."

Again, he wiped sweat from his brow with the back of his wrist.

"Yes, Sister. Can we be going now? I must be working hard on an idea."

"Yes, but first you must look at the front of the house too. We will drive around."

She started scrambling back down the path into the depths of the ravine, Nawzer sauntering behind, taking his time, making sure to not twist an ankle, now more convinced than ever she intended to kill him.

He vowed she would never get her chance.

Chapter 39—Arnold

ARNOLD AND DAVIDSON walked out of the lobby of the Henry M. Jackson Federal Building straight into 40-degree hazy drizzle and late-October biting chill. It was a penetrating cold that knifed straight through Arnold's black Fjall Raven as if it were made from sheer cotton instead of Gore-Tex. With a shiver, he stopped on the steps to zipper all the way up to his neck. Put on the hood as well. Davidson did likewise with his parka shell.

"Damn, it's cold! Not what I'm used to anymore," Arnold said, hunching his shoulders.

Davidson laughed.

"How quickly you forget. Perhaps now you understand my desire for a condo over there."

He started down the steps.

"So, how'd you think it went in there?" Arnold asked, catching up to him.

"Modestly well. You?"

Davidson stopped on the sidewalk and faced him.

"Totally agree," Arnold said, blowing into cupped hands. "This time *we're* on offense. Hey, change of subject...you up for dinner tonight? Uptown?"

Davidson seemed to consider it. "What time?"

"Does six work for you?"

"I can do that. What about Rachael?"

Poof.

Concern over last night just killed the buoyant optimistic mood of a moment ago. He'd described her blowup to Davidson on the ride downtown.

"That's the thing..." Arnold said, shaking his head. "I plan to call soon as we're done here, see if she's calmed down enough to even speak to me. My hope was that if you're at dinner it might, ah, soften things a bit."

"Good luck with that." Davidson began to turn away, but hesitated. "Sorry to cut this short, but I really need to be back to the office. I will either meet you at Uptown at six or back at the house later tonight, depending on the outcome of your call. It is still early. You still plan to meet with your decorator?"

"I dunno...depends on Rachael, she's now top priority. I need to smooth things out soon as possible."

"As I said, good luck with that. Catch you later."

With that, Davidson turned and walked away.

Arnold called after him, "Uptown's my treat, by the way...since I'm at Hotel Davidson."

"I accept," Davidson called over his shoulder.

As Arnold watched his friend continue along Second Avenue, an uneasy feeling sprouted in the very depth of his gut. Something...well, out of sorts. What? Nebulous, amorphous, frustratingly ill-defined. He suddenly found it difficult to breath. His heart accelerated. Wow, something definitely wrong. Not only that, but he was very afraid.

Of what? He glanced around, saw nothing threatening. Chance? Rachael? Davidson?

Shit!

Not knowing the reason for the anxiety only amplified it.

Shit-shit-shit!

He stepped back into the doorway, out of the breeze, dialed

Rachael. It rang until finally going to voicemail. Shit, she never ignored his calls.

Or...

...was that it? Something happened to her?

The feeling intensified. No, this feeling didn't involve Rachael. Yes, it was disconcerting for her to not answer, but this was about something else...

He dialed the vet clinic.

"Hey, it's Toby Taylor, Chance's owner. How's my boy?"

"He's fine. In fact, he's out for his morning walk."

"You sure he's okay?"

Pause.

"Yes. Why?"

The anxious fear morphed into a premonition: impending doom.

Do something! What?

"Are *you* okay?" the receptionist asked.

"Yeah, no, it's nothing, nothing...sorry to bother you...thanks."

He was teetering on the cusp of panic. Realized he was hyperventilating. He held his breath, counted off five seconds.

Calm down! Rachael.

He dialed again. It rang until going to voicemail again.

"Rach, it's me. Call me. Immediately! It's important. I know you're pissed but just let me know you're okay, that's all."

Shit! Why no answer?

She's said she traded days, so wasn't scheduled for work today, unless, of course, she traded back. Yeah, but even if she had, she wouldn't be there in the morning.

Shit-shit-shit!

She never ignored calls, not even those she didn't want to answer. He'd seen her even step out of the shower to answer a few. On the other hand, she was totally pissed at him....

Oh my God, it's Davidson!

Chapter 40—Nawzer

NAWZER SAT IN the passenger seat, studying what little he could see of the Jew's house behind the security wall: mostly a flat roofline and solar panels. Solid gates protected the pedestrian walk and driveway.

Pretty much what she'd described multiple times over months of emails and pictures.

"You see the two cameras? There and there?" Naseem asked, pointing.

He followed the finger's trajectory to two cameras on swivel mounts under the corners of the roof in front. He nodded. She also explained that additional cameras were strategically positioned at other roof spots, providing three hundred and sixty degrees of perimeter views. Nothing new here; she'd told him all this during the past two months. But the real point was that no one would go to such expense for such elaborate security to protect one computer. No, this degree of defense underscored the high value of the Jew's system. He fully understood this point.

"Nawzer! Look at what I tell you, it's important."

He made no attempt to mask his boredom. How much longer could he tolerate this shit? The bomb was built. It needed only a few finishing touches to the remote detonator. One day, perhaps two, then given the opportunity...problem solved.

"Yes, yes, I am seeing them," he said.

Naseem

She recoiled at his insolence but stopped short of saying anything because he was now looking at the front gate. Intently, too. What? Had she missed an important detail? She looked more closely. No, nothing seemed unusual or out of place. Nawzer nodded to himself and smiled.

"Do you see something?"

He steadied his iPhone and clicked off four pictures.

"I am seeing enough for now," he replied. "We can go."

"No! Tell me what are you seeing!"

"Drive. We must be going now."

Reluctantly, she released the parking brake and shifted to Drive. While passing the front gate, Nawzer took three more shots.

Chapter 41—Arnold

"WHAT HAPPENED?" DAVIDSON asked. "Did you speak with her?"

Arnold was now walking along Second Avenue heading toward the Smith Tower, iPhone to ear.

"Where are you?"

"I am about to exit Slate Coffee, why?"

"Something's *really* wrong. I mean really wrong. I can feel it. Where are you? Your exact location."

"I just told you: Slate Coffee. A coffee shop on Second Avenue, one block north of my office. Why?"

Arnold increased his pace.

"Stay right there. Do *not* move. Wait for me."

"Calm down, son. Everything is fine. What is going on?"

Yes, something was going to happen to Davidson.

He knew this as fact though he had never before had a premonition. It was a deeply disturbing, frightening sensation of undebatable realism.

"Just stay put, I'm coming to you. Do *not* hang up."

"Just slow down, Arnold. I am not going anywhere. Everything is absolutely fine. Believe me."

Arnold started jogging, phone banging his ear, breathing hard, running through a crosswalk as a driver laid on his horn, people turning to stare, the panicky feeling making his chest feel as if it would crack open. He was flat-out running now, past Metropolitan Grill.

One block to go. He blew through another intersection as the light turned red.

Then he saw it, a small shop next to a florist, Davidson to the right of the front door, coffee cup in hand. Davidson stepped from under the awning to meet him on the sidewalk.

"My God, Arnold. What. Is. Wrong?"

Arnold bent over, hand on knees, panting, fighting for breath, the panic beginning to ebb. Slightly. He shook his head, stalling to catch his breath.

Then finally said: "Something's definitely wrong. Bad wrong. Man, I got this crazy strong premonition..."

Suddenly he became aware of sirens. Growing louder. Davidson turned, looked behind them. Arnold looked too, just in time to see one fire engine and two black police SUVs barreling down Second Avenue straight toward them, then past, and stop outside Smith Tower. A second fire truck came screaming by ten seconds later, then a third, then the street and sidewalk was one huge congeal of vehicles and looky-loos.

He and Davidson remained side by side in the chilling October drizzle watching the unfolding scene one block away. He realized his anxiety was now gone.

Strange.

It was so damn intense only moments ago.

"Probably a heart attack," Davidson muttered without turning.

"I dunno...three fire engines? No Medic One? Doesn't seem right."

"Hmmm, point taken." Davidson nodded. "And the police..." Davidson had his cell out, dialing. A moment later; "That is very strange. Joyce does not answer."

Davidson crossed the intersection toward the crowd of

bystanders, Arnold tagging along at his heels. They wormed their way through the crowd to two cops blocking the front doors to the building. One cop stepped in front of Davidson.

"Sorry, Sir, no one's allowed in at the moment."

"But I work here. My office is in this building."

"Sorry, sir. Can't let you enter."

Davidson craned his neck to see into the lobby. Arnold did likewise. A fireman and a police officer stood in the center of the marble foyer, talking. All elevators were at lobby level with their doors open; an automatic recall triggered whenever a fire alarm occurred.

Arnold said, "Excuse me, officer, but can you at least tell us what's happened?"

The cop shook his head.

"Don't know for sure."

"Well, what? Any unofficial word?"

"I can't answer your question, sir, so if you don't mind, we're pretty busy here."

The Cryptophone in Arnold's pocket began ringing.

Oh, shit!

He tapped Davidson's shoulder, motioned to their left, held up his phone, and wormed back through the crowd, Davidson following, sticking close. Arnold answered the call.

Chapter 42—Arnold

"GOLD, FISHER. WHERE are you?"

"What? Hold one." Arnold stepped further from the crowd and plugged his free ear with his free index finger. "Say again?"

"Where are you?"

"Out front of the Smith Tower. Something's going on in there and the fire department won't let us in the building. Why?"

"Have a picture I need your eyes on ASAP to see if you can identify the individuals."

"Individuals? Who are they?"

"I want you to take a look first. How soon can you be back here?"

"Hell, I dunno....there's a lot going on at the moment. Joyce, Mr. Davidson's secretary isn't..."

"Look, Gold, this really isn't a request, I'm telling you. How long before you're back here?"

Shit, guess he's serious.

"Hold on a second." Then to Davidson: "Fisher wants me back there now. You okay without me?"

"No problem, go ahead."

Davidson turned his attention back to the building.

Arnold called over the crowd noise, "I'll call soon as I'm done with Fisher, see what's up," and started back along the route just taken. Then into the phone, he said, "Heading your way now. But what's the deal? Give me some sort of clue what's so interesting?"

Fisher hesitated a beat, which only piqued Arnold's interest.

"HPD stopped a vehicle coming from a cul-de-sac below your house, had two females inside. This was only minutes after your drone picked up activity across the ravine."

Holy shit!

"At the bottom of the ravine?"

He knew that area all too well.

"How the fuck should I know? All I know is it's in the general vicinity of your place. The cop was able to capture some pretty good shots with her body cam of the driver and passenger. I need you to tell me if you recognize either one."

"I should be in the lobby in three minutes."

"I'll be waiting."

Naseem

"What is so interesting?" Naseem asked.

Nawzer was studying the pictures on his iPhone, swiping back and forth between images. She had the car curbed on a side street three blocks from Arnold's house, engine idling, A/C fan humming, Naseem scanning the mirrors for police.

"We must be returning to the house, now," Nawzer said.

"The Jew's or Kasra's?"

Irritation and annoyance flashed across his face but vanished just as quickly.

"Kasra's."

"Why?" Such interest pleased her—his first genuine curiosity since landing—but his insolence was still pissing her off.

"I am needing more research."

"Research about what, Brother?"

She made no attempt to move the car and was determined to

sit here until he explained exactly was seemed so interesting. He was acting like a petulant child. She had missed something and this would be his way of getting back at her.

"It may be nothing or it may be something." He shrugged. "I am not knowing yet."

"A way past his security?"

"I am not knowing yet, Sister. This is what I am wanting to learn. Leave me to concentrate. Please"

Prick!

Clearly, he was savoring this temporary power over her. Temporary being the key word here. She swallowed a snide comment and pulled away from the curb. She'd give the prick one, maybe two days, then...

Arnold

"Wait!"

Arnold spun around, saw Davidson hurrying to catch up.

Davidson came abreast of him, said, "They have no idea how long it will be before I am allowed in the building, so I might as well tag along for an update on developments."

Arnold nodded, iPhone to his ear listening to Rachael's phone ring directly to voicemail. Yet again.

"Shit! Still no answer."

Davidson tried his office once more. No answer there either.

"That is strange," he said.

"What is?" Arnold asked, only half listening, increasingly worried, this being so out of character for Rachael.

"Joyce is not answering either."

"That could be easily explained. Maybe she had to vacate the office. We still don't know what the hell's going on over there, but sure looks serious."

"Perhaps. But I am still very concerned."

As they waited for a light to change, Arnold explained the

reason for Fisher's request.

The light went green. They continued on. A half block from the building, Arnold rang Fisher on the Cryptophone, told him to expect them in the lobby in a minute or two.

"These the best you have?" Arnold asked, swiping back and forth between five pictures.

"I consider us fortunate to have any of those," Fisher answered. "That was damn good work from that officer."

Arnold scrolled back to the first shot in the series.

"I totally don't recognize the driver...but this other one...man, that hat isn't doing us any favor. Blocks out most her face. Best I can say is, yeah, that's possibly her."

"Her. As in Naseem?" Fisher asked.

"Yes."

"You can't say probably?"

Arnold thought about that.

"Naw, can't go that far, not with that hat masking so much of her face. I'll stand pat with possible."

"All right then."

Fisher's phone rang.

He held up a just-a-minute finger and answered with, "Fisher."

Arnold watched Fisher's expression morph into forced deadpan.

Shit, something's up.

The uneasy gut feeling from earlier came crashing back. Bad news.

Fisher slowly replace his phone and looked directly at Davidson.

"Afraid I have bad news, Palmer."

Strange. Agent Fisher seldom addressed Davidson by his first name.

Davidson recoiled.

"For me?"

"There was an explosion in your office. Apparently, your secretary's been killed."

Davidson froze, his face draining of color. He stared at Fisher.

Fuck! I knew it. That feeling....

"What happened?" Arnold asked.

Fisher cleared his throat.

"There was an explosion. Both SPD's and SFD's initial impression is that a pipe bomb was used, but they're still collecting evidence. Because we have every reason to indicate this was a terrorist act, our agency's now taking point. We'll be involving ATF too."

"Naseem!" Arnold blurted, reflexively.

Fisher stood.

"Both of you stay put. I'll be back soon as I can. We need to talk."

Then he was out of his office.

Chapter 43—Naseem

"*THIS IS A* gift from Allah," Nawzer said, sitting at the kitchen table, intently working his laptop, Naseem opposite him, scanning news stories on her own machine.

She glanced up.

"Ah, so you are a believer again."

"I am never losing my faith," he replied too defensively.

"For not even a little bit? When you are fucking your *blond* girlfriend?"

She enjoyed the embarrassed flush in his cheeks and his apparent fluster.

"What I am choosing to do with my own time is none of your business," he finally replied.

"I understand your urges and thank Allah they involve only infidels." After all, who was she to judge, especially considering her prior work as an escort. "Tell me...what is this gift from Allah you have?"

"Not everything in American culture is bad," he said, leaning back in the chair with a mild tone of defiance.

Arms crossed, she too sat back, making a point of waiting for his answer.

Finally, turning his laptop toward her, he said, "Look."

She saw an enlarged, cropped photo of the front gate to the Jew's property but nothing of significance or out of the ordinary. Even closer inspection revealed nothing of importance.

Even though she knew he'd gloat over a minute detail she overlooked, after a resigned sigh, she said, "What's so important?"

"Sister, look very carefully at the front gate."

"Yes, I see the gate. What is so remarkable?"

She had tossed a half pound of poisoned hamburger over the gate perhaps two months ago but the Jew's dog refused to die.

"You are seeing the doorbell? The Amazon Ring?"

"Yes, yes, get on with it."

"It is wireless."

That smug tone of his echoed in her ears.

Fuck him!

She detested this juvenile game he was forcing upon her. She stared directly into his eyes.

He squirmed.

"I am remembering several months ago reading of these wi-fi connections...they are not being encrypted."

"Ah, so this may be a way past his firewall?"

He punctuated the reply with an enthusiastic nod.

"Yes!"

She relaxed, a smile crossing her face.

"Ah, then this *is* a gift from Allah. How soon before you have an answer?"

Nawzer swept his finger around the room

"First I am needing to establish a more secure network here before I am starting serious work. We are not taking any chances with the Jew finding out we are closing in."

"How long will that take?"

Nawzer pushed back the chair, stood, stretching his back and neck, shrugging his shoulders.

"One hour, perhaps less. But first, I am making us tea."

Chapter 44—Arnold

AS THEY WAITED in the conference room for Fisher to return, Arnold texted Rachael.

No answer.

All right already, I get it! You're pissed.

But to ignore repeated calls and texts? Simply was not in her nature. He had no doubt about it now: something was definitely wrong.

Davidson remained mute, a sphinx with a thousand-yard stare. What could he say to his friend that might be of comfort? Arnold slowly shook his head.

"Mr. Davidson, I'm so sorry..."

Davidson seemed to not hear.

Fisher poked his head in the office door.

"Need you two in the conference room."

Fisher introduced two other people already seated at the table as they walked in: Special Agents Woods and Tanner. Woods, a thin middle-aged white female, radiated a no-nonsense vibe. Tanner, a younger-looking African American male, struck Arnold as a tad less tight-ass.

After shutting the door, Fisher dropped heavily into the chair at the head of the oval table, said, "We need to go over the details of exactly what each of you did from the moment you left Honolulu."

He motioned Arnold to start.

"Mr. Fisher, before I do that, I'm *really* worried about Rachael."

"Who's Rachael? Your girlfriend?"

"Yes. I've been trying to contact her all morning but she's not answering calls or texts."

Fisher shot Woods a quick but serious glance.

Arnold quickly added, "I mean, this is not like her at all. I have a *very* bad feeling about this."

Nawzer

Nawzer put the finishing touches his cobbled-together small network built from two of his own, plus Naseem's and Kasra's laptops. Their internet download speed seemed glacial in comparison to the fiber-optic feed in his apartment. His encryption algorithm in his computer slowed the download speed further, testing his patience almost to the breaking point.

Naseem asked from across the kitchen table.

"What did you find out?"

"Nothing yet. I am now just starting. We are making mistakes if we are rushing. Patience."

"We don't have time for patience. What have you accomplished?" she demanded.

"The network is just starting working so now I am beginning to work also. Where are you wishing to start?"

"How sure are you of the doorbell?" she asked.

"I am not knowing until I am doing more research."

"Fine," she said, clearly frustrated with his circular argument. "Before you get too wrapped up in that, when did you last check the lawyer's email? You have not given me an update for several days and that is critical information to our plan."

He considered how to respond. In fact, it'd been ten days since he last took a look.

He said, "Before I am leaving Los Angeles."

At least that was truthful.

"How many days before you left?"

Nawzer shrugged.

"I am not sure....perhaps three?"

He gave himself a huge benefit of the doubt.

She motioned to his open laptop.

"Well then?"

Nawzer began to type.

"I am being certain that because of your phone call, the Jew is suspecting how we are finding him and is removing my access, but"—he shrugged— "one is never knowing. Perhaps you are upsetting him sufficiently to be overlooking this. I am thinking we are very lucky the Jew is not finding it months ago."

He chuckled at their good fortune.

Naseem apparently did not appreciate the humor.

"Perhaps you are right, Sister. Perhaps the Jew is not as smart as I am thinking, perhaps Allah *is* smiling on us."

"You would like that, wouldn't you," she said with a definite accusatory tone. "It'd mean returning more quickly to your blond-haired Melissa and your San Fernando bungalow complete with the infidel friends you've cultivated over the past ten years."

Nawzer sat back, arms crossed smiling, suddenly in no rush to accommodate her request.

"The Quran teaches us: 'O son of Imran, never be envious of people concerning the favors I have conferred on them by My grace; do not glower at them, and do not succumb to your envious self. Indeed, the envious man is indignant at the bestowal of My favor, and contests My apportioning of gifts among My creatures. Whoever is such, he neither belongs to Me nor do I belong to him.' Perhaps you need a Melissa in your life?"

Naseem

Momentarily speechless, she fought to not lean across the table and slap that smug smirk from his face. She knew any slight satisfaction it might yield would do nothing to help her plan succeed. For the moment, she needed Nawzer. So, instead, she swallowed her rage in search of an argument that might gain his cooperation.

"Think of it this way, Brother. The sooner you finish here, the sooner you'll be back home."

Nawzer held his defiant posture a few seconds before returning his attention to the computer. Two minutes later, he glanced up in surprise.

"I am not believing this. My trojan is still there."

"What?" Naseem asked, snapping out of a daydream.

"The Jew is not finding it. I am still having access to the lawyer's computer."

"Is this a problem?" she asked, confused.

"No, it is not being a problem, but it is giving me concern."

"Concern? Why?"

"I am thinking the Jew is not so stupid, so I must be asking myself why he is not discovering it?"

"Not to worry," she said, with a flip of her wrist. "The Jew has made stupid mistakes as long as I've known him, otherwise we never would have found him. I think you are worrying about nothing. Now, you must concentrate on the doorbell."

Nawzer did not look convinced.

Nawzer

"I am hoping you are right," he said to Naseem before returning to the task.

The sooner he finished the doorbell project, the sooner he would put the final touch on the remote trigger for the bomb. And soon as that was complete, he'd devise a scenario to kill Naseem with it. The act would give him tremendous satisfaction in addition to restoring the dignity he'd lost from being subjected to her constant verbal humiliation.

Yes, she could sit across from him, haughty and smug now, but just wait.

See how widely Allah smiles then!

Chapter 45—Arnold

"WHAT HAPPENED THEN?" Fisher asked.

"After I double-checked to make sure her apartment door was locked, I left the building and took an Uber to Mr. Davidson's."

"What time was that?"

Arnold shrugged.

"Hold on...the app'll tell us the exact time." He opened the Uber record on his iPhone. "It was, like, 12:59 when it dropped me at Mr. Davidson's, so...figure with traffic that time of night, it was...like, nine minutes earlier."

"And you say she was really mad?" Fisher asked.

"*Pissed* is a better word for it. I've never seen her so pissed."

"Which brings me to my next point: could not answering your calls simply be her way of emphasizing that anger?"

"No, absolutely not. She doesn't handle things that way. Believe me, I know!" An idea popped into mind. "Okay, so let's try this. Say you're right, say she's not answering *my* calls. Let's see what happens if you or Mr. Davidson call?"

Fisher shrugged.

"Not a bad idea, Gold. Worth a shot. What's her number?"

Arnold gave it to him. Fisher dialed.

"You're right. Straight to voicemail," he said.

Fucking anxiety gut-punched Arnold again, amped up now, rekindling his gut pain.

"I'm telling you, something's wrong," he insisted.

Fisher blew a long cheek-puffing breath.

"Yeah, you might be correct on that." He seemed to mull over a decision before turning to Agent Woods. "You two go ahead, interview Davidson while Gold and I take a run over to her apartment, do a welfare check. You good with that?"

"Absolutely," Woods answered for the two of them.

Fisher curbed the government hybrid in a yellow three-minute loading zone five feet beyond the bus zone. He flipped down the visor to display a law-enforcement sign rubber-banded in place on the off-chance the government plates were not enough for parking enforcers. Together they walked briskly through the glass doors into the lobby and straight to the front desk.

Fisher flashed the concierge his credentials.

"We're here for a welfare check on Ms. Rachael Weinstein."

"Unit 1202," Arnold quickly added.

The concierge was a beefy guy with closely cropped black hair, beard, and black jeans. The name KEVIN was engraved on the nametag pinned to the breast of his black polo shirt.

"Welfare check? What seems to be the problem?"

Fisher made a get-on-with-it hand motion.

"I'll call up." Kevin dialed, listened several seconds before hanging up. "No answer."

"That's the point, Kevin," Fisher said impatiently. "We need to do a walk-through of her unit to make sure she's okay. I need for you to accompany us."

"I'll get the key," Kevin said, disappearing into his office.

A few moments later, Kevin knocked loudly on Rachael's door, waited, knocked again.

No answer.

"Go ahead, open it," Fisher said.

Kevin paused tentatively before unlocking and cracking the door two inches.

With his mouth to the opening, he yelled, "Miss Weinstein, Kevin the concierge."

No answer.

Kevin pushed open the door far enough to lean his head in and yell, "Miss Weinstein, we're entering your unit now."

Silence. Kevin stepped aside for Fisher to enter but Fisher said, "This is how this works. Gold, stand here." He pointed to the threshold. "Look around and tell me if everything looks exactly the same as when you left last night. Do *not* step inside. Got it?" Fisher moved to the side of the door but remained in the hall.

As Arnold scanned the interior his anxiety deepened. Something just *felt* wrong. But he shook his head.

"Looks the same as it did last night."

"There only one bedroom?" Fisher asked. Arnold nodded.

Fisher pointed to the open door.

"That it?"

"Yes. But she had it closed when I left." Arnold quickly added, "So, yeah, you're right, that *is* different. Sorry."

"Stay right here," Fisher said, pointing to the threshold. "Kevin and I'll check it out." Then to Kevin: "Walk directly behind me and don't touch anything."

The reality of Arnold's fears hit home with a vengeance.

Please God...

Arnold watched Fisher step cautiously to the bedroom door and elbow it open. He hesitated, glancing around, then slipped inside. Ten seconds later he came out and headed toward the small island between the living room and kitchen, Kevin following like a bloodhound. Fisher's face showed no emotion.

Fisher and Kevin returned to the hall.

Fisher told Arnold, "I want you to take a quick look in bathroom, tell me if anything seems disturbed or out of place."

Chapter 46—Naseem

"I AM STILL not knowing if it is possible," Nawzer told Naseem.

"Why not?"

Was Nawzer as smart as she assumed? Had it been a mistake to keep him in charge of their IT needs? Or was the Jew simply too shrewd for him to handle?

She'd been forced to ask herself these questions far too frequently these past months. Too late now to replace him, especially with all the details he knew concerning their operation. She was, however, growing more cautious about accepting his opinion and increasingly worried that his apparent incompetence might inadvertently lead law enforcement to her. To mitigate her own risk, she had carefully crafted an escape should the situation acutely deteriorate. Escaping to fight another day was better than....

"This is because last year Amazon is becoming aware of the problem and are correcting it. The only way we are knowing if it is working is to be trying it directly."

"So?"

Why did the fool have to always be encouraged like a baby to take each step? Why must he insist on asking permission?

"Go ahead, try it."

Nawzer gave a sigh of impatient annoyance, straining her

patience once more. Since she took command of their cell, his misogynistic disdain at being forced to follow orders from a woman was more blatant. He even dropped an occasional jab that a woman who sold her body—regardless of whatever pseudo-noble rationalization she voiced—was an irreconcilable sin. His personal prejudices made little difference to the well-established fact that she was their leader. This and this alone made it his duty to show her respect and follow orders.

"No, you are not understanding. I am not being able to break into his system from here." He pointed to the kitchen table. "I am needing to be within twenty feet of his house."

"Why didn't you just say so? Let's drive there, then."

Arnold

"Nothing looks out of place," Arnold told Fisher.

"Absolutely certain?"

The reality of standing in the apartment under this circumstance continued to cause throbbing gut pain.

"Best as I can tell...I mean it's been, what, less than twenty-four hours?"

Back in the hall, Fisher made sure the front door was secure.

He asked Arnold, "She have a car here?"

"No. She takes a bus to work and an Uber home."

To Kevin, "The building have video surveillance on the entrances?"

"It does," he replied, a bit defensively, as if it were an absurd question. "Both for the lobby and garage. The system's in my office."

"Can you make a copy for us?"

Fisher started toward the elevators, Arnold and Kevin following.

"No problem. I'll burn a DVD." Kevin punched the down button. "Have a specific time period in mind?"

Fisher asked Arnold, "You left the building at midnight?"

Allen Wyler

"I did."

Then to Kevin, "How many cameras cover the lobby?"

"One for the front door, another for the elevator alcove."

"Fine. Give me both feeds from midnight to now."

"It'll take me at least thirty minutes once I get to my office."

As Kevin disappeared into his office, Fisher motioned Arnold to the seating area. He settled into the same couch Rachael sat on two months ago when Arnold reestablished contact after disappearing from Seattle. Arnold dropped into the same chair as that night.

"Let's go back over every detail. When did you first try calling her after you left here last night?"

"Let's see..." Arnold was finding it very difficult to concentrate, his mind jumping from one thought to another without a common thread other than worry. He shook his head and tried to force himself to think. "It was right after Mr. Davidson and I left your building, so that must've been around...I don't know, what time did the meeting break up?"

"Why not check your phone? You called on that, did you not?" Fisher suggested.

"Crap! Of course." A moment later he said, "It was eight thirty-six."

"Just to be clear, this was the first time you called her after leaving the apartment?"

"Correct."

"When she didn't answer, you try her at work?"

"No."

"Why not?"

"Primarily because she doesn't work days. She's too junior...so I guess I just assumed..."

Fisher's phone rang. He checked the screen, raised a just-a-moment finger.

"Hold one. Need to take this."

"The car that HPD stopped in your neighborhood, the one with the

160

two females?" Fisher asked after disconnecting the call. "We ran the driver's license and plate through DMV. Guess what we found?"

The question seemed both strangely unimportant and rhetorical, especially with all his mental energy focused on Rachael.

"Jesus, Mr. Fisher, I have no idea."

"The driver is a TSA agent at the airport. Ring any bells?" Fisher asked.

"Not off the top of my head. Why?"

"We're taking a deeper dive into to her. Right now, something about her doesn't pass the sniff test, especially the timing and location. Back to Rachael. Which hospital she work at?"

Fisher dumped the car in the patient loading zone directly outside the hospital front door, flashed his creds to the valet and said, "We'll only be a few minutes," and continued on into the lobby without missing a beat, Arnold scrambling to keep up.

"What floor she work on?" Fisher asked him.

Had she ever mentioned a specific number or service? Probably. But for the life of him, he couldn't remember.

"I don't know."

Fisher walked straight to a circular information desk manned by a white-haired woman in a maroon smock and the gold-inscribed nametag: GERDA, VOLUNTEER SERVICES.

He asked her, "Where will I find the nursing department?"

Fifteen minutes later, the nursing supervisor informed Fisher, "She's not on the schedule for this evening."

"What about tomorrow?" Fisher asked.

"Not tomorrow, either."

Fisher thanked her and left the office, reversing their route along the dog-legged hall back to the front lobby, Arnold feeling more and more desperate. He realized he'd been hoping against hope she'd miraculously be here at work, in spite of knowing how unrealistic this was.

"There's a Starbucks three blocks north of here," Fisher said, pulling away from the loading zone. "Let's stop in to refuel and regroup."

Arnold continued to stare out the front window, fighting to keep from imagining Rachael in some godawful indescribable room under equally indescribable conditions. The images sickened him, yet he seemed powerless to stop them.

"Okay?" Fisher asked, shooting him a glance.

"Why are you doing this, Mr. Fisher?"

"Doing what?"

"Devoting so much effort to Rachael? I mean, with all that's happened this morning, the bombing and all..." Part of him didn't want to hear Fisher's reply for fear of what he'd say, yet part of him desperately needed a reality check.

Were his fears real or was his imagination simply doing a major number in his head?

"Gold, we both know what the stakes are." Fisher glanced at him. "Or do you?"

Arnold shook his head, eyes misting up.

"Jesus! All my fault."

"C'mon, Gold, this isn't the time for self-recrimination. We need to work every angle we can and I need your undivided help."

"Sorry...it's just, I keep thinking of what it must be like..."

"You have no idea what's actually going on with her. I don't either. That's why we need to keep pushing this. Hard. Keep that in mind."

"Want me to pick something up for you?" Fisher asked, unfolding himself from the car, which was again curbed in a loading zone.

The thought of caffeine, or anything else, for that matter, nauseated him.

"Christ, my stomach...I can't..."

He stayed in the passenger seat staring out the front window.

"Suit yourself, but if you change your mind...I'm grabbing a fresh-brewed, so this won't take long. Use the time to put together a list of every family member and friend you can think of. You can start calling them on the drive back to the office."

Chapter 47—Naseem

THEY WERE WORKING their way slowly and carefully up the rocky ravine, partly because Nawzer insisted on hand-carrying his laptop instead of toting it in his backpack as she suggested, but also to minimize noise that might attract attention of the neighbors. Heat radiating off exposed lava made the microclimate a tangibly humid mini-hell.

"Wait," Nawzer whispered.

Naseem stopped, glanced back at him.

Leaning into his uphill leg, panting, face dripping, he swiped at his forehead with the back of his wrist, uncapped the bottle of Evian from his cargo shorts and emptied it in his mouth.

"No, don't toss it," she cautioned, worried about leaving DNA, in spite of the low odds the bottle would ever be traced back to them.

You never knew what law enforcement might look for if it were suspected they'd been here.

He glanced at the empty bottle, nodded, stuffed it into his pocket, swore under his breath, straightened up, inhaled deeply, ready to resume the climb.

She started the rocky incline again, Nawzer following, pausing every few steps to swipe his forehead again and again in an attempt to keep drops from his eyes. Finally, she halted at the spot directly below the sturdy concrete pylons for the steel I-beams supporting the Jew's back deck.

Praise be to Allah; the overhang gave them a small patch of shade in which to work.

Nawzer shrugged off the rucksack, settled cross-legged on a relatively level stretch of path to await the laptop to boot. Two minutes later, he nodded to Naseem.

"I am being ready."

She dialed Kasra's cell phone.

"Go ahead, Sister, ring it."

She waited, phone to ear, visualizing Kasra approaching the Jew's front gate to press the doorbell.

A moment later, she whispered to Nawzer, "Done."

"Again."

Naseem repeated her instruction, listened, nodded to him one more time.

"One last time," he said.

The sequence was repeated. Grinning, Nawzer flashed a thumbs-up.

Naseem whispered into the phone, "Disappear now, Sister."

Arnold

"You tried her parents?" Fisher asked.

"Not yet. They're not usually home until"—he checked his watch—"about now."

Arnold had called every one of Rachael's friends he could think of. No one had spoken to her since day before yesterday. Each negative answer amped up his anxiety another notch, impossible as that seemed. He was now convinced his gut was eating itself and half-expected it to erode straight through his abdominal wall.

"What about Facebook?" Fisher asked.

"Already checked. Radio silence for the past two days."

Ding. Arnold glanced down at his iPhone.

"Jesus fucking Christ on a crutch!"

"What?"

"It's a security alert. Someone just rang my doorbell. Hold on, I'll pull it up."

Arnold retrieved the video.

"Holy shit, you're not going to believe this. The driver? The one the cop stopped in my neighborhood?"

"Yeah?" Fisher said, sounding hopeful.

"She's at the front gate."

He handed over the phone.

Fisher studied it before returning it with, "I'm on it. Right back." He ran out of the office.

Naseem

"You get it?" Naseem asked Nawzer.

"Yes, I am seeing the Ring now," he said, meaning the doorbell.

"Good. Can you get into his wi-fi through it?"

"Patience, Sister, please. I am trying now."

She watched him type, frown, type more. Then a bigger frown. He seemed to be waiting for something. Suddenly the laptop's hard disk began working overtime.

Nawzer punched the power button to turn off the laptop.

"Fuck!"

"What?"

Nawzer began furiously pressing various key combinations.

"Fuck-fuck-fuck!"

"Nawzer, what's happening?"

He skewered her with murderously angry brown eyes.

"I told you!" he yelled.

"Told me what?"

With both hands Nawzer slammed the laptop against a large protruding chunk of lava, jumped up, and stormed down the path.

"Stop!" she yelled, no longer concerned with attracting attention.

Nawzer made no sign of acknowledging her command. Naseem scooped up the broken computer and scurried after him.

"What is happening?" she called.

Arnold

"You're smiling. You find something out about Rachael?" Fisher asked.

Arnold flinched at Fisher's sudden reappearance.

"I wish! No...nothing like that," replied Arnold, thankful for the momentary, amusing distraction of what might be going on if this was another attempt by Nawzer at breaking into his system.

But Fisher brought him right back in the present awful situation.

"Okay, so what is it? I need some cheering up," Fisher said.

"You know what the Amazon Ring is, right? The doorbell?"

"I've seen the ads. Why?"

"Well, when it first came on the market, I picked one up figuring it'd be a kick in the butt to fool around with. Never took it seriously on accounta it not being encrypted, so it's an open invite for neighborhood kids who want to play hacker. A couple months ago, when Naseem showed back up, I mounted it on the front gate as a decoy. Anyone who knows me would know not to use it."

"And?"

"Well, it's loaded with a totally awesome virus." Arnold checked his watch. "So, if—as we have every reason to suspect— that woman is working with Naseem and Nawzer and that was another lame-ass attempt to hack my security, Nawzer's computer should be totally trashed."

Fisher started for the door again.

"In other words, Nawzer's in Honolulu?"

"I'd bet on it."

"I'll send a heads-up to our LA office. They've been trying to establish a better handle on that shithead the past couple months. If he *is* on the island, it might narrow down a few things. In the meantime, call Rachael's parents."

Alone in the conference room again, Arnold quickly edited a script on his Surface, to make sure his wording was scripted to lessen the risk of messing up and sending them the wrong message.

Calm down...be cool. Don't blow this.

He started the recorder on his iPhone, cleared his throat, said, "Hello Mrs. Weinstein, is Rachael there?"

He then listened to the recording. Not even close. Took three more practice runs before he believed his little speech was good to go.

Naseem

They sat in the hot car interior, windows lowered, A/C turned up; the broken laptop discarded in the back footwell.

"Do not lose faith. Allah is with us," Naseem said.

"I am losing faith with those words. How can you be saying this after what is just happening?"

As much as she preferred a hard, disciplined style of command, she knew to soften her words this time. Losing Nawzer's help now would further delay progress.

"Do not lose faith. Allah can test us at any time. He rewards those who stay the course in the face of adversity."

"This is easy for you to be saying. I am the one shouldering all responsibility for this."

She bit her tongue. That couldn't be further from the truth. She, and she alone, shouldered every ounce of responsibility. She inhaled and paused before answering.

"Nawzer, my brother, you must not let your heart be so heavy. You were able to enter the lawyer's computer once before. You must find a way back in now, because it is there that you *will* find a key to unlock the Jew's system. I am certain of this."

He shook his head.

"I am not seeing how."

"Do as I just said. Make another attempt at the Jew through his lawyer."

"But how? It has not been working."

She smiled, happy to be able to throw his tired line back at him.

"Patience. We must have patience. We shall think and pray. A solution will come. You are very clever. You will succeed. Do not lose faith. You have friends who are able to provide counsel. They can help you hack in the lawyer's computer, and when you do..."

Chapter 48—Arnold

"HELLO, MRS. WEINSTEIN...Rachael isn't there by any chance, is she?"

"No, Arnold, she's not. Why do you ask?"

Uh-oh. Best to stick close to the truth as possible.

"We had a little, ah, disagreement last night and she's not answering my calls or texts...I really need to speak with her to try to patch things up."

"If she's not answering you, I suspect she has her reason, dear."

And left it at that.

"When was the last time you heard from her?"

"Why would you ask something like that? Something *is* wrong. What?"

Shit!

He was deviating from the script.

"No, nothing like that. It's just..."

Just what?

"Look, if you hear from her, tell her I need to speak with her."

"Should I be worried, dear?"

Oh, Christ!

"No, nothing like that. She was just upset with me, is all. It's really nothing, Mrs. Weinstein. Seriously. Look, I gotta go."

170

Arnold set the cell phone on the table. How could he have pulled that one off better? He suspected he'd done nothing but upset her.

Shit!

Just then Fisher, Wood, Tanner, and Davidson walked into the conference room, shutting the door behind them.

"Get hold of the parents?" Fisher asked as the group spread out to sit around the table.

Arnold shook his head.

"They haven't heard from her either."

Fisher cleared his throat.

"I feel your concern. We all do. Yours as well, Palmer." He sent a glance in Davidson's direction. "But at the moment, we need to focus attention on how to move this entire investigation forward."

He motioned for Woods to continue.

"Preliminary analysis indicates the explosion resulted from one pipe bomb that detonated at approximately nine-oh-one a.m.," the agent said. "Review of the lobby video shows an unidentified female wearing an Amazon smock enter the building at eight-fifty-one, ten minutes prior to the explosion. She was carrying a rectangular package estimated at approximately twelve by three by three inches, which is an atypical package size for Amazon. We suspect this was the bomb. She was next seen exiting the building eight minutes later."

Woods opened a manila folder and slid an eight-by-ten glossy color photo across the table to Arnold.

"Recognize her? See anything familiar?"

The photo—taken at a downward angle, obviously cropped with enough graininess to suggest enlargement—captured a female in an Amazon smock and ball cap with a protruding black ponytail. Arnold studied the image closely before returning it to Fisher.

"Ah man...I can't make out a damn thing at that angle."

"It's the best one we have," Woods said. "We've been working with Amazon. No deliveries were made to that building since three-fifty-two p.m. the previous day. Moreover, they show no deliveries to that specific office in the past week. Mr. Davidson confirmed that."

Davidson, who still looked shocked, managed to nod. Arnold had never seen him so emotionally drained. He wanted to reach out and put a reassuring hand on his shoulder.

"We checked with FedEx, DHL, UPS, and USPS. None of those carriers made deliveries to the building since yesterday. All of which makes it very likely"—he tapped the photo—"that this is the person who delivered the bomb." Woods turned to Tanner. "John."

"Photo analysis suggests the unsub is five feet, seven inches, one hundred thirty pounds, dark complexed with black hair. All of which is consistent with—but not indicative of—Asian or middle Eastern descent."

"A cursory examination," Tanner continued, "of Mr. Davidson's clients over the past year was conducted."

He nodded at Davidson.

Davidson—staring into space—took a moment to realize the question was directed to him.

Without addressing anyone in particular, he replied in a barely audible voice, "I cannot think of anyone who might be responsible."

"All of which leads us to believe," Fisher concluded, "that this is Farhad's work. It's certainly her preferred method for doing business." Then, glancing around the room, "Anyone have anything else to add?"

"Yeah." Arnold said. "What about Rachael?"

Fisher seemed to weight his next words carefully.

"We have nothing definitive to either support or rule out our suspicion that she is Farhad's hostage. Having said that, I can't think of anything else we can do tonight that might shed significant light on this question."

He drilled Arnold with his eyes.

"Can you?"

"Yeah, absolutely. Ask Verizon to locate her phone."

Fisher nodded.

"That process requires we jump through various legal hoops. That's presently in the works, Gold. The earliest we can expect to hear from them is sometime tomorrow. Probably in the morning."

Fisher scanned the other faces one more time.

"It's been a long stressful day for everyone and we're all tired. I suggest we get back at it first thing in the morning when our minds are refreshed. Our strategy's still solid and continues to be our best shot at sorting out this mess."

Chapter 49—Arnold

ARNOLD AND DAVIDSON were walking slowly south along Second Avenue toward the parking garage, having not exchanged a word since leaving the conference room to be escorted down the elevators to the Federal Building front doors. Davidson remained strangely detached from his surroundings. That made Arnold as concerned for him as he was for Rachael.

He glanced at his watch.

6:45PM.

Unbelievable! Where had the hours disappeared to?

Yet, in retrospect, a ton of things occurred since their morning meeting with Chang and Fisher. Still, for him at least, every minute seemed shrouded in surreal dissociation.

This couldn't really be happening, not to them.

Yet, he knew it was.

Christ, Davidson seemed totally emotionally trashed. And vulnerable. In need of protection.

Step up, dude. he needs someone.

"You okay?"

Davidson kept walking.

"Where we going?"

Without turning, Davidson said, "I am heading straight home

to pour a glass of wine and devote some quiet time to processing Joyce's death."

Whew! The first cogent words out of the man's mouth since answering Fisher's last question.

"I totally get how you must feel."

Davidson stopped and stared at him.

"No. You cannot possibly understand. We worked together for years...And to die that way...my god!"

"You're right, I don't...Sorry," Arnold said, feeling totally out of sorts at searching for comforting words, having not experienced similar situations before today. "I just don't know what to say other than I *really* am sorry, Mr. Davidson."

Davidson shook his head and resumed walking.

"I know you are. Sorry, I..."

"Okay, how about this," Arnold offered. "We haven't eaten a thing since morning. How about we pick up some takeout on the way home, maybe a couple dishes from Uptown?"

Davidson shook his head.

"We can pick something up for you. I have no appetite."

"Naw, you're right. Actually, I'm not really hungry either, it's just...well, I mentioned Uptown to Rachael last night before things blew up and...well..."

"No harm in taking a look. It is on the way. Pick something up for yourself if you wish."

It was seven-thirty by the time Davidson curbed the Tesla in loading zone in front of the restaurant. Arnold jumped out, ran in, scanned the patrons.

No Rachael.

Yu-Mei, the owner was standing at one of the booths, chatting up a group of customers.

He did not want to interrupt her, but...she turned, heading toward the cash register with a credit card, saw him, said, "Take any table you want."

She inserted the card into the reader.

"No, I'm not here to eat. I'm looking for a friend." He handed her his phone with a picture of Rachael on the screen. "Has she been in here tonight?"

She accepted the phone, studied the photo a moment, returned it.

"No, I haven't seen her."

He knew Yu-Mei delivered takeout in the neighborhood herself, so may not have been in the restaurant if Rachael stopped by looking for him.

"Could you show this to your staff, see if anyone else saw her? Please, it's very important."

"Sure. Wait here."

Arnold scanned the bar to his left. No Rachael there either.

"No one's seen her," Yu-Mei said, returning the phone.

Shit!

Soon as they entered his kitchen, Davidson grabbed a partially consumed bottle of cabernet on the wet-bar counter to the right of the built-in wine cooler, pulled the cork, and without a word, removed another bottle from the cooler, uncorked it, set both bottles on the island in the center of the kitchen. He placed two Riedel glasses beside the bottles and divided the remains of the old bottle between them.

He stood on one side of the island, Arnold directly across from him.

"Help yourself," Davidson said sliding one glass toward Arnold.

Davidson raised his glass in a solitary toast.

"Poor Raymond."

He sipped, set the glass back on the counter, stared toward the city view behind Arnold.

Arnold settled onto a stool on his side of the island.

"Raymond?"

Davidson continued staring several seconds.

Then: "Joyce's husband. Someone from SPD notified him. Christ! I should have been the one to do that." He shook his head sadly. "I dread talking to him."

Arnold realized he had been so self-adsorbed in worry over Rachael during the day that he'd ignored the emotional fallout that Davidson was suffering over Joyce's murder.

Jesus! What a lousy friend he was turning out to be.

He wanted to reach out and place a reassuring hand on his friend's shoulder, but sensed Davidson wouldn't accept it.

"I'm *so* sorry, Mr. Davidson..."

"Palmer. Please."

Davidson downed the remains of his glass in one gulp, replaced it on the island and started pouring from the new bottle. Arnold had never ever seen him chug wine. After another sip, Davidson grabbed the bottle and his glass and headed into the living room, dropped on the couch, set his glass and bottle on the coffee table in front of him, and leaned back to stare at the ceiling.

Arnold settled into the club chair directly across the table from him, wracking his brain for some appropriate words of condolences, something to soothe Davidson's obvious grief.

"Are you and Raymond close?"

Admittedly lame, but better than nothing.

Davidson stared a moment before returning attention to his wine. This time he only sipped before replacing it carefully on the table, then glanced at Arnold.

"No, not particularly. I—sometimes *we*, when Martina was available—took Joyce and him to El Gaucho or Morton's for dinner for the Christmas season, but otherwise..."

"You think by not being the one to break the news to him, you shirked some sort of obligation?" Arnold offered tentatively.

Was this prying, overstepping a boundary?

Davidson seemed to consider those words.

"Perhaps...perhaps."

"You think you'd any feel any better right now if you had?"

177

Again, Davidson considered the question.

"Probably not. But I have a deep sense of loyalty to him. Joyce was with me from the start...helped me set up the entire office, small as it is. Filing, billing, appointments...I trusted her implicitly with..."

Davidson trailed off to take another sip.

Arnold followed his lead.

"I will really miss her..." Davidson finally said, standing. "Excuse me a moment." He headed into the kitchen, a moment later reappearing with a paper towel in hand, dabbing his eyes. "Sorry."

"For?"

"I am not usually a person to display emotion."

"Know what?" Arnold teetered on the cusp of saying "Palmer," but for some reason, he just couldn't. "I'd be a goddamn total mess if anything happened to..."

Fuck!

For a moment his mind had been totally distracted from...

Davidson leaned back in the couch.

"Go ahead with that thought. I need a change of subject. What did you and Fisher learn about her?"

Arnold summarized the steps taken in their attempt to locate her. When he finally wrapped up, Davidson refilled their glasses.

"That leaves us with only two possibilities," Davidson said. "She is either hiding and ignoring contact with anyone, or she is Naseem's hostage. Does this square with Fisher's thinking?"

"Yes, but we both believe Naseem has her as a way to force me to hand over SAM..."

Verbalizing this unspoken fear only intensified the anxiety gnawing deep into his gut. What was Rachael feeling? Terrified? Was she even alive?

If I could just figure out a way to find Naseem for Fisher...

"I mean..." He was up, pacing tight circles, Davidson still on the couch transfixed in his own state of mind. "...you're right, she could be hiding. I don't know. But for some pessimistic reason I automatically gravitate into the worst-case scenario. Why is that? It's paralyzing me. It's making me totally ineffective in helping Fisher. I don't get it."

Davidson said nothing.

"What the hell can we do?" Arnold asked.

"The only thing we can do," Davidson answered. "Work with Fisher to the best of our abilities. Do not forget: we *do* have a plan. A solid one. There is no reason to abandon it."

Davidson pushed out of his chair and headed wearily into the kitchen. Arnold continued to pace but less frenetically now. Another meeting with Fisher was scheduled for first thing next morning.

For what? They all had their assigned tasks, right? Oh crap!

He was so consumed with worrying about Rachael that he'd forgotten to work on the malware they intended to embed in the bogus PDF.

Davidson returned, drying his hands with a dish towel.

"I am retiring early tonight. Same drill in the morning?"

Arnold's glass remained on the table beside the partially consumed bottle of wine.

"Same drill." Arnold picked up his wine glass. "In the meantime, I'll work on my assignment. Try to get some sleep. I know tonight will be difficult for you, but..."

"Just cork the bottle when you are done. I left the cork on the wet-bar counter."

Chapter 50—Arnold

ARNOLD SCHLEPPED HIS rucksack and wine into Davidson's home office, dropped heavily into the desk chair, put his laptop and wine on the desk, and fired up the computer. As it booted, he swiveled toward the magnificent city view and tried to clear his mind from the cacophony of the day but couldn't stop worrying he'd missed something in tracking down Rachael.

What's Rachael feeling right now? Fright?

What could possibly be done to find her? He slowly, meticulously reviewed each step they took today, but found concentration difficult. So he stood at the window admiring the view, hoping to calm his anxiety. Fisher was the professional at solving these problems, so he should provide whatever help he needed. Their only hope, he concluded, was to secure a trace on her iPhone and Fisher was already jumping through the legal hoops to do this. Yeah, under normal conditions he could probably hack into Verizon's records to expedite the process. But given his present state of mind, he didn't want to risk muffing it. He'd just have to wait until Fisher received an answer from Verizon. Perhaps by morning.

Shit!

Waiting was killing him.

With the computer booted, he updated his antivirus software, then logged onto his Dark Web email account under the alias, Massa Aurum (his nod to the Latin for gold) and forwarded a copy of the malware from Davidson's computer to another hacker—a guy who specialized in trojans—requesting information on its origin and potential traps.

Although he suspected the code was straightforward, he remained concerned about being sucked into a trap. Especially now. You never quite knew what to expect when dealing with an asshole like Nawzer.

He paused for a sip of wine, but then looked at the glass in his hand. The alcohol might only fuck him up more that he already was, so...He carried the bottle and glass back into the kitchen, rinsed out the glass, and corked the wine.

While awaiting a response on the trojan, he decided to put all his effort into writing the code for the malware to be embedded in the bait PDF.

Chapter 51—Arnold

"RISE AND SHINE," Davidson called from the kitchen.

Arnold realized he must have fallen asleep sometime after two a.m. He distinctly remembered checking his watch around then, having tossed and turned since flicking off the light just shy of midnight. He sat up, rubbed his eyes, detached his Apple watch from the charger. 5:59 a.m. What, maybe two, two and a half hours sleep? He felt like rewarmed dogshit.

"I'm going to grab a quick shower."

He hoped that would reinvigorate him some.

"Just as long as we are on time to meet Fisher," Davidson called back. "You know how he is."

Freshly showered and shaved, wearing new underwear, Arnold lugged his rucksack into the kitchen and dropped it on the floor next to the island.

"Here," Davidson set down a mug of freshly brewed black coffee for him. "Sleep at all?"

"Not much. You?"

"I finally resorted to Ambien, but even then, slept, maybe, four hours at most."

Davidson looked worse than Arnold felt, especially his dark-rimmed eyes at half-mast, bags beneath them.

"I plan on a stop at Starbucks for breakfast and another coffee in route to the garage. We can walk to Fisher's office like yesterday," Davidson said, rinsing out the coffee pot and mug.

"No argument from me on that one."

Arnold tentatively tested the coffee. Perfect temperature. Davidson probably poured it when he was showering. He downed the mug in two large gulps.

"Your return flight still set for tomorrow?" Davidson asked as he steered into downtown traffic before taking a bite of his Starbucks breakfast sandwich. It was a quarter to seven.

"It is, but I plan on staying here until this Rachael thing is settled. I can move into a hotel, if that's an issue."

"Do not worry about that, Arnold. I just wonder what more you can do at this point. If this turns out to be a ransom play on Naseem's part, would it benefit you to be home where she can contact you?"

"Good question...that's just another thing we need to iron out with Fisher."

He glanced at the warm sandwich in hand and realized he'd lost his appetite. Or maybe never had it. When had he last eaten...lunch yesterday? Breakfast? Arnold took a bite of sandwich and chewed. Tasteless. He washed it down with a sip of an equally bland latte.

"You were scheduled to meet with your designer yesterday, were you not?"

Shit! Forgot completely about her.

"Yeah, matter of fact...but I mentioned something to her about not knowing how long I'd be tied up, so..."

He let it hang.

He choked down another bite of sandwich, decided enough of this shit, balled the remainder in the wrapper. He'd dunk it in the trash on the way out of the parking garage. Davidson appeared to be having better luck with his.

* * *

Arnold slung his rucksack over his shoulder and shut the car door.

"You always keep that with you?" Davidson asked.

True.

Arnold carried the backpack with him constantly since the night he fled from the basement of his home into the ravine.

"You never know when you might need it. It's a firmly ingrained habit now. Maybe if this Naseem thing stabilizes I'll give it up, but until then..."

This time Chang met them in the lobby to escort them through the security scanners and up to the conference room. Fisher was already at the conference table when they entered, open laptop in front of him, a venti Starbucks cup to his right. He had darkly rimmed eyes and a full day's worth of stubble, and looked only minimally better than Davidson.

Christ, the man looks worse than I feel.

"Gentlemen." Fisher motioned wearily to the chairs opposite him.

"Been at it all night?" Arnold asked as they tucked into chairs.

"I have. We obtained an order for Verizon to check Rachael's phone but it's turned up nothing. Must be turned off."

"Shit," Arnold muttered, shaking his head.

Rachael, I'm so sorry....

"This is discouraging," Davidson said.

Fisher nodded.

"Yes, but it's also why it's so important to stay focused and on task." He raised a hand before Arnold could say a word. "I understand you're upset. I share your concern and it's fair to say everyone in this room feels the same, but given the situation, our only hope for finding her quickly is to stay the course."

"But—"

"No buts," Fisher said emphatically. "Bear with me. Now, *if* Farhad does have Ms. Weinstein—and we don't know this for fact—it's likely she'll leverage this to force a settlement for your system. Agreed?"

Arnold nodded.

"Yeah, it's a reasonable assumption."

"Although it's very probable she knows you're presently here in Seattle, she'll try to contact you on your Honolulu landline."

"This is where I take issue," Arnold said, having anticipated Fisher's logic. "If she has access to Mr. Davidson's files—which we know she does—she knows my cell number."

"If that's the case, why did she call your landline the other night?" Fisher said.

"I have no idea...but if she does have Rachael, it stands to reason it's here in Seattle, not Honolulu."

"True," Fisher admitted. "But everything indicates Naseem is still there and not here, so that's where any negotiation will have to occur."

"I don't follow."

"Think, Gold. You've said yourself that the system's booby-trapped. She must know that. If Nawzer's over there, then part of the reason is for him to be able to learn your system. That's not going to happen if you're here in Seattle. Understand what I'm telling you?"

"He *is* right, Arnold," Davidson added. "More than ever, you need to act rationally instead of emotionally. Listen to him. This is his area of expertise."

Fisher said, "Your flight's been moved up to one o'clock."

Arnold was stunned.

"Today?"

"Today. I know you were scheduled for tomorrow so we sweet-talked Hawaiian into changing your ticket. Which means"—Fisher glanced at his watch—"we should wrap this up straightaway so you can work your magic with Davidson's computers before you leave. Right, John?"

Chang nodded.

"That's the plan. Here is the PDF case file."
He handed Arnold a flash drive.
"Great! We all agree," Fisher said, standing.
Meeting over.
Fucking guess so.

Chapter 52—Arnold

ARNOLD AND DAVIDSON didn't speak from the time they exited Fisher's office until they were a half block away from the Smith Tower front doors. Davidson stopped abruptly, took hold of Arnold's shoulder to stop him too.

"I understand your emotional turmoil, son," Davidson said. "At the moment, I am just as lost as you."

He exhaled through pursed lips.

"This will be my first time back in the office since..." He paused to swallow. "Agent Fisher made a very good point back there...anything we do to help him helps apprehend Naseem, and that helps both of us. I want to see her brought to justice just as much as you. Keep that in mind. How well you perform upstairs will be our best shot at achieving our goal."

"Thanks, Palm...uh, Mr. Davidson. Sorry for being so self-adsorbed back there...I know how difficult this is for you too."

As they walked off the elevator on Davidson's floor, Arnold asked, "Have a bug detector in there?"

He knew Davidson kept one at home and in the car, but wasn't sure about the office.

"As a matter of fact, yes. You think I should use it before you do your work?"

Yellow CRIME SCENE DO NOT CROSS tape crisscrossed the office doorway. Davidson pulled it off and wadded it into a mass. The office door remained unlocked, so he pushed it open a crack but didn't enter or look inside.

"You'd think they'd secure the door," Arnold muttered, waiting to see what Davidson would do.

Davidson slowly pushed the door the rest of the way open with the toe of his shoe, exposing the reception room, then edged onto the threshold while scanning the interior.

Arnold followed, peering over his shoulder. EMT detritus—disposable blue gloves, plastic wrappers, a few dressing wrappers—were scattered on the floor along with papers, pens, and the desk lamp. The glass in several frames directly to the right of Joyce's desk was shattered, probably from shrapnel. An overturned desk chair shoved to one corner. An unfamiliar, slightly bitter odor clung to the air.

For several seconds Davidson remained perfectly still, before finally muttering, "It's in my office."

A moment later Davidson was sweeping the office with the bug detector.

"Looks like nothing to worry about," he said, righting Joyce's desk chair and rolling it back to the footwell.

For another few seconds he simply surveyed the office.

Finally, he said, "You can work at my desk. In the meantime, I will reach out to a janitorial service to have this room cleaned soon as possible. I plan on leaving with you. I plan to secure the file cabinets while you work."

Arnold checked his watch.

"Better get started."

In the inner office, Arnold dumped his rucksack and black Tumi bro-bag on the floor to the left of Davidson's desk and settled in, though his mind wasn't yet on the task. He'd Uber to Sea-Tac and spend his wait-time working in the first-class lounge. There was still a ton of details to iron out. He wished he'd spent more time working last evening, but also knew that had been impossible in his frame of mind.

"What's your password?"

Davidson was at the window behind him, staring out over the view.

"What?"

Arnold repeated the question.

"DavidsonLaw. D and L uppercase."

Arnold leaned back in the chair, stretching out a kink in the right side of his neck. Out of some silly well-ingrained habit, he hunched his right shoulder when working, especially during mouse-intensive tasks, which comprised a good percentage of time. He'd made numerous attempts to break the habit, but always seemed to revert to the worst possible posture.

Although he pegged Nawser as a farm-team-level hacker, the man was certainly no village idiot. With that in mind, he worked carefully and methodically with focused concentration, minimizing any chance of error. Especially worrisome was becoming distracted with thoughts of Rachael. One stupid mistake could sabotage the entire plan. But he'd accomplished his tasks.

Arnold pushed out of the chair and reached for his bro-bag.

Davidson asked with obvious surprise as he walked back in.

"Finished already?"

"Yeah, things went smoothly, pretty much as expected."

Arnold rocked his neck side to side while massaging the muscles.

"No problems?"

"Nope. Just like we thought, both machines had it. Didn't find any other issues, so I simply removed the trojan, updated your antivirus but I left enough holes that he can find a way back in, then planted the PDF, just as planned."

Although antivirus software had been installed in both machines at the time of purchase, it was a preloaded trial subscription that expired four years ago.

"Did you discover how it ended up in there?" Davidson asked.

"No. Not enough time for that now. I'll look into it at the airport, but odds are we'll never track down the source. Besides, if Nawzer was smart, he made sure it autodeleted as part of the installation. It's an effective way of covering your tracks."

Davidson nodded.

"While I was at it, I tightened a few bolts on your wi-fi." Arnold made a sweeping gesture around the office. "It wasn't encrypted."

Davidson's brow furrowed.

"Should it be?"

"Absolutely. That provides just one more level of security."

"Does that mean I must to do something special when I intend to use the computer?"

"Nope. Nothing will look or feel different, but you do need to install the encryption key on your home computer. I emailed you the key so you can do it tonight. It's easy. Just follow the simple instructions on the email."

Davidson's concern seemed to lessen but not completely resolve.

"I realize this may sound stupid to you, but if it's encrypted, how can—"

"How can Nawzer access your computer and stumble across the PDF?"

Davidson nodded.

"Yes."

"If I made things too easy, he'd be suspicious," Arnold said. "This way, if he wants back into your machine, he'll be forced to try tricking you in another phishing attack and *that's* how we're going to nail his sorry ass."

Davidson brightened.

"Got it. Nice."

"We'll get the bastard."

"While you were working," Davidson said, "a thought crossed

my mind. I have friends in law firms that might benefit from your services. Might be that you could easily to turn this into a real business." He cocked his head. "Gold Associates. Offices in Seattle and Honolulu. That has a nice ring to it, does it not?"

An "aha" jolt of excitement hit.

"Wow! Certainly, something worth serious consideration...if we can get through our present... clusterfuck."

Arnold nodded toward the window and pointed at the roof of a neighboring building.

"In spite of what we just did, someone can easily eavesdrop on your cellphone conversations. See those places...there, there, and there. A Stingray at any of those spots would have no problem with it. Point is, don't use your cell here or at home for that matter."

Using a Stingray in Davidson's neighborhood might prove conspicuous.

"Understood," Davidson said.

"And unless it's a flaming emergency, text before calling, just to make sure we're clear. I'll do the same. We good?"

"We are."

Arnold shouldered his backpack. He'd call Uber from outside on the sidewalk.

"Finally, do *not* click on anything in an email or text until I'm back in Honolulu and ready to go. We good?"

"Understood."

With a sigh, he put a hand on Davidson's shoulder.

"I am so sorry about Joyce, Mr. Davison. I can't tell you how sorry I am."

"Thank you."

While the Uber sailed along First Avenue South toward Sea-Tac Airport, Arnold called Chang on the Cryptophone to update him on what was just accomplished with Davidson's computers.

"Totally tubular, bro!"

"Totally tubular? The fuck's that supposed to mean?"

Chang laughed.

"Have this friend who, for some strange reason, is totally wrapped up in Eighties surfer shit...guess it was a rage thing back in the day, their equivalent of 'totally awesome.' Dumb as it sounds, I've sort of grown attached to it."

Sounded flat-out stupid to Arnold, but he demurred.

"You warn Davidson what to watch for? I mean, in no uncertain words?" Chang asked.

"Yeah, he totally gets it. I think he's embarrassed about the mess his office security's in."

"He should be. Anyhow, sounds like we're on the launch pad waiting for ignition. All we need now is for our friend to take the bait."

Chang's words began to fade into background noise as Arnold began to worry about Rachael again. The gut pain was back and was hurting like a sonofabitch.

"Sorry. What'd you just say?"

"You okay?" Chang asked.

"Worried is all...don't know if anything's turned up on Rachael, do you?"

"Sorry, bro. But as I was just saying, Fisher's Honolulu flight should land two hours ahead of you."

Fuck. Almost missed that completely. Pay closer attention, dude.

"Guess I can ask him in person, then," Arnold said.

"Good luck and good hunting."

"Totally tubular, dude!"

Hmmm....he was actually sort of warming to the phrase. Senseless as it seemed.

Naseem

Naseem's phone dinged, indicating a text. From Kasra, informing her the Jew's return flight had been moved to today instead of tomorrow.

Smiling, Naseem deleted the text. Soon the Jew would taste the bitterness of having something precious taken from him.

Yes, she was looking forward to this.

Chapter 53—Naseem

NAWZER SWORE UNDER his breath.

Naseem glanced up from her work.

"What did you say?"

They were on opposite each other at the kitchen table, individual laptops on the chipped red Formica, the thick heavy air scented with turmeric and cumin in spite of it having been three hours since he brewed their tea. Kasra was out at the airport on her TSA shift.

Nawzer shook his head, clearly frustrated, swore again softly.

"Tell me," she demanded.

"The lawyer's computer, it is no longer being available to me."

She sat back, hands clasped in her lap.

"What do you mean, it's no longer available? It is not there?"

"Yes, the computer is being there but I am not being able to be inside."

Naseem stretched and yawned, working out kinks from two hours of intense work. She understood the need to stand and stretch periodically during long periods of concentration but forgot to do so.

How can you remember such a trivial act when you focus on important tasks? Impossible.

"And this surprises you?" she asked.

Nawzer also took the opportunity to stretch.

"No, I am not being surprised. Annoyed possibly, but not surprised."

Naseem smiled.

"Praise Allah."

Nawzer stared at her.

"You think this is good? Are being serious?"

"I am. Why?"

"Why? We are not being able to see the lawyer's emails now," he said with a strong note of irritation.

"Yes, I understood that, but *think*," she said, tapping index finger to her temple. "This gives us valuable information."

"And this is?"

"We know that *someone*—most likely the Jew—has realized you can access those computers and took appropriate precautions."

"We are not knowing if it is the Jew," Nawzer replied. "Perhaps it is being the FBI. *This* is what is causing me to worry."

"Yes, this is possible. But regardless of who it is, this will be only temporary. It means you must be very cautious when you find another route back in. Think, brother! If the Jew or the FBI removed your access, it may because that computer contains information of great value to us. You must find a way to go back into those computers."

"Go back? How am I getting back in there? My access is being *gone*."

Nawzer bent over to touch his toes.

She shrugged.

"That is your job, Brother. Why not use the same method that was so successful last time? It worked before. Why won't it work again?"

"But now he is knowing his mistake. I am doubting he is making the same mistake again."

"Yes, but if it's Allah's will, and if you are clever enough, it *will* happen. Do not forget, we have powerful sympathizers who are as clever or even more clever than he is. Perhaps you should seek help from one of them?"

Nawzer nodded slowly, a smile flickering at a corner of his mouth.

"Yes, I am knowing a fellow who is being very clever at such things. I will be asking him."

"Good. Contact him immediately." Naseem nodded toward his laptop.

"Yes, Sister."

An hour later, Nawzer stood, smiling broadly.

Naseem glanced up from an email and crossed her arms, waiting to hear what he had to say. Nawzer simply stretched more.

For the love of God!

"What?"

"As you are saying," he said with a sly smile. "Our friends are being very helpful. We are now praying to Allah for a result."

"Ahhh...you are back in the lawyer's computer? So soon?"

"No. This is not what I am smiling about. My friend is being very generous and is sending me a very clever trap. I am sending it now the Jew's lawyer. We should know within hours if he is making the same mistake."

Chapter 54—Arnold

WITH ONLY A rucksack and bro-bag, Arnold blew straight through baggage claim and on out the doors to Lot D and his waiting car. He tossed the rucksack and bro-bag in the back footwell, fired the ignition, and made for the line of cars waiting to exit.

While waiting to clear the gate, he dialed the vet's office to say he was fifteen to twenty minutes from picking up Chance.

Once on the freeway, a vague eerie sensation burrowed into the base of his neck, right between his shoulder blades, forcing him to glance at the rearview mirror.

Okay, sure, there were cars behind him. So what?

I'm being followed. That's what.

By? Naseem?

His asshole puckered.

Now what?

He knew enough from TV shows and movies to realize that good surveillance teams change up on subjects. Or was he just being totally paranoid?

Perhaps, but he couldn't shake the creepy eerie feeling.

"Fuck this."

Ignoring a blaring horn, he cut across the right-hand lane to take a fast approaching exit ramp, a diversionary tactic he'd seen on

TV. Secondary streets would make it exponentially easier to expose a tail, a strategy he'd picked up from a spy novel.

Fuck!

The creepy sensation wouldn't let up, despite being unable to spot anyone behind him. No helicopter above either. But this feeling was way too tangible to be totally imagined and was exactly like the night Karim hunted him in the alley behind the Green Lake house.

Do something!

Like?

The vet's office was only a half mile away. Pick him up or wait? On one hand, he'd feel more secure with Chance next to him. On the other hand, he didn't want to expose him to danger. Then again, Chance bailed out his ass last time someone seriously threatened him.

Screw it. They were more effective as a team. Chance sensed things he didn't.

Naseem

An alert popped up on Naseem's laptop: URGENT CONTACT.

She logged into the Dark-Web Skype equivalent, the one used for ultra-sensitive communication. Nabil was online waiting for her.

"What is it?"

"It didn't detonate."

Huh? "I thought—"

"No, not that, the one in the Jew's car," Nabil clarified.

"Ah." She paused to collect her thoughts. Could this be true? "Are you certain?"

"Yes, Sister. Kasra gave me the arrival time so I drove to where I could watch the garage exit. With my own eyes I saw him drive away."

"You are sure it was his car?"

"No doubt at all." Then, after an exasperated sigh, "If there was an explosion, police and the fire department would've responded.

Nothing happened. I tell you, for some reason it didn't work."

"Did you check the garage?"

"No. I am afraid to go anywhere near there, not now. I am worried."

An act of defiance on Nawzer's part? After all, the detonator was his responsibility. Was this a way of taunting her?

"Any idea why it failed?"

"Nothing at all."

She looked at the closed bedroom door where Nawzer slept.

"What do you want me to do?" Nabil asked.

"Nothing for now. Thank you."

Arnold

"You miss me, boy?"

Arnold was down on his haunches, arms outstretched, Chance's paws skittering in a useless attempt at finding traction on the smooth cement. Finally gaining momentum, all sixty pounds came careening full force into Arnold's waiting arms, almost knocking him back on his butt. Arnold managed to cup the pooch's cheeks in both hands to limit a mad flurry of wet doggie kisses and whines, then started in with his own greeting; a flurry of choobers and rabber-de-jabbers, the latter being intense stomach rubs.

A moment later the receptionist waved his Visa card at him. Reunion complete, Arnold pushed upright and signed the transaction.

"We'll miss him," she said. "He's always such a good morale booster for the other pets."

Arnold grinned, pleased with the kind words. Pet owners love praise. He was no exception.

"Man, I missed him! Even for just a few days."

He glanced down at his buddy who was looking back at him, tail still going like sixty. Nothing like a pooch!

* * *

Arnold stopped by one of his favorite convenience stores to score a ham and cheese on rye, a frosty La Croix, and four of Chance's favorite peanut-butter doggy biscuits.

Good to go.

On the way back to the car, he scanned the immediate vicinity, realized he probably looked totally ridiculous on account of having no idea what to look for.

Well, anything suspicious. Yeah? And what exactly does suspicious look like?

He wasn't exactly sure, but he figured was like porn: you knew it when you saw it. The nebulous feeling of being surveilled relentlessly smoldered deep within the muscles at the base of his neck, forcing him to scan, once again, his immediate surroundings. Not a damn thing appeared of place. Now this paranoia was beginning to royally piss him off: was he being victimized by some kind of Naseem mind-fuck game? Regardless, the nagging feeling couldn't be ignored.

After dumping the goods in his rucksack, he slid behind the wheel, fired the ignition and headed toward Chance's favorite park. He'd touch base with Fisher after settling in at the picnic table.

For the time being, though, his highest priority was to indulge Chance, which, truth be told, would ease the guilt for boarding him. Now all he had to do was find a way to make amends for lining Rachael up in Naseem's crosshairs.

They headed up the winding two-lane stretch of asphalt to their favorite view spot. That is, until a black Ford SUV came screeching around the corner, barreling straight for him. He'd avoided the area for weeks after. Then, after weighing conflicting emotions, decided he'd be nuts to allow Naseem to deprive them of favorite routines (well, within reason. There was also a case to be made for prudence). Chance loved this spot. So did he.

Fuck her and the camel she rode in on. Never again!

Her bullshit was going to stop.

Yeah? And exactly how's that going to happen?

That bitch has to die, that's all there is to it. Especially on account of Rachael.

You think big, dude. But you really have it in you?

With Chance exploring the new scents laid down since their last visit, Arnold settled in at the picnic table, set out his sandwich and can of water on the scarred wood tabletop, dug out his iPhone, and dialed Rachael. It rang straight through to the same canned message: the mailbox was full. No different from his previous attempts to reach her.

Chang mentioned that Fisher caught an earlier flight, so he must be in the city by now. Arnold called him on the Cryptophone.

Fisher answered with, "What's going on, Gold?"

Hmm...something off with Fisher's tone...what?

"John mentioned you were en route, so wanted to touch base, see if anything's come up with Rachael."

He watched Chance check out all the usual suspects: a couple palm trees, a clump of grass...

"No, no news to report. Sorry."

"Oh."

Yeah, something definitely going on with Fisher. His tone carried a note of evasiveness. What?

Dead air.

"Ah, Mr. Fisher?"

"Still here."

"Don't mean to sound nutzo paranoid, but, like, ever since getting into my car at the airport, I've had this super-strong-creepy-weird feeling of being followed."

More dead air. Something *was* up, and he was being left out of the loop.

Finally, Fisher said; "You've *seen* someone following you or you *think* someone's following you? Big difference."

"That's the thing...I can't really tell on accounta not being trained in counter-surveillance shit, so I'd have to say it's just a very

201

strong feeling."

"Heading home soon?"

Strange question.

How did Fisher know he wasn't at home? Was the FBI tracking his phone? Or his car? What the hell was going on?

"Why do you ask?"

"Just answer the fucking question, Gold. Are you?"

"I will be, soon as we finish up here."

"You familiar with the Times Supermarket on North School Street?" Fisher asked.

"The one in Kamehahameha Shopping Center?"

"Meet you in there. Whenever you and Chance leave the park and drive over. Talk then."

Fisher disconnected.

Fuck me!

Arnold was now totally and completely freaked. So, he *was* being followed. By the FBI. Why? And as long as he was on this particular subject, why go through all the James Bond secret-agent shit with the supermarket? Well hell, better get going. He pushed up from the picnic table.

"C'mon, boy."

They headed for the Mini.

Chapter 55—Arnold

ACCESS TO THE Kamehahameha shopping center was limited to two vehicular entrances, each off a cross street, making access tricky for first timers to the lot. The supermarket anchored a far corner of a medley of buildings and shops clustered into an irregular squarish mass. Arnold shopped this particular market primarily for the Taste of Times counter, which featured a nice variety of meal-appropriate dishes throughout the day; breakfast, lunch, and dinner. Crispy orange chicken was a dinner favorite of his. Then again, he had too many favorites.

He approached the store slowly, searching for a parking space close to the entrance, saw a car backing out and took the spot soon as it became empty. No sign of Fisher.

Arnold slipped out, closed the door, leaned in.

"Daddy has to go. Chance stays."

Chance moved to the driver's seat to poke his nose out the window and wait. Arnold gave him three quick choobers before heading into the store and straight to his favorite counter.

Long as he was doing the secret-agent schtick, might as well make it look legit and pick up dinner, right?

No Fisher. He turned his attention to the dinner selections, felt a presence to his right, turned.

203

And recoiled in shock.

"Jesusfuckingchrist, Mr. Fisher, you just scared crap out of me."

A voice from behind the counter asked, "You ready to order, sir?"

Arnold glanced across the counter at a short Asian woman, then back at Fisher.

"Go ahead," Fisher told him. "Act normal."

What the fuck?

Back to the saleswoman.

"I'll take the grilled guava spare ribs and string beans."

The woman reached for a takeout container and a serving spoon.

"One order?"

"Yes."

"Nice!" Fisher nodded approval at his choice.

"What the hell we doing, Mr. Fisher?" Arnold asked, still unnerved.

"Short version," Fisher said. "You've been under surveillance since first notifying me of Naseem's call. We picked up an unsub in a stolen Toyota that tailed you to the parking garage the day you flew to Seattle. The unsub was able to slip away and we lost him, but given Naseem's love for bombs of all types, we decided it might be prudent to check your vehicle. Guess what? We removed a pipe bomb on the undercarriage, directly under the passenger seat. Probably only big enough to kill your dog but strong enough to send a clear message."

Arnold's mind was suddenly mired in questions.

"Whoa whoa whoa!"

"Here you go," the clerk said, handing Arnold the packaged dinner.

Fisher nodded toward the cashier.

"Act normal, pay and leave. We're the only ones tailing you at the moment. Guess I could've broken this news on the phone, but felt it'd be better to tell you in person."

"Act normal—you shitting me?"

Fisher appeared dead-ass serious.

"Go ahead, leave, but call soon as you're home. I want an update on where we are in our plan. Remember, it's our best shot for finding Farhad and Rachael. In the meantime, know we have your back and are working this hard as we can. Just stick with the plan and keep the faith."

"Okay, but before I go..."

"No, nothing new on Rachael. Sorry. But, as I said, we're working that equally hard."

Fisher left Arnold standing in the checkout line.

Arnold opened his front door of his home to let Chance charge into the living room. Although he'd checked the security system before getting out of the car, you never knew...so a quick sniff-through by Chance just added a layer of reassurance, which he sorely needed.

Once inside, he locked the door and waited for Chance to clear the interior.

Although the A/C was programmed to kick in if the great room hit eighty degrees, he typically left the windows open so the trade winds could blow through the house on all but the hottest afternoon hours. Three days of being closed up with A/C running left a disagreeable, slightly moldy, metallic tinge to the air, so after dumping the dinner container on the counter, he raised the sunshades and opened the sliders to the deck and was immediately bathed in a lovely breeze. He then opened windows, especially in the master bedroom, to increase air circulation.

He refilled Chance's water and checked his dry-food dish. Good to go.

Fuck! A car bomb.

Part of him couldn't believe it. Part of him figured par for the course. His hands continued to shake.

Dear God, if they did that to me, what have they done to Rachael?

205

Out came a Maui Pale Ale from the SubZero. He twisted off the cap, tossed it in the trash, sucked down a long refreshing pull, and, for a moment, slumped against the kitchen island eying the chaise.

Safe to go out there?

Hmmm....Might be prudent to first check in with Fisher.

He flipped open the Cryptophone.

"What's happening with the PDF?" Fisher asked before Arnold had a chance to say hello.

"To tell the truth, haven't had time to look. It's only been, like," Arnold checked his watch, "what, ten or so hours since I planted it."

"Let me know soon as you have word. Remember, she's here and I fucking guarantee you she's not getting off this hunk of lava unless a marshal's on each arm as she's duck-walked to Con Air. You can put some money down on that one, Gold. That is, if you're into sure things."

"I'll believe it when it happens."

"Fucking pessimist."

Chapter 56—Arnold

HE STOOD AT the threshold between kitchen and deck, scanning the hillside across the ravine. Fisher assured him the area was clear, but he flashed on the image of Rios' head recoiling as the bullet struck. Better made damn sure. "SAM, launch RAID."

"RAID deployed," SAM answered.

Three minutes later RAID was back on the roof and the sniper spot cleared, yet the pucker factor remained strong enough to keep him from venturing out there.

That settled it. He glanced at the frosty ale in hand, decided alcohol probably wasn't the wisest choice, considering the work still in need of completion. He set it on the counter and replaced it minutes later with a steaming mug of hot chocolate on the desk to the right of the keyboard (without spilling a drop) and texted Rachael. Just on the off-chance...

Please, God, let her just be hiding. Don't let...

He called Davidson's cell, figuring by now he was either home or enjoying dinner out. Turned out he was just leaving the Metropolitan Market parking garage with a couple of fried chicken thighs and a tub of cole slaw from the deli. Arnold brought him up to speed on Fisher and the FBI surveillance. Davidson sounded relieved to learn of the protection.

"Any questions on next steps?" Arnold asked.

"No. My role is simple: wait for something suspicious to arrive in my in-box. Correct?"

"Correct. Notify me the minute it pops up."

If it does.

"Got it."

"I wish us luck," Arnold said before clicking off.

Next item of business: check the records from RAID's patrols during his absence. As previously scheduled, the around-the-clock routine security patrols had continued, with special attention to the ravine and the area in, and adjacent to, the sniper spot. The patrols launched randomly throughout the day and were of varying durations to prevent Naseem from identifying any sort of schedule, just in case she was contemplating a brute force smash-and-grab for SAM.

Next item: a deep dive into SAM, searching for the slightest hint of an attempt by Nawzer to breach his firewall while he'd been away.

Bingo!

Two attempts.

Both through Davidson's computers before the trojan was removed. Both while he was 30,000 feet over the Pacific heading to Seattle. Both unsuccessful. Both clearly in the wheelhouse of a second-string hacker. This buoyed Arnold's confidence. Surely, the dumb fucker would snap up the bait in Davidson's computer. Wouldn't he?

Leaning back, he tested the hot chocolate.

Ahhh, perfect temperature.

Next: one last deep dive into Naseem's phone call.

He strongly suspected she'd used a burner. If not, a spoofed number. Nawser might not be as technically savvy as he thought considered himself to be, but the dude wasn't dumb enough to overlook this elementary point.

After polishing off the hot chocolate, he started digging.

Yeah, dropping the U of H courses had been the right thing to do. No way he could possibly have finished that work with all that was consuming him now. Especially with his constant worry about Rachael.

Twenty minutes later Arnold called Fisher on the Cryptophone.

"What?" Fisher said upon picking up.

"Tried the number Naseem used on the call, and guess what?"

"Not in service."

"Exactly."

"No disrespect, Gold, but my techies got the same result. Just wanted to learn what happened when you called. Thanks for following up on that."

This didn't surprise Arnold.

"Anything else for me?" Fisher asked.

"Yeah, I'm about to take Chance on his evening walk. Any problem with that?"

"Where you planning to take him?"

"Just once around the block, then call it a night."

"No problem."

"Sorry, but just have to ask...anything on Rachael?"

"Sorry. Would've told you if there were."

Chapter 57—Naseem

NASEEM WATCHED NAWZER push back from the table, stand, clasp hands overhead, and hold an exaggerated stretch for ten seconds. Finally finished, he went to the stove to ignite the gas burner under the tea pot. Although she only caught his profile, he held that smug, arrogant expression she viscerally despised, the one he typically flashed before answering a technical question.

Prick!

"What?" she asked, fighting the urge to say something harsh.

"Nothing," he replied with questioning eyebrows. "I am only heating water for tea."

Feigned innocence. Typical. Infuriating. Another example of his incessant juvenile need to control discussions. No different from any other man she'd ever known: misogynistic, controlling, convinced of their superiority. Firouz, the sole exception. He valued her intellect and leadership; they were precisely the reason he designated her the group leader after he was detained.

"No, you have something to say. It's written on your face. What?"

She waited. Seconds passed.

Finally, Nawzer—his back to her—said, "I am sending another email to the Jew's lawyer. We are waiting now."

Chapter 58—Arnold

ARNOLD WAS POLISHING off his morning coffee when the TracFone—the one he and Davidson purchased at Target—rang.

God, please let this be The Call.

Heart sprinting, he picked up the phone.

"What up, Mr. Davidson?"

"I am the bearer of good news. An Amazon tracking notice just appeared in my inbox."

Arnold fist-punched the air.

Yes!

"Ah, which computer? Home or office."

"The office. It just arrived in my inbox."

Arnold's heart continued racing.

To make absolutely certain this was no false alarm, he asked, "You expecting a delivery?"

Davidson laughed.

"Would I be calling if I thought it legitimate?"

"Holy shit, this is probably it."

"What shall I do now?"

Arnold forced himself to take two slow even breaths and not answer without first thinking carefully, just like when he was playing chess.

Concentrate.

Don't be distracted by Rachael.

This might help find her.

"Do *not* touch your keyboard or mouse until you hear from me. I want to check in with Chang before we do a damned thing, just to be sure we're all on the same page and ready to go. Call you back soon as I have word. We good?"

"We are."

"Totally tubular! This should only take, like, two minutes, tops."

Chang's Cryptophone rang. "That you, bro?"

"Totally tubular news, I hope."

He went on to explain about the tracking notice that Davidson just received.

"Tubular indeed!" Chang said. "Has to be our man."

"Certainly hope so. The wait's been killing me."

Arnold reached for the cup.

Empty.

"Okay, okay...let me think...." Chang muttered. "We get only one shot at this, so...you're all set on your end? Locked and loaded?"

"Locked and fucking loaded, dude."

Then, as a failsafe—for both of them—Arnold described every step he'd completed.

"All right, then," Chang agreed. "Time to take this to stage two. Do your thing, but give me step-by-step downloads along the way. Okay?"

"You bet, boss."

"Every fucking step of the way." Chang echoed. "I'll put Fisher on notice."

"Mr. Davidson, I'm going to log on to your network now. Do *not* freak if you see some weird shit going on."

"Actually, I plan to walk over to Starbucks for a latte so you may work in peace. The suspense is killing me."

"Totally cool." Then: "No, wait! Don't leave just yet. I'll need you to open the tracking notice but only *after* I tell you to. Go ahead, hang up for now and I'll call the moment I'm set to go on this end."

"Understood. Bye."

Chapter 59—Arnold

ARNOLD COULDN'T HELP but laugh out loud at the tracking notice. Amazingly bush-league. Especially the two typos on top of the spoofed sender address. Fucking ridiculous. Nawzer must've bought it off another farm-team hacker at a bargain-basement price.

He sent Chang a copy, complete with three laughing-tears emoticons in the subject line in spite of hating those goddamned things. This one was just too good to not use a couple.

Then he called Davidson.

"I'm ready to roll on my end. Go ahead, click on tracking link."

"Hang on...okay, clicking...*now.*"

And boom: just as Arnold knew would happen, a chunk of malware embedded in Davidson's computer.

"Congratulations, you're now infected with a bad case of RAT."

A brief pause, followed by, "Is this good?"

"You bet."

"Because?" Davidson asked.

"On accounta we have our hooks in Nawzer now. Call you when I have an update."

He swapped the TracFone for the Cryptophone, where Chang was still on the line.

"Heads-up John, a copy of the trojan is heading your way."

"Totally tubular, bro."

Soon as the file was sent, Arnold switched from the right monitor to the left and logged onto the Dark Web as Massa Aurum in search of an online acquaintance, a white-hat malware guru whose on-line name was (undoubtedly a pseudonym) Troy. Damn! His lucky day; Troy was logged onto the first message board he checked. Arnold made a mental note to buy a Powerball ticket before day's end—assuming he caught a break in the action. His right screen remained zeroed in on the bogus PDF on Davidson's computer. Would Nawzer bite?

Massa typed: *Yo Troy, got a moment to check out some code?*

Troy: *Bring it on.*

He sent Troy a copy of the malware. Troy acknowledged receipt.

Massa: *Will wait for response.*

As the nervous minutes ticked slowly by, Arnold continuously scanned all three screens, waiting for something to happen.

Took Troy all of three minutes before he was typing: *Your basic trojan. cheap basic shit. probably coded in South Central Russia. why?*

Massa: *pulled it off a bud's machine. thanks. o you 1. later.*

He was typing Chang a report when he saw Nawzer pop up on Davidson's computer.

Totally tubular! Fuck the report.

He picked up the Cryptophone.

Arnold said, "Dude! He's in Davidson's machine as we speak."

"Outstanding!"

Arnold began a real-time sportscaster-style narration as Nawzer snooped the main directory. "Okay...okay...he's checking out...whoa, here we go, he zeroed in on the PDF..."

Agonizing seconds of silence.

"And?" Chang asked.

"And nothing. He's getting all cagey-cute, like...oops, dude's not even looking at it now."

"Damn!" Chang said.

"C'mon, c'mon...okay, okay, he's circling back..."

Then nothing.

"Still there, bro?" Chang asked

"Yeah. He's not doing a damned thing at the moment."

Tick tick tick...

"Yes!" Arnold yelled.

"He bite?"

"We got him, dude. Got to terminate. Call you back."

Arnold's fingers blurred over the keyboard. Seconds later he was inside Nawzer's computer with no idea how long it would be before the asshole realized he just been fucked in the commission of his own hack.

Arnold initiated a global data dump, indiscriminately and furiously downloading every file from Nawzer's computer to hard disc, SAM's motors churning at max speed, laying down gigabyte after gigabyte as they came flying through the fiber-optic cable, vacuuming up information fast as fucking possible. For the first time in the last thirty-six hours, Arnold held a glimmer of hope for finding Rachael.

After ten minutes, unable to contain himself a moment longer, he jumped up, shouted "M-o-t-h-e-r-*fucker*!" and started a totally ridiculous version of an Indian (tribe unknown) war dance, whooping, waving arms, and sending Chance streaking from the room.

Get a grip, dude.

He stopped, glanced around as if he'd slapped in the face.

The rational part of his brain made one sobering reality very clear; sooner or later, depending how observant and tight his security was, Nawzer would realize someone—probably Arnold Gold—just turned his computer into a digital colander. Retaliation might not be pretty.

He didn't worry about retaliation against him directly, because he was well-defended. But Rachael...certainly, Nawzer knew about her.

Oh, shit, what have I done?

His gut and asshole knotted. He began pacing tight circles, willing himself to calm down, to find a momentary distraction that might enable him to think clearly.

Yeah, and what would that be?

Well, how about a cup of hot chocolate? That always seems to work. He searched the house for Chance. Found him curled up on the deck, black snout between his front paws, eyes closed, seeking sanity. Kneeling, he rolled him onto his back and started in on some serious tummy rabber-de-jabbers. It was the best therapy for them both.

"Chance is a good boy....yes he is..."

He repeated the phrase over and over, desperately trying to make amends for spooking the dog.

Back in the kitchen, he nuked another mug of chocolate and ferried it back to his desk to update Chang.

"...as we suspected, they communicate through AnonMail-dot-Onion."

He referred to an anonymous encrypted email server on the Dark Web.

Arnold hit the Enter key.

"I'm sending you their encryption key now."

A moment later, Chang responded; "Ahhh, most excellent. I'll make sure Fisher recommends you for the White Hat Medal of Honor."

Funny! Hadn't heard that one.

"Look dude," Arnold said. "I now have a shitload of files to start wading through. Ping you when I know something important, like a password or two."

"Totally tubular, bro! Ciao."

Arnold cut the call, realized he was still flying so high from the hack and needed to seriously calm down and organize his thoughts.

Where to start?

He sat back to think as Nawzer's files continued stacking up faster than he could possibly sort through. Okay...okay, what, exactly, was he searching for? Had no clue. Under normal conditions he'd organize a systematic search, but now...there wasn't time. Rachael...

Slow down. Get a fucking grip before you do a damn thing. What are you really looking for?

He paused for a calming sip of chocolate and tried to ignore the rapidly increasing data dump from Nawzer's computer. Chance wandered back in and, with a sigh, plunked down next to Arnold's chair and curled up.

SAM beeped. He checked the right monitor, realized the download just finished.

Let the games begin. Back to offense.

First order of business: batten down security on Davidson's computers. He destroyed the lame-ass malware on Davidson's computers, then locked down the corresponding firewalls and activated a serious-as-shit antivirus package that'd certainly keep Nawzer out for good.

Second order of business: search the treasure trove of downloaded files for the crown jewel: Nawzer's password. He assigned SAM that task. SAM's software could search objectively and rapidly without being distracted by worries over Rachael.

Arnold's earlier excitement was calming to a manageable level, instilling in him increasing confidence. Between Fisher, Chang, and himself, they'd find Naseem. He was sure of this.

Then what?

Short of exchanging Naseem's freedom for Rachael, how in hell could they rescue her? Well, maybe the answer didn't reside with Naseem. Maybe it resided with Nawzer. Better yet, maybe the more effective strategy was to nail the person in Seattle working for Naseem. That person had to have Rachael. Yes, this made the most sense. This realization caused him to see how muddled his thinking was just minutes ago.

Hey, this is Fisher's expertise, not yours. Leave some of this shit to him and concentrate on those things that might help.

By the time he schlepped a fresh hot chocolate back to his desk, SAM had the password waiting for him. He promptly forwarded this to Chang.

Careful now, no mistakes.

He nestled into the gaming chair to review his progress.

Penetrate Nawzer's computer. Check.

Download contents. Check.

Share key contents with Chang. Check.

Okay, next step—the mother of all steps—was use Nawzer's computer as a gateway into Naseem's computer, and—best of all worlds—her cellphone. Do that and...

Unless, of course, Nawzer figured out he was hacked. In which case, he'd be totally out of luck. Meaning, he had, at best, maybe one, possibly two hours before being locked out.

Chapter 60—Arnold

ARNOLD HAD AN idea. Back at the keyboard, fingers flying, he logged into Nawzer's encrypted Dark Web email account. A quick scan of contacts quickly narrowed his choice to one likely candidate.

For the next several minutes he crafted a message and a spoofed email address. Once he was satisfied with the wording, he double-checked every detail to make sure his ruse held no obvious tell, then hit the Enter key, hurling the email out into cyberspace.

"Here's what I just did." Arnold explained to Chang the contents of, and logic behind, the email: an urgent request for Naseem to text back immediately.

"Fucking brilliant, bro! You're on a roll now."

"I'll ping the moment she bites. Assuming, of course, she does."

"She will," Chang assured him.

"Glad you sound too goddamn confident."

Way more confident than he was.

"I am." Chang said. "That's because we're dealing with a group of shitheads."

Arnold leaned back in his chair, steepled fingertips tapping chin, watching the digital timer on the monitor slowly...

Tick tock tick tock...

The waiting seemed so...what? Useless? Yeah, useless.

I should be doing something else, anything I can think of to help find Rachael.

Like?

What other option was there? Couldn't leave the house. Yeah, sure, he needed to buy food and take Chance for a walk...or a thousand other errands. No, he needed to sit right here tethered to SAM until Naseem responded to the text.

Which raised an interesting question: how long should he wait before deciding his little gambit wasn't going down the toilet? Shit, no way to know. Unless, of course, something compelling popped up on Nawzer's computer.

Okay, but at least get off your ass and move a little.

With a sigh, he glanced toward the ceiling and made a decision: if Naseem didn't take the bait by the time he finished making his next hot chocolate, fuck it, he'd take Chance to the park for a run and then, on the way back, drop into Times Supermarket for a few essentials.

The microwave beeped. He was setting the hot chocolate on the desk, when Naseem's response to the spoofed email flashed on screen.

Glory-fucking-osky!

Chapter 61—Arnold

ARNOLD WAS FINDING it annoyingly difficult to stay focused on the task at hand, his concentration fragmented by the excitement of potentially closing in on Naseem as well as the unrelenting worry about Rachael. He had to force himself to work slowly and methodically, double-checking every step for fear of blundering.

Yes, he was a gambler, but was he willing to make this bet? With Rachael's life hanging on the outcome?

"What you waiting for, bro?" Chang said. "Start digging, see what you come up with."

"Easy for you to say, especially since you're not the one with their ass on the chopping block. Computers? No problem. But iPhones...I'm not really grade-A with phones."

"Oh, bullshit! You da man! Besides, you have a hell of a lot more skin in this game than I do."

"Exactly! That's why I'm being so..."

"Such a pussy?"

When Arnold didn't reply, Chang added, "Look at it this way, bro: here's your opportunity to score payback for Rachael."

Arnold swallowed hard, nodded to himself.

Chang was right.

"Be back to you soon as I have something real."

Chapter 62—Arnold

ARNOLD SETTLED IN, having steeled his nerve; made sure his keyboard, mouse, and monitors were positioned exactly the way they felt most comfortable, adjusted his butt in the chair, (all superstitious behavior, he realized. Still...) took a deep breath, and started in.

Naseem's text reply gave him her phone number.

First order of business: determine if that number was valid or spoofed.

A few commands answered that question: Valid.

Next item: research the number in order to dig up basic information on the phone, like, model, serial number, and linked devices. Easy.

Minutes later he was armed with the following: it was an iPhone X linked to an Apple Watch and a laptop. A different phone—actually a newer model—from the one she was using at the time of the warehouse shootout.

Smart!

He would've dumped that puppy too. But the Apple Watch was an entirely new wrinkle. And gave him pause. Somehow, Naseem owning that watch felt out of character.

He shipped a copy of this new information to Chang along with a complete copy of her phone contacts. Then he asked himself: could there possibly be any additional information to harvest from the present data before turning his attention elsewhere?

Hmmm...what about the Wallet app in her phone? He flashed on the *"What's in your wallet?"* Capital One TV ad, and laughed out loud.

Which, in turn, caused Chance to nose-bump his elbow. He reached down, gave the dog a reassuring choober for good measure. He jotted *wallet* on a pad next to his mouse before he might become distracted by another flash of brilliance.

Okay, what about Naseem's iCloud? Was the phone also linked to that?

Totally tubular! Yes, it was.

Another jotted note on the pad. *Hang in there, Rachael, I'm coming!*

As a security precaution—to avoid inadvertently triggering a booby trap—he copied all the information retrieved thus far to two separate off-site systems. Then, one quick look in the Wallet app, and he had her credit-card number and two Bank of America accounts.

He paused while paranoia bells began ringing in the back of his mind. It was too easy.

Shit! Am I being played here? Was this a layup by Nawzer? Then: *Not his style, man.*

Then he was up again, pacing circles, wiping his palms on his cargo shorts and taking measured, controlled breaths. Not enough time to check with Chang. Every minute wasted increased the risk of being discovered. He had to press on, be careful, and have faith in his own judgment.

Back in the chair again, he rechecked security. All quiet on the Western Front.

Next item: dig further into the iCloud angle.

And dig he did. *Jesus Christ, are you fucking kidding me?* Her iCloud connected directly to her MacBook. *Her fucking MacBook!*

He called Chang with the news. "We be jommin, mon, doncha know!" Chang said in perfect Jamaican accent. Then: "I'll sic our financial gnomes on this shit, like, double pronto."

"Did I mention her phone's a Series 10?" Arnold said, not wanting to waste a moment, yet not wanting to omit important information. His anxiety was now up to slow boil, making it impossible to remember what he might've mentioned to him earlier.

"You did, why?"

"And it's paired to a Series 5 Apple watch?"

Chang hesitated.

"Good to know, but not sure how this helps us. I'll file it away, though."

"What's your next move?" Arnold asked, meaning the FBI.

"I need to confer with Fisher before answering that. However, from here on out, we will proceed with extreme caution. I suspect he's even going to want to run a few things past a magistrate for a ruling."

"Why?"

"Don't be naïve, bro. In spite of your intel being extremely helpful, Fisher and I know precisely how you're getting your hands on it and it isn't exactly on the up-and-up, so...we need to come up with a way to make it more...ah, acceptable should it have the potential of ending up in court..."

Court? No way that bitch was going to end up in court. Not if I can help it. Too much risk of...

"...so it can be deemed admissible."

"Fuck that! What about Rachael?"

"Calm down, bro. I'm not saying say we can't use it. I'm just saying we need to be very diligent in laying down an appropriate paper trail before attempting to use it in any meaningful way. I especially want to figure out how to legally obtain her GPS coordinates from her phone. In the meantime, why don't you, since you have access to it, find that out for us ASA-fucking-P."

GPS coordinates? Now?

Fuck, why didn't I think of that?

"No prob. Give me...oh...two minutes."

"Totally tubular," Chang said. "I'm switching you over to speakerphone while I patch into Fisher. If for some reason we drop the link, call back."

Once again Arnold's fingers were working at lightning speed over the keyboard.

"Okay, here you go..."

He gave Chang the phone's most recent GPS coordinates before uploading them into Google Maps.

Bingo.

The crosshairs centered on a small property fronting Merkle Street, an obscure dead-end in a community of single-family homes off Likelike Highway.

Chapter 63—Arnold

NERVES ZINGING, HEART rocketing along in excess of MACH 2, Arnold felt as if the top of his head was bouncing off the ceiling.

Take a break? You need it.

No. Making too much progress. Every new piece of critical intel brought them that much closer to finding Rachael.

Speed's good, but speed kills. Be very, very careful.

Much as he hated to lose momentum, he knew he should pause for a Zen moment.

Zen moment? What the fuck's that? And why am I talking to myself?

Just listening to this internal dialogue convinced him a break was needed.

Back in the gaming chair after a short walk with Chance, hot chocolate to the right of his mouse, Arnold called Chang.

Chang answered with a cryptic, "Go bro."

"Anything of note since our last chat?"

"Actually, a ton of shit's going down at the moment."

"Such as?"

"They're setting up for a knock-and-talk at the house you pinpointed for us."

Arnold sat up, now on the edge of the game chair.

"No shit?" Finally! Something happening. They were close now; Arnold could taste it.

"I'm on an open link with Fisher as we speak, listening to a blow-by-blow, so if I sound distracted, I *am* distracted. Just stand by and I'll keep you totally updated."

"Understood."

Arnold's gut now churned even harder than earlier.

Could this actually be the day the FBI captured Naseem? After two years of hunting?

"Go ahead and pull up the location up on Google Earth if it's not already on your screen," Chang suggested.

"Hold on, pulling it up now."

Arnold reentered the coordinates, zeroed in on the spot, then enlarged the picture of the house and property.

"Okay, looking at it. What now?"

"Using one or two screens?" Chang asked

"Three, actually."

"Al right then, I'm about to patch you into to a real-time video feed. Hold one."

Holy shit, real time?

He began nervously fiddling with the mouse, sliding it back and forth across the gaming pad.

"Is this usual?" he asked.

"Is what usual?"

"Allowing a... civilian to watch this sort of thing."

"You're asking the wrong person, bro. This is as new for me as it is for you. I'm just the geek assigned to the case...least that's what I was told. But Fisher wants you available for a possible visual confirmation if someone's actually inside."

Made sense. Also exciting to see the action. Then again...

"Okay, but it'll only take me a couple minutes to drive over...I mean, it's, like, maybe five miles from here." Soon as the words flew out, he flashed on the warehouse encounter and changed his mind about any in-person eye-witnessing of possible action. Besides, the house could be nothing but a waste of time. Might even be abandoned, for all he knew.

"I suspect he's well aware of that," Chang said. "The downside to this, of course, is we have no fucking idea what we're dealing with in there. I'm also damned sure every one of those shitheads is able to recognize you from at least fifty feet and we don't want is to tip our hand until absolutely forced to."

Okay, that made sense.

"You up and running on the live feed now?" Chang asked.

He checked the center screen.

"In living color."

"Excellent. Describe what you see."

It took Arnold a moment to correlate the Google satellite view on the left monitor with the live feed on the center monitor. The right monitor displayed Google Maps. Best he could tell from correlating the terrain with the surroundings, the camera was positioned one or two properties down and across the street from the target house.

"The target "—he slipped into the terminology he'd heard Fisher use in the minutes leading up to the warehouse raid— "appears located in a working-class residential area just north of downtown. The house itself is set into a fairly steep hill almost at the end of the street."

"Exactly. What else?" Chang asked.

Arnold studied the house more closely.

"It's a one-story structure. The property appears to end at a retaining wall with what...might be a six-foot drop into the neighboring property. There's a short driveway with two cars parked side by side."

"Okay, the visual's good to go. I'm now patching you into the comm line. You'll be split between both Fisher and me."

Chance was standing on Arnold's left side, tongue out, panting, sensing something important going on. Arnold reached down, gave him a few reassuring squeezes to the back of his neck.

"Good boy."

"You're live with Gold, now," Chang said.

"Gold, have a copy?"

Fisher's voice was in his left earbud, Chang's voice in his right.

"Copy that."

For some strange reason he figured "copy that" sounded more official than "ten-four." Did the FBI even say ten-four? From a slew of Discovery ID viewing, he knew police used the numerical code, but the FBI? Didn't sound right.

"All right then, here's what's going down. HPD's running the licenses on both vehicles outside the house. We should know the owners' names any moment. In the meantime, there's only one way out of there and that's the street you're looking at. It runs downhill, behind us. Uphill, it ends at the last property and that's at the base of a steep ridge. This means the house is contained. No one's getting in or out without us seeing them.

"At the moment," Fisher continued, "we're interviewing the uphill neighbors. I'm monitoring that, but so far, they haven't been able to provide any detail about occupants of the target house. They do, however, see various vehicles come and go at all hours, so it's not your normal scene for this hood.

"At the corner property at the bottom of the hill is a mom-and-pop travel agency. We have a surveillance vehicle on the cross-street outside it...hold one...yeah, yeah..." Fisher said, obviously carrying on another conversation.

Arnold was up, pacing, a pack of gerbils scurrying furiously through his stomach. Chance paced alongside, occasionally glancing up as if to ask, *You okay, Dad?*

He grabbed the chocolate and downed the cold dregs.

A moment later Fisher came back.

"Property records show the owner's a female with a Middle Eastern first and last name. We just checked and she's not the TSA agent driving the car HPD stopped in your area, but could be a relative or associate...we don't—hold one..."

A moment later.

"Gold, you catching this?"

Arnold hurried back to his desk and leaned on his palms to watch the live feed. One of the cars was backing out of the driveway.

"Yeah, I'm watching."

Without moving his eyes from the screen, he dropped back into the chair.

Once out of the drive, the car backed uphill several feet, braked, then started straight downhill, passing directly past the camera.

"Get a look at the driver?" Fisher asked.

Arnold assumed the question was directed to him.

"Yeah, but not good enough to know if I recognize him."

"Hold one." Fisher muttered something unintelligible, then: "We're emailing three shots of him. Please acknowledge receipt."

Chang whispered in his other ear.

"If you recognize him as one of Naseem's accomplices, it'll go a long way in obtaining a search warrant for that house. Fisher has a federal magistrate on speed dial with a templated request all set to go. Just say the word. We only need to add a few finishing touches."

SAM chimed with new email.

"Okay, the pictures just arrived."

"Good. Let me know," Fisher said.

Arnold brought them up on the right-hand screen, the center screen still running the live video. He was looking at four nicely cropped and focused shots, clearly taken through a telephoto lens. However...

"Ah, man..."

He flipped through the pictures: two head shots of the guy walking from house to the car, another of him behind the wheel as it approached the street corner, and one side-view as the guy drove past.

"What do you think?" Fisher asked.

Arnold was chewing his lip, waffling. Chance whined and nuzzled his elbow.

"Something very strange weird funky's going on with this..." A wave of frustration hit. "Can't quite figure out what, but..." Was he the only obstacle to learning if there was crucial information about Rachael inside the house? What would it hurt to say the man looked like...

"Is he or isn't he one of the terrorists, Gold?" Fisher pushed.

Chang whispered: "Even if he resembles..."

Okay, okay...you're not a hundred-percent sure who that driver is, but you know damn well her phone was inside that house so it must be connected, right?

Was? How long since he last checked its location?

"Gold, you still there?"

Christ, this was taking waaayyy too long...if Naseem *was* inside, she sure as hell knew by now what was going on outside.

Just fucking go for it, dude. If she's not there now, she was there.

"Yeah, he resembles one of them...but I can't come up with a name."

"Excellent! We're all over that warrant now."

"How long's that going to take?"

Chapter 64—Arnold

ARNOLD LEFT THE ear buds in while awaiting a progress report from either Chang or Fisher but took the opportunity to feed Chance, drain his bladder, and nervously nuke another hot chocolate.

How many cups did this make today? Had no idea. Didn't give a shit, either.

He was too damned nervous to do anything but worry about Rachael, fidget, pace, and detour now and then to the deck to gaze across the ravine to the sniper spot to refresh his memory as to just how evil Naseem actually was. Had she already killed Rachael? If she intended to use her as a bargaining chip, why hadn't she contacted him?

By now the fuckers in that house were probably well aware of the shitstorm brewing out on the street. They'd have to be brain-dead to not know. Then again, Fisher was smart enough to know that they were smart enough to know that...

All right already!

"Gold, you there?"

He ran back to SAM and the gaming chair, slopping chocolate along the way.

"I am."

Fisher said: "We have a search warrant for the house and an

arrest warrant for Naseem and Nawzer, so we're ready for a knock-and-talk. Chang, the live feed still rolling?"

"Roger that....hey, bro," Chang said to Arnold. "I'm switching your live feed to a different source. Here we go."

The view on the center monitor switched from the target house what looked to be the inside of a car.

"The hell am I looking at?" Arnold asked.

"It's the live view from our bomb specialist's body cam," replied Fisher. "Her job is to clear the inside of that house before we execute the search warrant. And that will depend on whether you recognize anyone inside."

Made perfect sense. Once again, he nervously slid the mouse back and forth across the pad.

"Any further questions?" Fisher asked.

"Nope."

Finally!

This was it. The day of Naseem's capture.

Okay, then what?

Rachael was probably still a hostage, presumably in Seattle. And that, he realized, was a huge bargaining chip for Naseem, possibly even a get-out-of-jail-free card. Not only that, but once captured, the court system afforded her due process, and any trial carried the very real risk of her skating on some bullshit technicality or argument by a crafty lawyer.

Like, what kind of technicality? Easy: how about the intel the FBI used as the basis for the search warrant? Based entirely on information he, Arnold Gold, obtained illegally from hacking Nawzer's computer.

That thought gave him serious pause. How many laws had he broken?

He now appreciated the reason Fisher and Chang were moving with caution. Perhaps they were just being reasonable. Perhaps he'd been too anxious to cut corners to bring down The Bitch. But in the process, had he totally torpedoed a successful prosecution?

What if Naseem *was* inside the house and elected to go out in a blaze of jihadist bomb glory? Yeah, that would solve a shitload of legal issues but might also make Rachael infinitely more difficult to find. And now that he was dwelling on this particular subject, if Naseem did die in the next few minutes, would her sympathizers avenge her death by executing Rachael?

What the fuck have I done?

Eyes closed, he grimaced. No going back now.

"Gold, you ready?"

"Yes."

Chapter 65—Naseem

NASEEM'S IPHONE STARTED in playing the marimba ringtone. She glanced at the face propped up in the cupholder. Nawzer.

He knew better than to call unless it was a matter of extreme importance.

Another glance in the rearview mirror and immediate surroundings. No sign of a cop car. All clear. She turned into a strip mall parking lot and nosed into a space in front of a nail salon where a beat-up panel truck shielded the car from the road, and answered the call.

"Why are you not using the burner?" Naseem demanded, making no attempt to mask her irritation, her nerves tattered bundles after three days of mounting stress and inability to sleep.

No answer.

"Well? Answer me!"

"It is being on the table."

Ahhh, yes...charging the battery. Forgot.

"This better be important. Speak. Quickly."

She was using the new phone, only two weeks old. Neither Homeland Security nor FBI—nor anyone else, for that matter—knew of it. Regardless, the FBI could surely gain NSA's assistance in finding her. She once read of NSA's sophisticated software and its ability to scan more than 534 million calls a year for keywords, making it almost impossible for a conversation to pass unnoticed unless cleverly disguised with code words.

"Our friends in the travel agency are calling. The house is being watched."

An adrenaline surge jetted through her arteries, instantly focusing her mind.

"Are you very sure of this?" she asked.

"I am having no reason to not be believing them."

Trust no one! Not even Nawzer. Especially Nawzer. Could he be setting her up? Was the FBI listening?

"Have you looked for yourself?"

"No," he admitted.

How did the FBI find the safe house? She had purposely taken carefully planned steps to remain discrete when establishing it. Her heart was pumping wildly now.

"Why not?"

Nawzer paused.

"I am calling you immediately after I am finding this out."

Stupid goat!

"Then look out the window, tell me what you see."

"Yes, I am doing this now."

She heard the phone rustle—perhaps from changing hands. A few beats passed.

"I am seeing three cars down the street. Four men in each. Oh...they are looking at me. Now."

"Move away from the window." Too late. They undoubtedly saw him. "No, wait. Keep looking, tell me what they're doing."

She remembered seeing a van as she drove down the street to the intersection but hadn't paid it any attention. Perhaps that had been a mistake.

Did Homeland Security have pictures of Nawzer? Probably not.
He hadn't been detained and questioned in LA...

Could she be absolutely certain of this?

Would he admit it if he had? He was only a techie, not a jihadist in arms...so, if law enforcement had questioned him why would he even bother to warn her? Hmmm. Perhaps he told them what he knew simply to save himself? After all, he'd grown too fond of his soft, decadent lifestyle with his nice flat and blond guppy-lipped whore...perhaps he'd made a deal with the FBI? This could easily explain how they located the safe house so soon after his arrival.

"They are getting out of their cars now and are walking this way. What are you wanting me to do?"

"You are the only one in the house?"

When she'd left, he was alone in the house. However, sympathizers often dropped in randomly during the day.

"Yes, yes, of course," he said, clearly nervous.

Ah, perfect. "And no weapons of any sort?"

"No."

She thanked Allah for allowing her to safely drive away from the house before these people—whoever they were—appeared. Perhaps Allah had inspired her to leave disguised as a man.

She realized Nawzer still awaited an answer.

"Simply open the door and greet them. Be pleasant. You know nothing."

What he did next would tell her just how much the FBI actually knew. Because if they arrested Nawzer...

"And if they are asking to come inside?"

"Respectfully request they show you a search warrant. If they do have one, tell them you must first speak with our lawyer, Ahmed. Ask them to wait outside until you've discussed this with him."

"Okay, as you are wishing...ah, Naseem?"

"Yes?" What was that nuance in his voice? Fear? Yes, fear. Which proved beyond doubt he was never a true jihadist, for a true fighter does not fear death. No, Nawzer was nothing but a techie, his commitment to the cause only as deep as his computer skills and the money he earned. This note of fear in his voice erased any question of deception. The FBI had somehow found her without his help.

Suddenly, she realized the reason: the Jew. The Jew needed to be dealt with immediately. She'd simply kill him, then disappear again.

"Be careful, Brother" she warned Nawzer. "They are closer than we suspected."

"And you are being careful too, Sister."

"I am always careful."

"I am hurrying, now, they are at the door. Quickly...disable the GPS on your phone so they are not finding you."

"My GPS? You mean in the car?"

She could simply walk away from it now, giving her an excellent head start.

"No. That one is being unavoidable. I am meaning the GPS in your iPhone. Turn it off. Now."

"How?"

She heard him yell, "Yes, yes, I am coming."

Then Nawzer was reciting quick instructions: "Go to home screen."

She switched to speakerphone to have the use of both hands.

"Yes, I'm there."

"Go to Settings."

Both thumbs working on the touch screen now.

"Yes."

"Find 'Privacy'."

"Yes, yes...Go on."

"Make sure Privacy is being turned *on*. Then turn *off* Location Services. Now you are using your phone without the GPS. I am going now."

"Wait! One more question. How did they find us?"

"I am not knowing for sure."

"Yes, yes." She was growing impatient with his inability to voice an opinion. Especially now. "Give me your best guess?"

No answer.

"Nawzer!"

After a resigned sigh, he said: "I am suspecting the Jew is using the malware on the lawyer's computer to be finding my computer. If this is true, then it is not so difficult to be finding you. This is the only way this is making sense."

Something in his tone triggered enough suspicion for her to believe he was holding back critical information.

"In other words, you made a stupid mistake, didn't you!" she demanded.

"No!"

The force of his defensiveness only shored up her suspicion. He *was* responsible. Under different circumstances she'd sort this out another way, but this was hardly the time or place to do so. If Nawzer was taken into custody for interrogation, the damage he could potentially inflict would be devastating. He'd quickly surrender every scrap of information he might have in order to save his decadent soft life. Their entire Dark Web network, for example. She made a mental note to destroy that immediately after killing the Jew. What else was now at risk? Not much. She'd have sufficient time to think through that question. When taking over from Farouz, she'd been meticulous in her effort to isolate Nawzer from allied cell activities. So the information he might be able to divulge, although damaging, wouldn't be as catastrophic as she first thought.

One thing was now certain: Nawzer was a lost asset, one easily replaced.

"Sister, what are thinking?"

She glanced at the phone, realized she hadn't disconnected from him.

"Answer the door, Brother. Good luck. Remember, Ahmed is our lawyer."

She cut the connection. For a few seconds she remained perfectly still, prioritizing her next moves. She'd find an internet café, access their Dark Web messaging system, and warn everyone to abandon it. Before doing that, however, she must kill the Jew.

And Nawzer.

She'd planned for this very contingency.

Nabil built a special bomb, one capable of being triggered remotely via cellphone just like the IEDs employed in Iraq and Afghanistan. She had stored that IED under the living-room couch, with its phone fully charged and ready to go.

Chapter 66—Arnold

"HAVE A CLEAR view?" Fisher asked Arnold.

Arnold leaned forward in the game chair, elbows on knees, nervously rubbing palms together.

"Roger that."

"Good. I want you to eyeball whoever answers the door. I want an immediate assessment. If you need a better view, just shout out. Don't be shy."

Christ! His heart was probably doing one-sixty now as he rocked back and forth in the chair. Everything was coming down to the next few minutes. Would Naseem be inside that house or not?

He watched Fisher's knuckles rap the door three times. No response. Fisher knocked again, louder this time.

Then Fisher whispered, "Hear that? Someone's in there."

"Nope, didn't hear it," Arnold said.

"Well, I did. Now we know we're going to be able to look inside."

Arnold fought the urge to ask if the voice was male or female but feared distracting Fisher.

Finally, the door opened. A man stood in the shade of the doorway blinking at the sunlight, the contrast on the camera too severe to capture enough detail to make a decision.

"Yes?" the man asked.

"FBI Special Agent Fisher." Fisher made a point of holding his ID for the camera to record. "Who are you?"

The man hesitated.

"I am not understanding what you are asking."

As Fisher repeated the question more slowly and loudly, Chang's voice popped up in his right ear; "Anyone you recognize?"

"Not in that light. Have him to step onto the porch," Arnold said.

Fisher waved the man out onto the small bare concrete pad that served as a porch. The man took two steps forward then stopped with full sunlight on his face.

Fisher repeated the question but the man simply stood tall, blinking in the light.

Meanwhile, the bomb specialist stepped around him to glance inside the house.

Arnold was able to see a small living room, kitchen, a hall leading to the right, t-shirts and shorts strewn randomly over every piece of well-worn secondhand furniture, open grease-stained fast-food containers dumped on the coffee table and floor, a sofa cushion on the floor in front of the TV, the interior in such disarray it made a pig sty seem like a Ritz-Carlton suite. Then he noticed pay dirt: four open laptops on the red Formica kitchen tabletop.

The bomb tech backed up to focus again on the occupant.

"Gold?" Fisher said.

Arnold said, "I'm not entirely sure, but if forced to bet, my money's on Nawzer."

"Because?"

"Nothing in particular, I guess, other than a just a very strong gut feeling."

Fisher held the search warrant up for the man to see.

"I have a search warrant for this house. May we come in now?"

The man blinked, backed up a step.

"I am thinking yes, but I am also thinking I am calling my

lawyer first. Please, I am needing one moment."

He raised an index finger as he backed up into the living room and stopped by the tattered couch.

"Here, take this," Fisher said, holding out a copy of the warrant while quickly craning to see into as much of the interior as possible without crossing the threshold.

Suddenly the image became blinding light, then blurred as the camera arced wildly toward the sky.

Next came the boom of a thundering explosion.

Chapter 67—Naseem

NASEEM BACKED OUT from the parking spot, turned the car toward the exit, waited for a break in traffic before nosing out, making sure to adhere exactly to the speed limit, her Glock 40 on her right, crammed between the seat and center console.

She knew the route to the Jew's house cold after two-plus months on the island. Her plan was simple: with the transmission in park, engine running, approach the security gate. Then ring the bell, and soon as the Jew stepped from the house, unload the full clip into him and the damned dog, drive back to town, dump the car in a parking lot, disappear. Simple. Easy. Effective.

With the Jew eliminated and Nawzer now gone, there was no longer a reason to remain holed up on this island. As for the Jew's system? Time to walk simply away and call it a lost cause. After all, it had produced nothing but grief and needless loss of her brothers' lives.

She knew of a sympathizer with a boat capable of transporting her across the Kaini Channel to Molokai. From there she could hop a commuter flight to Maui and from there another flight to the West Coast, or perhaps Japan or Australia. The greatest risk would be avoiding detection at the Maui airport, but that was a risk well worth taking as long as the Jew was eliminated. She smiled at the simplicity and beauty of the plan. Watching the Jew die would be a supreme pleasure.

She prayed for Allah to continue to smile on her.

Arnold

"The fuck happened?" Arnold asked, the live-feed image having blacked out after the flash. The moment the words flew out of his mouth, he realized how ridiculously stupid he sounded. Did he even have voice contact with anyone?

Seriously, dude? A bomb. Obviously.

"Hang on," Chang replied.

Well, that answered one question. Still in contact with one of the team. What about Fisher? He alive? And Nawzer? And Naseem?

Fuck! If Naseem was dead, how would that work for rescuing Rachael?

Okay, what could he do?

Well, his only contribution to the case so far—other than walking around with a Day-glo red target on his chest—was his computer skills. So...why not run down a few things. Before Chang patched him into Fisher's live feed, he'd been monitoring Nawzer's computer. He checked, but found it no longer online. Interesting; it went dead at about the same time as the explosion.

"Goddamned motherfucker!" a voice said.

Arnold sat bolt upright. Was that....Fisher?

"Goddamnit!" the voice said again.

Yeah, Fisher's voice, seemingly all right.

"What happened?" Arnold asked.

"Not now, Gold! We're in a situation here."

"Wait, I think I have something."

"I said, *not now.*"

"This could be important," and Arnold barged ahead, explaining the significance of Nawzer's computer.

"So fucking what!" Fisher replied. "A bomb just settled the

issue of whether or not terrorists were in there. The only thing we don't yet know is which ones and how many."

"Stand by, bro," Chang said. "I'm going to check her phone GPS. If that's dead too..." After a beat: "Yeah, her GPS's gone. The phone either went up with the blast..."

"...or she disabled it," Arnold added.

"Yeah, that's possible I guess, but what are the odds Nawzer's computer and Naseem's phone go dead at the same time if they're not right next to each other?"

"Right, but you don't know the exact sequence, do you!"

Silence.

"No, guess not."

Arnold paced, his mind humming along at rabid bat speed, the gut pain like sulfuric acid burning through metal.

"Something's been gnawing at me," he said. "I think the guy who drove away from that house wasn't a man. I believe that was Naseem in disguise. Someone must've warned her."

"Seriously?" Chang asked.

"Seriously. And know what else? Bet you she's heading here right now. To kill me."

"Hold one. I'll give Fisher a heads-up on this, but HPD's already got a BOLO on that vehicle, so I don't know what else they can do at the moment."

Fisher was back in his ear.

"You *think* that was her or you're *sure* that was her?"

"Abso-fucking-lutely convinced!"

"Why the change of mind all of a sudden?"

Arnold thought about that.

"Not really sure but at the time something just didn't feel right about it. But if she isn't in the house, she's heading this way fully intending to try to kill me."

"I suspect you're right, that that was her, but we don't have a shred of corroborating evidence. But for now, there's a BOLO on the vehicle. And if she is in the wind, the last place she might head is to your place."

Several chunks of information were clicking into place.

"What you thinking, bro?" Chang asked.

Oops.

Forgot that he hadn't cut either comm link.

"Okay, here's the thing...she bought an Apple watch, right?"

Chang sounded like he was catching on to where this was headed.

"Yeah?"

"If I remember correctly, that model is GPS-enabled. Give me a sec to pull up the specs."

Fisher asked: "And we know this because?"

Arnold responded as he typed.

"When I hacked her phone, I found her Wallet app with her credit-card number in it, so I scanned all her purchases since the warehouse thing."

Chang: "Send me the link, bro."

"Yeah, yeah..." Arnold replied, not really paying attention now, fingers in a crescendo of clicks, the screen flashing page to page, working through various steps until... there it was.

"Okay..." Arnold continued, "I've got that GPS up now and it's *moving*. She was *not* in the house. John, you should be getting the link now."

He zapped it to Chang.

Heart racing, palms sweating, his eyes glued to the monitor, he uploaded the information into Google Maps. Problem was, the watch, like the iPhone, could be easily turned off. Or, if she realized it included an active GPS, she could simply toss that puppy out the window. In the meantime, however, he'd continue to feed Fisher her location.

Chapter 68—Naseem

NASEEM STUCK STRICTLY to speed limits while also keeping an eye on every vehicle in her immediate vicinity. So far, she'd not yet seen one police car.

Good! Allah was smiling on her.

Knowing this strengthened her resolve.

Nawzer no longer presented a problem. This was a greater relief than she'd assumed. No more worrying what would happen when he was interrogated. Yes, her group would need to quickly replace him, but she already knew a good candidate. There were other minor housekeeping issues to tend to soon as possible— destroying their present communication system, for example— but these were all trivial matters, really, because within hours, the group would easily migrate to a new safe site. However, every one of these items would have to wait until she killed the Jew.

She felt the Glock 40's reassuring cool black steel in her lap, with a full magazine in the stock plus one in the chamber. More than sufficient for the task ahead. And if the police caught her afterward? No problem. Two more full clips were stashed in her purse. She'd practiced rapid reloads until she could literally do them blindfolded. Yes, if need be, she was equipped and mentally prepared to leave this life in the glorious spirit of a true martyr.

So far, her clever and timely escape from the safe house seemed destined for glorious success. Especially the ease with which she'd driven directly past that suspicious van at the end of the block. As it turned out, she passed right under the FBI's arrogant noses. Had they realized their blunder yet? Perhaps. If so, other law-enforcement agencies would be searching for this car, but her confidence was strong and she would succeed.

With her head start, she believed that nothing, absolutely nothing, could prevent the satisfaction of seeing the Jew die.

Fingering the Glock again, she smiled.

Yes, she'd certainly enjoy this.

Arnold

Arnold was pacing again, mind wresting to remember an important thought dislodged by the drama of the explosion...something to do with the car Naseem was driving...some obscure fact...should've jotted it down immediately. Goddamnit!

What?

If he only had something to jog his memory.

He stopped pacing, said, "John, do me a favor and run down that car's VIN. Okay?"

"Why? What you thinking?"

Holy shit!

There it was again, in vivid fucking Technicolor. He jotted it down before it was shoved aside by another thought.

"No time to explain. Just get it, okay?"

Ideas began begetting ideas, one right after the other in bam-bam-bam succession. Yes, this *was* important.

"On it, bro."

His cell rang. *Not now!*

He glanced at the screen ready to dump the call (*just another telemarketer?*). No! Wait!

Caller ID showed: RACHAEL.

Chapter 69—Arnold

ANOTHER OF NASEEM'S spoofs? Or, could this really be her?

The cell rang a second time.

"Got that VIN for you," Chang said.

Shit, forgot all about that.

"Great! Hold on," Arnold said.

The phone ran again.

You gotta take it, even if it's Naseem.

Arnold thumbed Accept, slowly raising the phone to his ear. "Yes?"

"Sweetie, it's me. This will be brief. I'm okay, I—"

"Where are you? I've been worried sick."

"I know, that's why I couldn't do this any more without calling. It's just that I...I was so afraid being alone in the apartment...and there was this creepy woman watching me when I left work...just know I'm okay where I am. I need you to understand and not worry. I'll call tomorrow and every day until I know for sure Naseem's arrested and we're all safe. I love you, Arnold."

"But—"

The line went dead.

Arnold stared at the phone for several seconds before slowly setting it down next to the keyboard. Could it be true? Was she really okay and safe? Well, it *was* her voice. No doubt about that. She didn't sound stressed like he imagined a hostage might be. But the main thing was, she was alive!

Chance nudged his elbow.

He leaned over, gave him a series of choobers, chanting, "She's alive, boy! She's alive!"

"What?" Chang was back in his ear again.

Arnold shook his head to clear it. *Where was I?*

"You want that VIN now, or what?"

"You bet!"

Massa Aurum, aka Arnold, logged onto a Dark Net message board looking for a master hacker, an online friend, Radical Dood. He ran a quick scan of active participants and holy shit; prayer answered.

Arnold typed: DOOD, NEED HUGE FAVOR.

Seconds suddenly went glacial. The only question in his mind now was just how long before Naseem turned up at his front gate. Still no sign of the HPD presence Fisher promised. The hairs on the back of his neck were bristling.

C'mon, Dood, c'mon...

NO PROB AURUM. WHAT?

CAN U HACK CAR GPS?

His fingers were now slick with sweat as drops rolled down his face and chest.

C'mon, man, c'mon....

Naseem

Naseem's peripheral vision suddenly caught red-and-blue flashing lights in the driver-side mirror, coming fast behind her in the left-hand lane. Then she heard the siren. She edged the car to the right side of the road, slowly applied the brakes, and reached for the Glock. She curled her fingers around the cool grip, index finger on the concave trigger guard. Because Glocks don't have safeties, all she needed to do was point and start shooting with a simple squeeze of the trigger.

Was this how her Jihad would end? A firefight against police? How very insignificant and unworthy. But, if this was Allah's will, then so be it.

She mouthed, "Allah Ackbar!"

Arnold

DEPENDS—WHAT MODEL?

He forwarded the info to Dood, along with: *CAN U DO IT? NO PROB. WHY U WANT IT?*

Chapter 70—Naseem

THE COP CAR blew past, barreling on through the red light, pushing sixty in a thirty-MPH zone, vanishing around a curve ahead.

Silence.

Naseem slumped back in the seat, head resting against the steering wheel, sweat soaked and limp. She realized she was holding her breath and exhaled. The car behind her honked. She glanced up. A green traffic light. She was blocking this lane.

With the Glock once again tucked snugly between her thighs, she pushed her trembling foot on the accelerator, cleared the intersection, turned into a gas station and proceeded slowly to a spot away from the pumps and alongside three tandem garbage bins. She set the brake, killed the ignition, and slumped into the seat, arms limp, head back, eyes closed. She practiced meditation breathing and waited for her heartrate to decelerate. She needed calm.

Fucking Jew! His fault.

Two minutes passed before she began to feel sufficiently collected to continue the short drive to his house. She opened her eyes, leaned forward, checked herself in the mirror.

What a mess!

She slapped her cheeks, puckered her lips twice, finger-combed her luxurious black hair. There! Composed sufficiently to finish the task. About four miles to go.

As she fired up the engine a thought hit: Did the Jew anticipate she'd do exactly this? Was that cop heading there now to protect him? No purpose would be served by a gun battle there. Besides, if, as she suspected, law enforcement was searching for this car, they might concentrate their effort around his neighborhood. Driving anywhere near there might not be wise. What other options did she have? The obvious, of course: wait to kill the Jew at a more appropriate time.

Yes, that would be wise. Once again, she praised Allah for protecting her.

She'd wait one, three, maybe even seven days. With each passing day, the Jew would grow more careless and the police less vigilant, forced to turn their attentions to other pressing matters. And as far as her own safety? The island was large, with more than enough places to hide.

She believed the Jew stay would not leave the island either. His fancy home tethered him here, unlike the destroyed Seattle home he had fled. *The police can't protect him forever.* Revenge would taste just as sweet, if not sweeter, a week from now. Allah would make certain of that.

But what if that police car was responding to a different call, one more important than the Jew? Perhaps the Jew was still alone in the house.

Thinking more rationally now, Naseem saw the numerous flaws of her heat-of-the-moment plan. Given his elaborate surveillance and security, was it even realistic to believe he'd open the door when she rang the bell? No! Shooting him at his house would an impossible plan. It'd be far superior to attack him and the dog during an evening walk when the park held no other visitors.

"Allah Ackbar!"

Or…if the police were not near his house at the moment, could she lure him out by perhaps proposing a peace settlement? A part of her wanted him dead now regardless of the risks involved. Another part of her wanted to wait, to execute the plan methodically to minimize unforeseen issues so she could continue her real jihad.

What to do, what to do? The key issue was whether or not the police were anywhere near the Jew's house. She put his address into the dashboard GPS, zeroed in on it, and reviewed surrounding roads and neighborhood as she'd done so many times the past months. She laid out a spot and route that'd allow a quick view down his street and a quick escape if need be.

Then she'd wait for evening, for him to drive the dog to the park.

She'd follow him and kill him there tonight.

Her spirits rose. "Allah Ackbar!"

Chapter 71—Arnold

DECISION TIME: EXPLAIN the situation to Radical Dood?

Dood just made it agonizingly clear that he'd only fork over the information if Massa told him exactly what he intended to do with it.

What the hell am I going to say?

No good cover story came to mind. Every second he wasted doing nothing was, well, wasted.

Make up your fucking mind, dude.

Fuck!

Who the hell *was* Dood? White or black-hat hacker? Undercover FBI agent? Good guy? Bad guy? Did it make a rat's ass of difference?

Seconds continued to flash by at Mach 2. Arnold sucked a deep breath, decided on a Hail Mary.

TRACKING A TERRORIST FOR THE FBI

Dood: *NO SHIT?*

TOTALLY

Dood: *COOL! DOES THE CAR HAVE DRIVER ASSIST?*

Christ, Dood, exactly what I'm trying to find out.

HOW DO I KNOW?

DOOD: *GOT THE VIN?*

He sent Dood the vehicle identification number.

Then he was up pacing circles, Chance at his side, glancing up with an occasional whimper.

Arnold tried to choober him, but found it impossible while keeping one eye on the screen, so...

DOOD: *GOT IT.*

Chapter 72—Naseem

HEART RATE FINALLY down to a comfortable range with breathing under control, a determined yet resigned calm settled in. Naseem glanced around as if awakening from drugged sleep. Nobody seemed to be paying any attention to her.

Praise Allah!

She gave a long sigh of relief.

She ejected the magazine from the Glock, double-checked that the clip was full, pulled the slide and ejected that round. She crammed it back in the clip, slapped the clip firmly back in the stock and chambered a fresh round. She was now assured the gun was ready if need be.

She mentally reviewed her revised plan a final time. She'd circle the Jew's neighborhood, spiraling closer to his house, searching for signs of a police presence. If none were seen, she'd park at the corner of the street he typically took when heading to the park. If he kept to routine, he'd appear a half-hour before dusk. If not? There was always tomorrow or the day after. Only the end result mattered, not the specific day.

Satisfied the plan was solid, she merged back into traffic, heading for the Jew's neighborhood.

He'd die today.

Arnold

GO AUDIO

Arnold disabled the webcam before linking up to Dood. For security reasons, he never allowed anyone but Rachael to see his face or any part of the house interior. None of his internet acquaintances even knew where he lived. Besides, who the hell was this guy? Friend or potential threat? Was involving him only setting himself up for a major disaster? Did he have any other choice? Not if he wanted Naseem out of the picture for good and Rachael safe. So, what the hell...he needed to go all in at this point.

"You there, Dood?"

"Loud and clear. You?"

"Likewise."

Arnold was now on a live audio link with the notorious hacker.

"Okay, here's how to access that GPS..." Dood began.

The real-time GPS coordinates for the car Naseem was driving appeared in the corner of Arnold's the right-hand monitor. Presently, they were not moving and were approximately five miles from his house.

"Got 'em yet, Massa?" Dood asked.

"I do," Arnold replied.

Dood said, "Me too."

"How the hell—"

"I'll explain later. You ready?"

"Yeah, give me a sec."

Arnold quickly relayed the GPS coordinates to Chang instead of directly to Fisher, figuring this route would buy a few more minutes of fucking with Naseem before law enforcement could intervene. That was, of course, if Naseem hadn't simply ditched the car and was now somewhere off in some remote jungle area of the island kicking back with a Mai Tai. Because if the car was simply dumped...

The GPS coordinates began to move. If Naseem was driving—

which he believed to be the case—she was headed his way.

"Too cool for school, Dood."

Arnold was awed. The dude possessed a mastery of skills that elevated him to an entirely different plane than the other hackers he knew, a level only a full-time hardcore professional might possibly attain. He was a Yoda in possession of some totally unequivocally amazing shit at the tips of his fingers.

"You cool with this so far?" Dood asked.

So far, it was easy. Nothing more than watching a cursor on a map.

"Straightforward, Dood. What next?"

"You need a bit of background info. Presently, the U.S. doesn't allow *fully*-autonomous vehicles on roads. Not yet. This car is only *partially* autonomous and uses lasers to sense immediate surrounding—"

"Dood, we don't have time."

"Fucking listen, man. This is important."

"Okay, sorry."

Jesus!

He wanted to scream.

"Cool it, Massa. This *is* important....as I was saying, you can control acceleration, braking and steering, but there's a catch."

"Okay..."

"If the driver takes his hands off the wheel for two seconds, the car sounds a warning and the sensors keep it centered in the lane. If the hands aren't immediately placed on the wheel, the car brakes to a stop. Keep that in mind."

"Okay, got it."

"Your mouse is your control. Left-click plus scroll accelerates, right-click for brakes. Sweep left or right for steering. We cool?"

Arnold quickly parroted back what Dood just said.

"Okay mission control," Dood said, "she's all yours."

Chang's voice popped up in his other ear.

"Yo, bro, whatever you're doing, stop it. Now! A pursuit team's about a mile out and closing."

Oh, shit!

He forgot that he and Chang were still linked up.

"Fuck no! She'll just ditch the car and disappear. Again."

"So what? We'll find her. Let *us* deal with this, bro."

The hell you will.

No fucking way was he going to risk another of Naseem's vanishing acts. This epic fucking saga was about to end for good in the next several minutes.

Arnold put a real-time Google map up on the middle monitor with the GPS coordinate crosshairs superimposed in the center, pinpointing the car's location. Once again car appeared to be stopped but now, with the map revealing where, he saw it at an intersection.

Holy shit! Only *three* miles away.

Dood said, "Shit, man, you have full control of that vehicle. What you waiting for?"

Arnold leaned closer to the screen, mouse in right hand, keyboard next to his left hand, waiting for the car to take off from the stop light.

"Why you doing this for me, Dood?"

"I know what you're about to do, Massa."

"No you don't!"

"Yeah, I do and I've always wanted to see if I could really fuck someone up this way. I'm totally into this."

Arnold swallowed. Fuck the light. Fuck the intersection. Tossing aside all concern for intersecting traffic, he floored the accelerator.

Game on!

Chapter 73—Naseem

FOOT LIGHTLY ON the brake, Naseem calmly waited for the light to turn green while constantly scanning the rearview mirror and intersection for any hint of a problem, the Glock still clamped tightly between her thighs. So far, no police. Good.

God is great!

KHNR—*690 on the AM dial, your best news/talk radio for the greater Honolulu area*—" was loud enough to catch a public-service alert describing her car if broadcast.

Talk radio admittedly wasn't as good as a police scanner, but it was her only option given the circumstances.

Suddenly the car took off, burning rubber straight into the busy intersection. Tires screamed as a beat-up candy-apple red Chevy skidded to a stop just shy of T-boning the passenger door. Frantically, she pumped the brake pedal.

No response.

The car continued accelerating. She screamed.

Eyes wide, hands clutching the steering wheel in a death grip, knuckles blanched a pasty shade of white, Naseem's right foot flattened the brake pedal to the floor.

Then the car was flying along Pali Highway, pushing fifty, seemingly with a mind of its own. She tried to swerve right. No response. Tried to swerve left. Again, no response.

She screamed once more, pumped the brake pedal full-force.

Arnold

Arnold realized that controlling the car was like playing real-life XBox. Only this wasn't some hi-def fantasy gaming animation on the monitor. This was hard-core real-ass happening-now shit. The enormity of his power struck full-force. Naseem was totally under his control. Here was his chance for payback!

Superimposed in the upper right corner of the map display was Naseem's pulse as recorded by her Apple watch. Man, oh man, that fucker was skipping along at 162 beats per fucking minute! *Scared shitless!* Exactly how he felt crouched in between dumpsters in the dark alley, praying Karim wouldn't shoot him to death as he'd done to Howie. Or when regaining consciousness as the burning Green Lake house came crashing down around him.

Naseem's vehicle was now doing a steady sixty, heading straight toward a left-hand curve in the road.

Shit, do something before she flies off the road and you'll kill an innocent bystander. Don't dare hurt anyone else.

He decelerated just enough to careen around the curve, then goosed it back up to a terrifying sixty. He couldn't resist yelling, *"How you like me now, bitch!"*

"Yo, Massum, don't forget, all he needs to do is let go of the wheel and that car comes to a dead stop."

Holy shit. Was Dood still linked up?

He was sure he'd cut the connection.

"HPD is on her," Chang said in his right ear.

Holy shit! Chang too?

He was sure he'd cut those links too. Obviously not. But he was too busy driving to do anything about that right now.

He flashed on the infamous live TV coverage of the LA cop caravan "chasing" OJ's white Bronco over the miles of freeways between Orange County and his Brentwood home.

Speaking of which, point in case; look what happened to that bastard after they caught him! A crafty lawyer played the jury so smoothly that OJ skated.

That shit's not going happen here.

"The hell's going on, Gold?"

Fuck! Fisher too? Completely forgot about him.

He decelerated Naseem to forty just long enough to cut the links with Fisher, Chang, and Dood. At last! Just him and Chance now, the pooch nuzzling his elbow, whimpering, sensing something big happening.

"Good boy, Chance is a good boy."

He wanted to choober the dog as a touchstone to reality but didn't dare lift a finger from the mouse or move his eyes from the screen.

You really going to do this?

What choice do I have? I'll never get my life back if I don't. But...

What about Rachael? And Howie and Rios? Don't they all deserve some payback?

The intersection to Hu'uanu Pali Drive was coming fast. He slowed the vehicle just enough to barrel through the turn, then floored it again, shooting her up the incline, away from the residential area.

"Who is he?"

Fucking Radical Dood was in his right ear again, loud and clear.

How the hell he do that?

He was sure he'd cut that connection.

"She's a she. And she's a fucking terrorist," Arnold shouted.

"You shitting me?"

"No! Already told you. I shit you not."

"Seriously? I mean totally?"

"Seriously!"

"Whoa...in that case, let's totally fuck her up!"

Chapter 74—Naseem

THE TURN ONTO Hu'uanu Pali Drive came screaming toward her, way too fast. She shrieked again, hand clutching the steering wheel so tightly her fingers ached, right foot furiously pumping the brakes, eyes wide, glued to the curving two-lane asphalt ahead.

Nothing she ever learned about controlling a car worked.

Something seriously wrong with it. Think!

The car slowed slightly just before the tires skidded through the turn, then she could hear the engine accelerating as the car blasted up the winding incline.

I know this road!

The same one her Brothers took in the botched attempt to run down the Jew. Suddenly she realized what must be happening: the Jew!

In a flash of clarity, she knew with absolutely certainty that the Jew was, in fact, Jinn, Al-Shaitan, the Devil. How else could a simple human employ such supernatural powers?

No! I refuse to let Al-Shaitan kill me!

Jump? Just open the door and jump?

No, at this speed you'll be killed. What's worse? Flying over the edge in the car?

She opened the door to roll out but the seat belt held her. She fumbled frantically for the belt release.

Too late!

Wide-eyed, she watched in stunned horror as the curve came rushing toward her.

Then the car was airborne, momentary flying out over the ravine, and slowly arced nose-down until it crashed into scrub-covered lava at the bottom.

Chapter 75—Arnold

ARNOLD SLUMPED IN the game chair, staring blankly at the mug of hot chocolate cupped in his hands, totally exhausted, mentally drained, without a tangible thought other than vague uneasy relief.

The epic ordeal—if that's what you could call his two-plus year battle with Naseem—was, at last, finished. He won. Time to wipe his hands and walk away. But that, he knew, would be impossible. His life was forever changed. Once again, he'd murdered a human being. First Karim, now Naseem. Yes, self-defense, both. Still, murder was murder...

A vague awareness nudged him.

He tried to ignore it but it persisted, more acute now, finally breaking through to him: a banging on the front door.

The sound, he realized, had been going on for...a long goddamn time. Not only that, but Chance was out in the hallway barking.

Slowly, carefully, he set the heavy white Navy surplus mug on the desk and tried to push up from the chair but dropped wearily back. The knocking started again. He sucked in a deep breath and was finally able to stand on lead pipes.

"All right already!" he yelled. Then, more softly, "It's okay, boy...I'm coming."

Deep within his mental fog, he recognized the face...just couldn't remember the name.

"Yo, Arnold, you all right?"

Knew the voice too. Having heard it not all that long ago either.

Get your shit together, dude. It's game's on. For fucking real now.

"Yeah, shit...I..." He leaned against the doorjamb and palmed his face. "It's just that..."

It's Tanaka, you dumb shit. Remember?

"Hey, yeah...Detective Tanaka."

Arnold offered his hand, his mind finally starting to levitate into a reasonable semblance of coherence.

As they shook hands, Tanaka said, "We need to talk."

"What...oh sure, come in." Arnold stepped aside.

"No, Arnold. I want you at the morgue to identify a body."

"A body?" Arnold said, trying for surprise.

"Yes," Tanaka replied, studying him closely.

"Who do you think it is?"

"That's what we want you to tell us. We *believe* it's Naseem Farhad. Can you do that? Like right *now*?"

Arnold blinked, wiped his face again, nodded. "Yeah, sure, guess so...give me a second to grab my car keys."

"Know where the medical examiner office is?" Tanaka asked as Arnold opened the car door, letting Chance in first.

Arnold shook his head. "No, not really. Figured on using the GPS."

The GPS...how ironic!

"It's eight-thirty-five Iwilei Road. Follow me. That'll make it easy."

"Sorry, but I need to stop along the way...for him." He nodded toward Chance. "We haven't been out of the house today and his bladder needs the break."

"Make it quick. Fisher's chomping at the bit to wrap things up."

Arnold noticed the sky was rapidly closing in on evening.

Jesus, what time was it?

He checked his watch and felt even more guilt for ignoring Chance's needs so many hours.

Chapter 76—Arnold

ARNOLD DROVE TO the park closest to the morgue but ended up giving Chance a few bonus minutes. Yes, Fisher wanted to wrap things up, but Chance had been ignored way too long today and needed some quality doggie time. It wouldn't kill Fisher to wait five or ten more minutes. After all, Arnold had been the one to give him Naseem's location. That saved him time, right?

But there was more to it than worrying about Chance's well-being. With each passing minute came increasing dread of actually looking into the lifeless face of the person he killed. Assuming, of course, the individual in the morgue was actually her. And now that he thought about it, just how certain was he that Naseem was the one driving that vehicle?

After all, everyone had seen a man leave the house and drive away in that car? What if she'd given that man her phone as crafty diversion to help her escape via another route? Or, what if she'd handed the car off to another terrorist once out of the house? Short of looking at the victim, there was no way of knowing.

Oh my god.

Had he totally fucked up?

He sat on the grass to mentally review the information available to him at the time. What, if any, concrete objective evidence did he have that Naseem was actually in that vehicle?

Well, okay, the phone...but...

...but what?

The watch?

Equally weak.

Fisher was right. He needed to look at the body. There was no other way.

Up on shaky legs now, he called Chance, and returned to the car, figuring Chance could continue the run after he'd visited the Medical Examiner's office.

Chapter 77—Arnold

ARNOLD STOOD OUTSIDE the door of the Mini and assured Chance of his return, then double-checked the windows and the doors before heading to the front door of the building. Time to get on with it.

The Medical Examiner's Office was a sun-bleached two-story block of white stucco. Approaching the glass doors, Arnold realized the building was only blocks from the warehouse where the infamous shootout went down.

How long ago did that happen?

Two and a half months? Yeah, give or take. Felt more like a fucking millennium or maybe even another lifetime. The joke was, that in the intervening days and weeks, a feeling of security had slowly enveloped him, lulling him into an unfounded belief that Naseem's threat had vanished.

How innocently naive those unsuspecting days now seemed. He'd even started planning a future, modifying his lifestyle as he grew closer to Rachael. All his dreams were splintered with one goddamned telephone call, her first word imploding his fantasy like a house of cards. She just kept popping up in his life like a fucking Whac-a-Mole.

Rachael...where was she? He still had no idea. Would he hear

273

from her today? Perhaps try her phone as soon as he finished the morgue thing? Yeah, that's what he'd do.

Tanaka and Fisher, in a white polo shirt and khaki pants, stood just a few feet inside the doors waiting, Fisher making a display of anxiously checking his watch as Arnold pushed through the door into the lobby.

"Took your own sweet time, didn't you, Gold," Fisher said.

He joking?

Neither law-enforcement officer offered their hand.

Guess he's serious.

"Been a stressful day for all of us," Arnold replied. "Let's get this over with."

"Fine with me," Fisher said, motioning Tanaka to lead the way.

The detective headed toward the back of the building.

Arnold remained motionless, staring at a disposable white plastic sheet covering what he assumed to be the supine female body laid out on the stainless-steel gurney. Another man in a white plastic full-length apron, mask with eye shield, and rubber gloves pulled back enough of the drape to expose the person's face, but Arnold couldn't bring himself to look up from the polished concrete floor. This simple task was turning out to be more difficult than imagined.

"Yo, Gold? That her?" Yes or no?" Fisher asked.

Arnold glanced at the FBI agent.

"You plan on verifying the identity with DNA, right? Why do you want my opinion?"

"We most definitely will, but I don't know if there's a suitable reference on file. Besides, that process can take months before we get the results. That's why I need visual confirmation *now.*"

"I saw on CNN that after they took out al-Baghdadi, they had DNA verification within minutes."

"That was an entirely different operation with way different priorities. They have enough juice to expedite a test like that. This isn't the same level of fugitive."

Arnold nodded and forced his eyes toward the exposed head and then was staring at a death-mask. Yes, a face was there, but a face distorted by death's absolute muscle flaccidity and unnatural skin hue. He shivered. Partly on account of only wearing shorts and t-shirt in a severely air-conditioned room, but also from muscles contractions scintillating up and down his spine. Her corpse was seriously creeping him out.

"Gold?"

This woman on the morgue table was not Breeze, the Las Vegas escort who played a starring role in his debut into manhood by uncloaking the biggest mysteries of sex. Nor was she the woman for whom he'd wanted to buy a trophy purse. That person stayed in Vegas.

He flashed on the moment Breeze goaded him into proving SAM could predict outcomes, a decision that paralleled the folk tale of blues singer Robert Johnson standing in a dusty Mississippi crossroads weighing the Devil's offer of fame in exchange for his soul.

No, stretched out before him lay Naseem, the female jihadist who'd forced him into a life-or-death struggle for eighteen months. He reassured himself that whatever life lessons she may have taught him in no way diminished the evil in her heart. Naseem reaped exactly what she'd sown.

Your own fault, dude. You're totally responsible for every single one of the deaths—especially this one. If you hadn't shot off your fucking mouth...

Well, that wasn't entirely true either. Karim shot Howie and either Naseem or, more likely, one of her minions blew Rios's brains out. Only God knew unequivocally who'd murdered the two terrorists in the warehouse.

Grand total: five people dead.

He blinked, shook his head, tried to concentrate on the task at hand.

Just get this over with.

But this thing today...this guilt wracking him now would eat at his heart the remainder of his life.

He nodded.

"Yeah, that's her."

To his surprise, saying the words released a complex mix of emotions: joy from knowing the epic battle was finally over, yet remorse for the way it concluded.

"Just so we are clear, you're absolutely certain *this* woman," Fisher said, pointing at the body, "we see before us is the person you know to be Naseem Farhad. Yes or no?"

"Yes. That is, to the best of my knowledge, Naseem Farhad," he said with new conviction.

"Okay. Thanks. You're done here. I'll walk you out."

Fisher started for the door back into the hall.

A thought began to gnaw at him. Just how much did Chang and Fisher hear of his conversation with Dood?

As they were passing through the lobby, Arnold stopped, looked Fisher in the eye.

"So, this matter is totally finished? I'm free to go?"

He figured that if Fisher were going to mention Dood, this would be the time. If Fisher took a pass, he'd simply get the fuck out of the building, take Chance back to the park, and on the way home, stop someplace for a sandwich and diet Pepsi for dinner.

"No, Gold, we're not finished. Not by a long shot. I have several additional questions. Let's take it outside."

Uh-oh.

Arnold didn't like the sound of that.

Chapter 78—Arnold

FISHER STOPPED THREE feet from the double glass doors, in the darkening shade of the overhang, Arnold grateful for being back in warm humidity again. By any typical standard, a beautiful dusk. However...

Fisher rubbed his bare arms.

"I hate morgues," Fisher said. "Damn storage rooms...colder than polar-bear turds. Always."

"I have no frame of reference for that."

Fisher nailed him with a hard, cold stare, held it a few beats.

"You have anything to add about Naseem's, uh, *accident?*"

Uh-oh...what exactly did the man know? Better yet, what did he think he knew?

He couldn't remember at what point in the action he cut Fisher and Chang off the comm-link. He tried to think back, but with so much going on in quick succession...

Naw, I dropped that link. Didn't I? Yeah, but Dood got back on, didn't he!

Yeah, well, Dood was Dood, dude. Fucking Dood operated on a much higher plane than Chang. Maybe even somewhere up there beyond the rings of Saturn.

"I'm waiting," Fisher said.

Arnold saw absolutely no upside to answering. Besides, he had this mental image of Davidson's disembodied head hovering just over his right shoulder whispering, *Do not answer that.* He sucked a tooth and decided the best answer was a question.

"Why do you ask?"

He fully expected Fisher to ignore the bait.

"Several reasons."

He tried for his best innocent tone.

"Such as?"

"First, there you have motive. You weren't exactly overjoyed knowing she intended to kill you. Self-defense is sufficient motive for doing something, shall we say, proactive."

"Well, you're right on one thing," Arnold said. "I certainly didn't want her to kill me. So what? Wouldn't you share that prejudice?"

Fisher just continued drilling him with his hard-ass stare.

Arnold added, "I don't know a damn thing about how she died other than something about some sort of tragic accident."

"Oh, for Christsake, Gold, give me a fucking break! Expect me to believe she *accidently* drives off the same road her buddies tried running *you* down on? You really expect me to believe that two-ton load of shit?"

Davidson's voice whispered in his ear again.

Do not say a word.

Neither man moved nor broke eye contact.

Fisher finally said: "Chang claims you were talking with another hacker when the shit hit the fan. Any truth in that?"

Ahhh...Chang knew more than he realized. Now what? Deny it? How'd that play if Chang had a recording of the conversation? Time to bluff.

"Absolutely. I needed help getting her GPS coordinates for *you.* So what? That makes *me* responsible for her accident? How's that supposed to work?"

Watch out. Don't get sucked down a rabbit hole.

"Fuck if I know, Gold. That's why I'm asking. But off the record, if you and your pal were responsible—to any degree—for that accident, then con-fucking-gratulations. I can't think of a more poetic way to kiss her terrorist ass goodbye. But here's the rub: we just lost our best lead for finding your girlfriend."

"Oh, *shit*! Sorry! With all that's going on, I forgot to mention she called me yesterday."

"Say what?"

"Yeah, it was, like, super brief. All she said was that she's okay and would call again today. I mean, she said she's hiding someplace."

"You're convinced it was her?"

"Absolutely. The call came from her phone and it was totally her voice, and, yeah, it was her."

"She happen to say where she is?"

"No. Just that she's fine. I believe her."

Fisher studied him for a moment before nodding.

"When and if you hear from her again, tell her she needs to call me immediately. I have a few questions. Until we nail down several points this remains an active kidnapping investigation."

"I plan on trying her cell when I take Chance back to the park."

"Any chance she'll answer?"

Arnold shrugged.

"No idea."

"Then go ahead, try it now," Fisher said.

She didn't answer.

Chapter 79—Arnold

PHONE IN HAND, Arnold sat at the picnic table bathed in the mercury vapor light as Chance was off doing his doggie thing. He was anxiously waiting for Rachael to call.

She *was* going to call, wasn't she?

The phone finally rang and Caller ID showed RACHAEL. He put the phone to his ear, said, "It's over, Rach."

"What is?"

"Naseem's dead. She died in a horrible traffic accident this afternoon during a police chase. I just finished identifying her..."

He gave her Fisher's number and asked her to call him straightaway, then call him back.

Later that evening...

Arnold was stretched out on the chaise, the back angled at a comfortable forty-five degrees, the evening air a blessed eighty degrees. A Kona Big Wave was perspiring on the table to his right, and Chance was tucked into a snug ball of tan fur on the deck to his left, muzzle between slightly twitching paws. Doggie dreams. Perhaps a good squirrel chase. Yeah, nothing better than flat-out running after a terrorized squirrel.

He reached down, gave him a few behind-the-ear choobers just for drill. Man, he loved that pooch. *Thump thump thump.*

His eyes wandered across the ravine to the sniper spot.

"Sorry, boy, didn't mean to wake you."

Thump thump thump.

He took another sip of chilled effervescence laced with a slight tropical hop aroma. Incredibly light and refreshing. Perfect for this time of evening.

He struggled to consciously express the low-level foreign mood that had begun floating through him since identifying Naseem's lifeless body. Foreign. Novel. Pleasant.

Secure!

Yeah, that was it; Secure. Mental peace. (*Oh please! Fucking gag me!*)

Well, shit, how else to describe it?

Rachael was scheduled to arrive in two weeks to search for an apartment. What more could he ask for? Well, having her live with him would be better, but if this is how she wanted to handle their relationship for the time being, fine with him. Time would sort all that out.

He thought about Davidson too. How close they've grown since first encountering each other the night of Howie's murder, as he was being questioned at the SPD West Precinct. More than just a client/attorney bond. They seemed to be family. Arnold believed they'd see each other whenever they were both in Honolulu or Seattle. At least this was his hope.

And Fisher? He thought about Fisher and the multiple hardships they'd faced together over the past two years. Part of him would actually miss the man. Another part wished their paths never crossed again. As far as Fisher the person? For that, he harbored mixed emotions; on one hand, the man had surely helped him. On the other hand, Fisher used him as bait, twice knowingly putting him in harm's way. Well, that chapter of his life was finally closed.

Should he be grateful that Fisher wasn't pursuing an

investigation into Naseem's death? Yeah, perhaps. Then again, what hard evidence could he possibly have? Nothing. Possibly, like Dood, Chang had reestablished the communications link when things started going down, but so what? All he could possibly have was an audio recording and, perhaps, Dood's Dark Web name. Good luck tracking down Dood. And to what end? Was Dood going to admit a damned thing? Not!

After bringing Chance home from the park, he reviewed in detail all earlier recordings, paying particular attention to the moments leading up to Naseem's fatal crash.

Frame by frame, he'd reviewed the audio and video. Then repeated the process until he was completely satisfied that he'd missed nothing. Then, just to absolutely unequivocally put his mind at rest, he watched one final time. He now understood the actual chain of events.

The clincher came when Dood said, "Whoa...in that case, let's fuck her up, Massa!" For, it was at precisely this point that Dood took over control of the vehicle's auto-assist, cutting Arnold completely off. Meaning Dood was the one who drove Naseem over the embankment.

He sat back, mulling this over again. Comforting to know, but so what? Although he didn't actually drive Naseem to her death, he took ultimate responsibility for getting Dood involved. That part was undeniable.

Why didn't I tell Fisher this? Good question.

His iPhone chimed. Someone at the front gate.

His gut knotted. *Fuck!*

Wait a minute...probably just the pizza...

Forgot completely about ordering it, what, thirty minutes ago?

He pushed out of the chaise and headed for the front door, relieved and diffusely annoyed at not having been more forthcoming with Fisher. But in the final analysis, the nightmare was, at last, over and he could resume life as Arnold Gold. Soon as he finished with the delivery guy, he'd call Rach again. She was his highest priority now. Pizza? Hell, if it got a little cold, so what? Cold pizza was the sole reason God invented microwaves, right?

After setting the warm pizza on the counter, he grabbed the phone from the charger and headed back out to the chaise.

Chapter 80—Arnold

"YOU ASLEEP YET?"

"Not yet, just reading," Rachael answered.

Liar. He could hear the sleep in her voice and felt a bit guilty for awakening her.

"Need help packing?"

A slight hesitation, followed by a cautious, "Wouldn't turn it down...why?"

"Good, because I just booked a ticket to fly over tomorrow. I need to check on few things about the house and make up for the meetings I missed last week. Oh, and this time Chance is coming with me."

How long would he be in Seattle? No idea.

But it really didn't matter because he couldn't bear the thought of boarding him again. Besides, Chance would soon be shuttling between both homes, so why not start familiarizing him with the old Green Lake neighborhood?

Two Nights Later

Drizzle caught the mercury vapor streetlight at the perfect angle to produce a Northern Lights-like halo sheen, inserting a flash of beauty in an otherwise drab and dreary scene. Forty degrees of shitty evening weather that made late October seem endless while increasing Honolulu's appeal at this time of year.

Two-home living (well, actually three, if Rachael rented an apartment instead of moving in with him like he was actively lobbying for, but...) would soon be their lifestyle.

He and Rachael walked hand in hand, Chance sauntering next to her, the two having bonded immediately. This pleased Arnold immensely.

The neighborhood flooded him with tattered sepia-toned memories, most good, some still terrifying, like the evening the nightmare began: the gunshot, hiding in the alley, or, worst of all, regaining consciousness as the fire raged, then fighting to free himself from being tethered to the desk.

Time heals, he constantly reminded himself each time one of these memories resurfaced.

But Christ, how long would that take?

Howie's face appeared in many of the memories.

I'll never forget you, brother. Never!

Then they were pushing through the front door, approaching the familiar gray laminate counter, into the same heavy, humid air smelling of yeast, grease and tomato sauce. Probably the same customers as *that night*, except tonight a Seahawks game was on the large 4K OLED Samsung on the far wall.

The cook turned from the pizza oven, glanced up at him, flashed a broad smile, and called, "Yo! It's been a while, man. You been on vacation or something?"

Allen Wyler

Acknowledgements

IN NO PARTICULAR order, I thank the following people for their help writing this story:

Ken Robert, Cyber Security Solutions Architect

Jonathon Tomek, Cyber Threat Intelligence

Detective James Laing (Ret.), King County Police Department

One retired FBI agent who, for personal reasons, prefers to remain anonymous. You know who you are.

Jim Thomsen, editor

CPSIA information can be obtained
at www.ICGtesting.com
Printed in the USA
BVHW080158180920
588936BV00007B/759